Proof of Purchase

A JACK GRANT MYSTERY

PROOF OF PURCHASE

RICHARD B. SCHWARTZ

MIDNIGHT INK
WOODBURY, MINNESOTA

Proof of Purchase © 2007 by Richard B. Schwartz. All rights reserved. No part of this book may be used or reproduced in any manner whatsoever, including Internet usage, without written permission from Midnight Ink except in the case of brief quotations embodied in critical articles and reviews.

First Edition
First Printing, 2007

Book design by Donna Burch
Cover design by Gavin Dayton Duffy
Cover photo © age fotostock/SuperStock
Editing by Connie Hill

Midnight Ink, an imprint of Llewellyn Publications

The Cataloging-in-Publication Data for *Proof of Purchase* is on file at the Library of Congress.
ISBN 13: 978-0-7387-0829-4
ISBN 10: 0-7387-0829-1

This is a work of fiction. Names, characters, places, and incidents are either the product of the author's imagination or are used fictitiously, and any resemblance to actual persons, living or dead, business establishments, events, or locales is entirely coincidental.

Midnight Ink
2143 Wooddale Drive, Dept.0-7387-0829-1
Woodbury, MN 55125-2989
www.midnightinkbooks.com

Printed in the United States of America

OTHER BOOKS BY RICHARD B. SCHWARTZ

Novels
Frozen Stare
The Last Voice You Hear
Into the Dark

Memoir
The Biggest City in America

Criticism
Samuel Johnson and the New Science
Samuel Johnson and the Problem of Evil
Boswell's Johnson: A Preface to the LIFE
Daily Life in Johnson's London
After the Death of Literature
Nice and Noir: Contemporary American Crime Fiction
[Ed.] *The Plays of Arthur Murphy,* 4 vols.
[Ed.] *Theory and Tradition in Eighteenth-Century Studie*s

For Judith Alexis

along the brittle treacherous bright streets of memory comes my heart, singing like an idiot, whispering like a drunken man who (at a certain corner, suddenly) meets the tall policeman of my mind.

—e. e. cummings

ONE

However it ends, it always starts with tears.

I had been looking for her for four and a half weeks. Usually they're found much sooner than that, or never found at all. Her body had come to rest twenty yards from the shoreline of a small gray lake that's not even named on small-scale maps, a single rough-edged dot beside Route 18 in the San Bernardino forest. Midway between Crestline and Lake Arrowhead, it sits on a sloping, dusty ledge, just south of the highway. You park in the burn or you belly your car on the underbrush and partially exposed rocks at the edge of the tree line, then walk a few hundred yards through the wild grass and pine scrub. A local group still stocks it with bluegills, crappies, and any pan fish the federal government is anxious to give away. Most people prefer to fish Silverwood, Gregory, or Arrowhead. Bigger fish; better parking.

Back in the late fifties the American Legion and V.F.W. used to hold functions there: a quiet lake, a few hours of adventure for the city kids and an afternoon outing for their parents—all bathed in warm, shadowy sun, a steady wind off the mountains, and the smell of smoky grills and thoughts of deep steel tubs of cold beer in icy longnecks. Back then they parked above, along the main highway. It was still safe; they didn't have to dodge the teenagers in their trucks and the drunks in their 4 x 4's, taking the mountain turns at straightaway speeds and scaring the hell out of wayward tourists lured to Lake Arrowhead by come-on ads in L.A. hotel magazines.

A local eccentric named William Clyde Brattle had had a wooden gazebo built at the east end of the lake, complete with a brass gift plaque bolted above the center arch. The recipients of his philanthropy liked to call it The Bandstand, though there was barely enough room on it for five people to stand side by side without hitting their heads on an arch or nicking their elbows on a splintery section of frame. The top and sides are covered now with brown and yellow lichen and the flooring has been lost to rot, earth, and undergrowth.

The poor started coming here when there was no one left to bother them. They come up for the day and try to catch their dinner in the lake, first turning over the ground for redworms and night crawlers as the kids run off and throw pebbles or pinecones. Just before sunset they picnic in the trees below the shore. Grandma and Grandpa sit in foldup chairs in the shade and watch the rest—aunts, uncles, cousins, neighbors, friends, whoever could be squeezed into the back seats of their old sedans.

―――

When they found it there were piercing, hysterical screams. A finger at first, just above the rust-brown bed of dried pine needles—

the right, index finger, pointing up through the trees and toward the sky. Then the hand and arm and what was left of the head and torso and legs. Each time Oscar or Carlo or Frederico Montalvez cleared another handful of dirt someone yelled "*que horror!*" or "*malisimo!*" Nice people, the Montalvezes. Conscientious. Trying to do their part to serve the cause and clean up their tiny portion of the world. Just there for the day from Covina with another family from East L.A.—a day away from the lube pits, the griddles and grease traps, the machine shops, the crack vials, the sprayed walls, and the desperate eyes.

Frederico never expected to have his two-year-old daughter Teresita stumble upon the finger of a dead woman's body in a shallow grave, then try to shake hands with it.

———

No one had thought the drought in the mountains would end as quickly as it did, especially not the woman's killer. The sudden spring rains had brought up the lake level, spilling into the trees, and loosening the dry earth. Then the desert winds dried up the standing water, exposing what remained of the shrivelled finger of the right hand of Cynthia Bladen. There was even a trace of dried grass from the shoreline—the broad, sharp-edged kind we used to tear in strips and lay between our thumbs to make whistles. When they found her it was wrapped around her finger like a wedding band. Married to the earth now, lost forever in its first deadly embrace.

———

Bladen, Cynthia A., 37. Beloved daughter of Rachel R. Simonds and the late James W. Simonds of Chestnut Hill, Massachusetts. Devoted wife of Donald N. Bladen of Los Angeles. Dear mother of Charles Bladen, 5, and Amy Bladen, 3. Mrs. Bladen was a graduate of Columbia College and Law School, a partner in the law firm of Briggs and Billings, and a member of the First Episcopal Church of Westwood. She was active in professional, church, and community affairs. A memorial service will be held next Saturday evening at 8:00 p.m. in the garden of the family residence. There will be no visitation.

And no open casket.

———

A few other things too. Five feet, seven inches. Most of what could have been a model's body still evident. Short brown hair, green eyes, and thin brows. Character. Brains. Class. Excellent health. No conceivable reason for her life to end so quickly in an act of grotesque violence.

And one other thing. Cynthia Simonds and I had dated seriously before her seven-year marriage to Donald Bladen. I don't know why, but my name was still there in her Rolodex. Luck or fate, maybe the remains of something more. When her husband called and left a message on my machine to call him back, he was angry and upset. He told me she was missing and that it was urgent he talk to me, that if I was listening I should turn off the goddamned machine and pick up the receiver. When I returned to my apartment and played back the message I felt surprise and a lot of other things, some of which I hadn't felt in a long time. I thought about it for nearly an hour before I called back. When I finally did, he told me Cynthia had been missing for over a week. He said he wanted to see me right away; he wanted to talk to me; he wanted me to forget everything else I might be doing and find her.

He and I had never met or talked before her disappearance. By the time Donald Bladen had begun seeing Cynthia I was already out of the picture, living thirty miles away and dating a surgeon named Laura Weeks. And yet, the moment he saw me his gray eyes were searching mine with that special form of loathing that comes to those who need the help of someone with whom they have shared the feelings of the same woman. He grasped my hand in his and it felt stiff and dead. He never mentioned how he knew about us and I didn't ask.

He ushered me into his house, closed the door, and demanded to know why I had taken so long to return his call. Before I could answer he started to list his other demands. At that point I would normally say something that rich people weren't used to hearing in their living rooms, but I let him talk. I knew how he felt because I knew how much he stood to lose and I don't usually curse a man—even a man I dislike—when I see that his hands are shaking. I also knew the odds of his wife being found alive and happy; I didn't tell him how bad they were.

After fifteen or twenty minutes he was apologizing, calling me *Mr. Grant*, and sobbing into a succession of watery drinks that he kept clutching tighter and tighter with each sentence. I turned away, looking at a black and white picture of Cynthia in a silver frame on their ebony piano, waiting nervously for the glass to shatter in his hand.

As we talked and I began to pursue realistic possibilities with him I continued to wonder how he knew about me and his wife.

By then he had collected himself, made a fresh drink, and sat back down on the yellow silk couch behind his glass coffee table. The table was still covered with condensation rings but he put the glass square in the middle of what looked like a soggy Venn diagram. He didn't seem to notice the stack of cocktail napkins on the end table next to the couch. Instead he paused, looked at me hopefully, and asked if I would do whatever I could to find his wife. He kept referring to her specifically in that way: as *his* wife. I promised I would help.

A month later Frank White called me with the news of Cynthia's death. I drove to Donald Bladen's home and told him that his wife's body had been found. He told me he didn't want to hear any of the details. He said he didn't want to identify the body and he didn't want to talk to me further. He said it was obvious that I hadn't done enough and that he wanted me to leave. This time the gray eyes were streaked with red. He was staring blankly at the floor, clutching his hands together to keep them from shaking.

TWO

I WAS DRIVING INTO the sun and trying my best to see through the glare, the fog, and a dust-smeared windshield. I turned on the windshield washer, watched the smears get worse and worse, finally realized the reservoir was out of fluid, and went back to thinking about Cynthia Simonds Bladen. I was thinking about our first meeting when I pulled out of the driveway earlier. Now, twenty-five minutes later, I was thinking about our last. It wasn't difficult to recall: an uncomfortable, kiss-off dinner date with a lot of rambling talk about love and friendship that neither one of us ever really believed. We had started with rumpled clothes and refrigerator wine six months before; we ended with a window table above the Sunset Strip and an awkward formality. I had blocked out most of the talk, but I still remembered the food: shaved Norwegian salmon with lemon slices, Veal Oscar, and Puligny Montrachet from a far better year than the two of us were ever likely to have together.

I thought at the time that it could have been worse. It usually is.

A lumpy black Dodge passed me and cut in tight, playing chase-me with a green Econoline van and a '61 Chevy with a spiderwebbed windshield. There were days when I would have leaned on the horn and thrown a White Owl award or an Italian salute. Maybe worse. Like most women, Cynthia hated that in me. At least I always kept my service automatic locked in the glove compartment or trunk. Not all do.

It wasn't the fact that Cynthia and I weren't drawn together so much as the length of the list of things that was pulling us apart. She was racing along the Wilshire corridor and through the skyrise canyons downtown, coming up fast on a partnership tender, watching her flanks and weighing her options; I was trying to decide between having another operation on a sorry right leg that had been introduced to half of a Chinese grenade on the outskirts of Da Nang, or simply learning to smile hard and correct my golf stance.

I had some other things to decide also, but none of them were any more pressing. A light colonel's pension was adequate if not generous and I had found an insurance company called Valley Mutual that was willing to send me a check every time I sent them the name of a sinner, the steadiest of work—Southern California sinners not being in short supply. Cynthia was dressed for legal action, working breakfasts, lunches, and dinners; days, nights, weekends, and holidays. I, on the other hand, was finally wearing what I wanted to wear, going where I wanted to go, and doing most of what I wanted to do at the time I wanted to do it.

She was Boston with blueish blood; I was north shore Chicago with blueish collar. She was twelve years younger than me on the clock, twenty or thirty if you were digging your caliper points into the layers of scar tissue on the soul. I tried to come up with a mental list of the things we absolutely had in common, but I could never get past two items: we were both slightly above average in height and we both wished our apartments had been fitted with double sinks.

If some matches are made in heaven, this one must have been dreamed up by some spiteful demigod who got bored watching the celestial gates swing and decided instead to get into cruel jokes and cheap laughs, watching pathetic mortals fall in and out of love while he rummaged through his bag of barbecue chips and searched for a fresh tub of dip and a second six-pack of Corona.

Most of all I couldn't stop thinking about the salmon. The chef had sliced it so thin you could read the small print on the wine label through it; then he had arranged the pieces—along with the lemon slices—in the form of flowers. I don't know of any birds or bees that would have landed on them, but I remember being impressed at the time and thinking that each salmon flower should be taken apart gently and respectfully. They were like my relationship with Cynthia, I thought, except that they tasted a little stale and the chef had had his fingers all over them. He did remove each of the pips from the lemon slices though, which I thought was a nice touch.

Cynthia started getting philosophic about our relationship. She was touching one of the flowers in our table's bud vase and she told me she was thinking about how miserable it was that all things have to die, especially the best things. I was tasting the salmon and thinking about how all things have to die and then be eaten. I was also wondering whether or not the chef had washed his hands recently. Like I said, north shore Chicago.

I drove past Duarte, heading east on the Foothill Freeway toward San Bernardino and a final goodbye to Cynthia Simonds Bladen. By the grace of God and the Department of Highways I was driving against the traffic. Each lane on the other side was jammed, probably as far back as Pomona. The air wasn't soup yet but it was mixing with the fog to become dishwater gray consommé, seeping across the mountains, darkening trees, houses, and whatever else it could envelop before the late morning sun could begin to cook it away.

You would have thought that there might be less traffic these days, with the state of the economy, but there's never less traffic in Los Angeles. When you hit bottom here you land on the hood of a car or the bumper of a truck.

This time we had all started with such high hopes. The information age would boom forever, especially with the new generation of organic-material processors. The showdown between the C-Chip and the O-Chip turned out to be a non-event. Everybody went 'C' and the endless skies were the brightest shade of blue. Billions of eensy-beensy wires in billions of eensy-beensy molecules. Until the molecules began to rebel and the chips began to fall in unexpected ways. Beta technology may have been better than VHS, but VHS won and we all got over it. In this case, nobody could get over it, because nothing was working. The computers had given us a world where nearly every business was living between the wallpaper and the wall, with no room for error. When they began to suffocate there was nothing left to do but return to previous technology, and the search for it and the implementation of it was enough to push most new companies and many of the old ones into the pit.

The NASDAQ graph looked like the face of an unforgiving Everest and the Dow like a waterslide in a cheap amusement park. After the economy died, Cynthia followed, and for some reason or other she seemed to take a lot of me with her.

———

The Toyota dealer just above the freeway on the southern edge of the San Gabriels still had his two-story, inflatable plastic panda in place, squatting above his showroom like a baby on a training pot, held in place by a half dozen rigid guy wires. A fairly shitty panda, actually; with outsized ears and mismatched eyes, it looked like an olympic mascot designed by the North Koreans. I couldn't figure out what the hell it was doing there. Pandas don't come from Japan, like Toyotas, and this poor bear didn't even have a handful of bamboo to nibble on. He just sat there, with that 'Look at me, I'm cute' expression. Except he wasn't. More like a hypertrophied beach toy that you might get free with an 8-gallon minimum fill-up at an all-night station in Inglewood or Compton.

At least the head didn't bobble or the eyes follow you like an Elvis car doll or cheap Infant of Prague statue. He just sat, stared, and grinned.

I snaked down through San Dimas on the 210, hitting the San Bernardino outside Pomona and then drove on through Ontario, dead east. I could have gone straight, following the Foothill Freeway onto Foothill Boulevard and into San Berdoo, but I wasn't up for the start-and-stop and I had seen enough ersatz adobe, instant-tradition red tile, and inflated pandas to last me until the return trip. Foothill Boulevard looks like the paint and plastic nursery where the world's strip malls are conceived, born, and raised. They split like quivering cells, a metastatic east-west chain of economic wishful thinking.

The farther you go the worse the air gets. Lawrence of Arabia may have liked the desert because he thought it was clean, but he hadn't been to ours and seen the San Gabriels and San Bernardinos trap the smog on its journey away from the basin. Every few years somebody dredges up the old idea of digging a tunnel through the mountains and putting in the mother of all fans to suck out the filth. Why not? Send it all to a way station in Barstow and then kick it toward Las Vegas. Let the touts bet on how long it would take to get there and how much of it would be able to complete the entire journey. Shit migration. I wondered what federal agency would be responsible for monitoring its progress.

The Angelization of San Bernardino is progressing well. They've got much more than their fair share of traffic, dope, gangs, weaponry, and the other modern amenities of Southern California life. The people in Riverside and Ontario try to keep a safe distance. The people in Palm Springs try not to think about San Berdoo at all.

Like a lot of others, I was there to look at a corpse and talk to a police lieutenant. At least that brought people to town.

THREE

I was scheduled to meet with the locals at 10:45. I checked my watch and it was only 10:10, so I drove into the lot of the restaurant at the Ramada, turned off the engine of my Taurus rental (my wounded Celica recuperating at the Toyota hospital) and locked the door. I looked around the lot, saw mostly dusty pickups and rust relics, and checked to make sure I really had locked the door and rolled up the windows as tight as they would go.

The bar was generic black shag and red vinyl. The tables were glossy oak with a half-inch of polyurethane protecting the franchise furniture from greasy fingers and idle cigarettes. Mine hadn't been wiped off in awhile. I got tired of trying to signal for a waitress, left a few fingerprints as mementos and got up and walked over to the bar.

"What do you need?" the bartender asked, looking at me through puffy, black eyes as he forced out the words. He was wearing a stained, red, ruffled shirt under a short black poly waistcoat with the bottom button popped. His name was stitched into the pocket: *Barry*.

"Coffee, black," I said, "with some Jameson's on the side. Make it a double so I can keep topping it."

He didn't answer. He poured the coffee, filled two jiggers, lined them up at the corner of my saucer, and walked to the far end of the bar and started to wipe glasses. I didn't see any soap or water.

I floated some Jameson's across the steam wisps at the surface of the cup and thought about Cynthia and what was now left of her. After a few minutes I began to think about Laura Weeks, Cynthia's successor; I had lost her too. At least she was still around, if not for me. When I finished the second shot I signaled to Barry and ordered a third.

"That it?" he said impatiently.

"Are you expecting an early crowd for lunch?" I asked. It was 10:35 in the morning and except for a guy in a booth reading a paper I was the only customer in the room.

He stared dully.

"Give me a little peppermint schnapps on some shaved ice," I said.

"We just have ice cubes," he said, meaning it was too early in the morning to go to any more trouble.

"OK," I said. "That's fine."

What a sweet-tempered, accommodating person I can be when I suddenly remember I don't have enough change for a tip.

I tried to count the fingerprints on my glass, then I swirled the schnapps around in my mouth and worked it through my teeth. I let it lay on the back of my tongue for a few seconds, and then swallowed. Spiked Scope. Nature's most nearly perfect food.

The police department was housed in a two-story, stucco cube with a bell tower that looked like an oblong candle on a square birthday cake. Either this was the architect's rough draft or it was thrown together by his assistant just as the whistle was blowing. The clock hands on the tower were running five minutes early. I could have had another drink.

I introduced myself to the desk sergeant and told him I had an appointment with Lieutenant Craig. He looked at me, then looked back down at the pile of paper in front of him, and said mechanically, "Up the stairs to your left, first door on the right."

The outside of the building might have been a boxy attempt at some sort of recognizable style (I think they call it *brutalist*), but the inside looked and smelled like every station house in the world: gray walls, flickering fluorescent bulbs, scuffed tile, green file cabinets, black wire mesh cages, the distilled essence of sweat and caramelized burnt coffee, all of it housing a lot of people in cheap clothes pushing tall mounds of paper.

I knocked on the door marked 205 and no one answered. I knocked again, louder. Still nothing. I turned around and walked through an open door. A frowning secretary was trying to understand the voice on a dictaphone tape and type at the same time. She said "Shit" louder than she was aware and moved her foot to rewind the tape. Della Street in the real world. I moved around the side of her desk in front of the terminal in an attempt to get her attention.

She saw me but kept on typing, said "Shit" again, not quite as loud this time, and finally reached up and pulled the earphone out from under a wall of spritzed hair that moved in unison at the touch. She looked more like a middle-aged Barbie than Rosemary Woods.

"I'm looking for Lieutenant Craig," I said. "My name is Grant. I have an appointment."

"Across the hall," she said, "Room 205."

"Nobody answered when I knocked," I said.

"Why don't you just go in and wait?"

Good question. Before I could answer she had the earphone back in and was hitting the dictaphone start button with her toe. Her hair was standing out a half-inch or so farther now. She seemed to be aware of the fact because she typed a word or two and then reached up and tapped it back into place as if she was brushing at a fly.

———

The "office" was actually a conference room with nothing but a coat rack, an eight-foot table, and six foldup chairs. The walls were bare and the brown industrial carpeting looked as if it had been walked on by five million people with dirty shoes. It was at the stage where there were a half dozen or so black patches with no visible rug fabric left, just swooshes of greasy wear.

I propped open the door with the coat rack. Then I pulled out what seemed like the cleanest chair in the collection and moved it two spaces west so that I could be seen from the hallway. I ran a Kleenex over the seat twice and then sat down.

Five minutes passed. Then another five. I was ready to try the secretary with the lacquered hair one last time when a San Bernardino police lieutenant walked through the doorway, moved the coat rack, and let the door swing closed.

"Craig," she said. "You're Grant."

"Yes," I said. "How do you do?"

"What have you got for me?" she said, abruptly.

"Mostly questions," I said. It was clear we weren't going to waste any part of the morning working our way through a list of protocols and pleasantries.

"I don't have time for questions," she said. "This isn't a news service."

"I was hoping I could see the Coroner's report and find out what you've turned up so far."

"Didn't you hear me?" she said. "I already asked—what have you got for *me?* I've got a murder to solve and I'm not going to waste any of my time dispensing official information to a private who doesn't have anything to trade in return."

"I knew the victim," I said. "I knew her personally."

"How well?"

"We used to go out . . . several years ago."

"And?"

"And what?"

"How *well* did you know her?"

"A hell of a lot better than you did, lieutenant."

"Sit still," she said, "I'll be back."

Before I could respond she was out the door. Nobody was giving me time to answer. Or maybe I was just a second or two out because of the Jameson's. After about three minutes she returned with two styrofoam cups of black coffee. "Here," she said, "you could use this."

"What does that mean?" I asked.

"Grant, you smell like a vat of peppermint oil. That means one of three things: (A) you came in here expecting somebody to kiss you; (B) you used the room freshener instead of deodorant; or (C) you're trying to cover up the smell of whiskey or gin. (A) and (B) I would consider long shots; the smart money is all on (C) and I don't like to waste any of my time talking to drunks."

"Drunks sometimes tell the truth," I said.

"I know," she said, "why do you think I tried to find out first whether or not you knew anything?"

"Were you ever in the Army?" I asked.

"Why?" she said.

"Because the only people I've ever known who talk with that (A), (B), and (C) stuff were either Army instructors or college debaters."

"Didn't you mean to say (A), (B), and (C) *shit?*"

"I was being polite," I said.

"Don't," she answered. "I'd rather hear the truth."

"Well?" I asked.

"Well what?"

"Were you ever in the Army?"

"I thought about it," she said, "but decided against it."

"Because they wouldn't let you serve in combat?"

"That's right."

"Combat's dangerous," I said.

"So is being polite at the wrong time," she said, sliding back her jacket, putting her hands on her hips, and exposing the 9 mm automatic in a plain brown holster. She also threw her breasts forward slightly, as if she were showing me all the lethal things she had in a single gesture. She also seemed to be waiting for me to make some flip comment to that effect. When I let it slide she seemed disappointed.

"Here's the deal," she said. "I'll tell you what I can. You give me everything you've got now and everything you turn later. If I find out you're holding out on me—with anything, anything at all—we're finished."

"OK," I said, "but let's start off honestly. I already held out on something."

"You were going to make some crack about my chest. I invited it."

"I wouldn't normally use the word *chest* in that situation," I said.

"That's better," she said. "Now we're getting somewhere."

FOUR

"Let's go to my office," she said. "I just use this place for first-time meetings, especially when I know they aren't going anywhere. The room doesn't really hold out any hope or make any promises. Makes it easier to cut through the crap quickly and put the bulging eyes and enquiring minds back on the street. Not that I'm secretive . . . ."

"You just don't want to invest any time in bad risks or pain-in-the-ass civilians."

"Exactly."

She asked me if I wanted any water or coffee. I took the water. The glass was cleaner than at the Ramada bar. We walked down the west corridor and stopped at an unmarked door next to the stairwell. She produced a key from her jacket pocket and slipped it into the lock. "After you," she said, and stood aside. Her office was decorated in monk's cell-modern—simple tables and chairs with ramrod-straight files and minimal decorations. The furniture was oak, not pine, but nobody would mistake it for the frippery from the corporate line. No flags. Also no pictures of the president's, chief's, or mayor's smiling countenance. No yellowed news clippings, no stained coffee cups or overflowing ashtrays, no pencil stubs or grit-and-oil-tipped ballpoints. And no citations or commendations. Anywhere.

"Tell me something," I said.

"What?" she asked. There was an edge to her voice, the kind she reserved for the pain-in-the-ass civilians.

I thought better of it. "Forget it," I said. "It's none of my business."

"What?" she asked.

"OK, where are your citations? You can't wear both a skirt and a lieutenant's bar without a decent pile of them, at least not around here."

She looked at me and thought a moment before answering. "I don't play that shit," she said. "It's a crutch. When you look at the wall and start believing you're that smart or that brave you're already in too deep to get back out. If you don't start each day as if it's your first you cut the odds of ever making it to the second. I like things clean and simple: *Life* . . . and *death*. *Us* . . . and *them*."

"Life and death are pretty straightforward, but sometimes it's hard to tell *us* from *them*."

She looked at me again, not yet sure of the side where she might put me. "Not in San Berdoo," she said.

She unlocked the top drawer in the steel metal file on the left side of her desk and took out a brown accordion folder. There was a pad of yellow Post-its, a pad of routing slips, and a neat stack of

5 x 8 arrest cards on her blotter. She moved them to the side, put down the folder on its spine and pulled out an 8½ x 11 manila envelope. "The Coroner's report," she said. "Got anything on your stomach besides the peppermint sticks?"

"No," I said, looking for the slightest trace of a smile as she ran her thumbnail under the metal fastener. There wasn't any.

"It's short and to the point," she said, folding the cover sheet over and sliding her left index finger over the crease below the staple. The pages fell into place without much coaxing. She had been through it before, searching the manure pile again and again for the elusive golden pony. Her voice was professional and flat.

"Female caucasian, age 37. Sixty-seven inches in height, one hundred twenty-three pounds in weight after blood loss. Based on state of decomposition, death occurred approximately five weeks prior to discovery and autopsy. Body clothed upon discovery, buried in shallow grave of loose earth. Death occurred as a result of loss of blood, following severing of carotid artery. Instrument used not yet found, possibly a surgical scalpel. Death occurred at a different location than that of the makeshift burial; no significant trace of blood was found at either the burial site or on any of the victim's clothing. Either the clothing was removed prior to the victim's death or cleaned afterwards; alternatively, substitute clothing could have been provided after the death occurred.

"No visible trauma to hands, arms, or legs. No sign of significant struggle on the part of the victim. All fingernails intact. No remaining trace of flesh, blood, or hair beneath the nails. No evidence of significant disease. No evidence of pregnancy and no remaining semen residue or evidence of trauma suggesting sexual violation."

She paused, turned the page, and looked at me blankly. Then she began reading again.

"One other invasion site was found on the body. An even rectangle of flesh measuring seven and one-quarter centimeters by five and one-half centimeters was excised from the victim's left breast. The section excised included the nipple in its entirety and a major portion of the areola."

She looked up. Again the blank stare. "It looks like a censor's strip in an old movie," she said, "right across the nipple. Except it's not so neat anymore, since time and the insects got to her." I felt something seep into my stomach and slowly bubble into my throat. It was bitter and stale. Craig put down the report and spoke.

"What do you think of a murderer who's not happy just taking away his victim's life, but has to cut and mutilate her body too, especially in that way?"

I realized I was clutching my glass, just like Donald Bladen. "This one can't be allowed to walk," I said.

"But first he has to be found," she answered. "I've been looking and I've been thinking. And I've been rereading this report until I have every word memorized. I've looked at the body and at the coroner's photographs of the body. I've touched it and felt it and smelled it. I've gone over it four times looking for things that might have been missed. The lab techs are starting to look at me as if I'm violating this woman all over again. And each time I finish there is still nothing there but what the coroner listed. It's really very simple in its way—a dead woman with a slashed throat. No, not even slashed—neatly sliced. But I keep coming back to that nipple . . . that wasn't necessary. It was gratuitous violence. For the slashed throat he has to die; for the slashed nipple he has to pay.

"But before you can find him you have to understand him and how do you make sense of this? It wasn't a matter of sudden biting and chewing. It was surgical. He lingered over it and enjoyed it, but it was controlled. Why did he feel he had to do that?"

I didn't try to answer the rhetorical question. She continued anyway.

"Why do the freaks always have to add that touch of degradation? Why can't they be satisfied with their victims' deaths; why do they have to grind their feet into their eyes and bite and cut them; why do they have to sodomize them and soil them?"

"I don't know," I said. "The stock answers are never really enough."

"You see that blank wall?" she said.

"Which one?" I said.

"The one across from you, the one directly opposite my desk."

"Yes," I said, turning slightly in its general direction.

"Whoever did this to her I want to see hanging there."

"Maybe there's more than one person involved."

"Better still. I've got lots of wall space left."

FIVE

SHE FINISHED HER COFFEE and calmed down. "Tell you what," she said. "Take an hour and think about this. I've got some paper to clean up here. We'll eat lunch and talk. After you have some time to mull this over and let it sink in I'd like to hear what you think."

"Where?" I asked.

"Down the boulevard . . . a half-mile east. There's a bowling alley. They've got a greasy spoon in the back to help sober up the bowlers before they get back on the highway. The lanes are old and grooved; makes the locals feel like pros. A real dump—you'll probably like it. Nobody'll be there on a weekday. We can talk."

"In an hour . . ." I said.

———

The *Twenty-First Century Lanes* were straight out of 1954. Somebody had tried to dress them up with a bank of recessed fluorescent bulbs and a green neon sign that now crackled like a backyard bug fryer. Two heavily wrinkled sheets of mylar had been placed to the right and left of the alleys, positioned, presumably, to make eighteen strips of paint and wood look like an infinitely receding line of full-family fun. The actual result fell short, since the wrinkles made the half dozen bowlers there look like herky-jerky robots passing in and out of invisible folds of space.

The smell in the air was a blend of chalk dust, flat beer, and smoldering stale tobacco. Everyone on the lanes was wearing multicolored rental shoes with gray velvet numbers stitched across the heels. They all made a point of drying their right hands over the ball-rack fans before inserting their fingers into the balls, taking up their stance, and addressing the pins. It was the only motion they had down pat. They must have seen it on television and figured it would help make more pins fall.

I ordered a Rolling Rock in a bottle. The bartender had to search for awhile to find one. You don't see it often on the coast, but the bar had a display sign over the cash register. He emerged from the cooler like a deep-sea diver just short of the kick-in of the bends; his arm was extended and his hand clutched around the last bottle. Its label was torn and it was covered with white scuffs. When he offered it, I passed on the finger-smudged glass.

I turned around and focused on a young woman who jumped up and down every time she threw a ball that made it the length of the alley without falling into the gutter. When she jumped a lot of interesting things moved. She looked like a younger version of Laura, except that her hair wasn't combed and she was smiling a lot.

When I finished off the Rolling Rock I switched to Coors. A guaranteed supply there. The young bowler threw a 7-10 split and jumped even higher. It was probably the first time she ever knocked down eight pins at once; she spun around immediately and looked to her date for a signal of approval. He handed her his beer and she gave him a kiss. Then she took a drink and kissed him again. He hugged her and let his hand slide down to give her a pat and feel. She didn't seem to mind. There was foam on the side of her mouth, widening her smile.

A minute later when he was busy trying to pick up a 4-7 spare she was standing behind him with her right hand nervously extended over the fan. She was anxious, ready to go again. It probably distracted him but he didn't say anything about it. I figured he wanted to reserve the right to stand right behind her too; the view would be a hell of a lot more interesting than anything else in the bowling alley.

He missed his spare, gave her a pat and squeeze of encouragement, and sat down. She thought long and hard, released the ball, and nicked the 6 pin, taking out the 10 and tickling the 9, which wobbled for a second but finally survived. Her face dropped. From eight pins to a paltry two. So it goes. She still had her long legs and green eyes. For most people that would have been more than enough.

I looked at the bottle in my hand and realized it was empty and time for number three. The bartender already had one open for me and was looking for number four to put on deck. He wasn't counting; the cash register did that. Seeing the stains on his fingers and the waves of circles under his eyes I didn't figure him for the judgmental type.

Lieutenant Craig came in ten minutes later. For a change I looked at *her* legs. I was impressed. "What's that," she said to me, "your fourth or fifth?"

"My third," I said. "Did you bring any mints?"

She just looked at me. "Give me a ginger ale," she said to the bartender.

He handed it to her. When she reached for her wallet inside her purse he waved his hand mechanically. She dropped her arm and took me into the back room. The short order cook and the lone waitress were sitting at the counter, smoking cigarettes and drinking coffee. They were sipping from white china cups with no saucers. Just another thing to wash. The waitress looked up sleepily and the lieutenant said, "Later. Give us a couple of minutes first."

She took a long drink of her ginger ale and asked, "You like women who take charge, Grant?"

"Depends," I said.

"On what—whether you're at work or in bed?"

"No. On whether or not they know what they're doing—wherever they happen to be."

"Good answer," she said. "Buy you a fourth beer?"

"Sure," I said.

She signaled the waitress and ordered a beer and a second ginger ale. When she came back with them a few minutes later we ordered sandwiches and coffee.

"So tell me," she said. "What do you think?"

Suddenly the taste of death and decay was back in my throat. "I think Cynthia Bladen had too little luck and too much pain."

SIX

"And that's it?" she said. "I give you an hour and that's all you come up with?"

"Well, what is there really?" I asked. "You get a lot of breast mutilators with mother problems, but they're not usually satisfied with simple cutting. They want to bite and chew, like you said. Remember the case of the guy in Oakland?"

"Lawrence Galvin."

"Right. His mother didn't wean him until he was, what, two and a half? He used to walk around next to her trying to nurse, stretching and reaching like an abandoned calf. Suddenly she found a new boyfriend, gave the kid a plastic glass, and told him to piss off. He didn't take it too well. Finally he got old enough and big enough to do something about it.

"His file at Quantico is as thick as the Northern Virginia yellow pages. They never get tired of studying him. Textbook case. He went after every woman who resembled her. He couldn't stop killing her and he always took out his revenge with his teeth."

"I know. But people like Lawrence Galvin tend to be savage. They don't surgically remove a neat rectangle of skin. When they get finished with their victims they look as if they've been set upon by pit bulls and Dobermans."

"Only one of a number of problems," I said, "not the least of which is the fact that it looks like something that was planned and executed very carefully, not an act done in a flash of rage or madness."

"But there *is* a pattern," Craig said. "Look at the clean dress. You've got to take great pains to keep the blood off when you're slashing a throat. Either you go straight to One-Hour Martinizing after you're done or you strip the victim naked first. There's no alternative. Either way, the killer had to also give her a bath after he was finished."

"Right. It was planned down to the last detail."

"So he could enjoy it."

"Yes, I think so," I said. "Maybe he's a stalker. He watches and waits and thinks. There's also the obvious fact that Cynthia couldn't be the killer's actual mother. Her children are in nursery school. Assuming a killer in his twenties or thirties, Cynthia would have had to look something like what the killer's mother *used* to look like. Unless, of course, his mother was very well preserved."

"Or *her* mother," Craig said. "Don't rule out the possibility that we're dealing with a woman."

"Right. We haven't even opened *that* door," I said. "Mothers and daughters . . . not always a pretty picture, though they don't usually go so far as to slice off nipples."

"Mother-daughter stuff runs deep," Craig said.

"Damn right. You know Mary, as in *William and Mary*?"

"Colonial Williamsburg, right?"

"Right. She was the wife of the new king but the daughter of the deposed king; that meant she succeeded her own mother."

"So?"

"Well, right after the English gave James II a one-way ticket to France and invited William of Orange to take over the job, his wife Mary did something she had obviously been anxious to do for a long time—she walked into the palace and sat herself down on her mother's throne, took a deep breath and gloated like a son-of-a-bitch. Not that her majesty would express it in quite those terms. Mothers and daughters, lieutenant."

"How did you know *that*?"

"When I'm not swimming in vats of peppermint oil I read history."

"Not bad," she said.

"Thank you," I said, surprised by the fact that she was actually capable of giving a compliment. I didn't respond at first, but instead continued to look at her, and slowly came to the realization that I was actually staring into the lieutenant's large brown eyes. I tried my best not to make it too obvious, but I wasn't sure that I had succeeded.

Craig signaled the waitress for a refill on the coffee. She lumbered over, poured us each a cup, and asked us a second time if we wanted any half-and-half. We said no and she walked back to the counter. On this pass I saw her name tag: *Libby*. Craig just nodded her head, tried the coffee, and started to ask me about Cynthia.

"Does it hurt to talk about this?" she asked.

"Truth?"

"That's the deal."

"Yes," I said. "As a matter of fact it does."

"Good. That'll help you remember."

"I thought people blocked out things that caused them pain."

"Only in the movies," she said. "In real life the pain focuses the memory. You go over the same ground again and again, trying to change it, trying to understand it, trying to hold on to what was good."

"You sound like an expert," I said.

"On what—memory or pain?"

"On both."

"I do pain," she said. "You can help me with the memory."

SEVEN

I HADN'T SEEN ANYONE drink as much black coffee in one sitting as Craig did since I was an active member of the peacetime army. I suddenly remembered the specially engraved coffee mugs and the homemade ashtrays fabricated from sawed-off 105 shells with .50 calibre rounds welded to the centers. Before claymore mines were taken out of the army's inventory, commanders and first sergeants would put them at the edge of their desks with the words **Front to Enemy** facing any visitors who happened to stumble into the day room.

Craig was drinking with a cup and saucer, not a stain-encrusted mug, but her fingers were perfectly steady and she was holding every ounce like an industrial-strength sponge.

I had switched over to ice water. Libby wasn't very happy about the fact that she had had to go back to the fountain to get something that wouldn't generate an additional tip. She brought it in a malt glass: insurance against the prospect of her having to make a return trip.

"So tell me about Cynthia Bladen," Craig said.

"I'll tell you what I know," I said. "We dated for awhile, but the legal fast-track kept taking her in too many different directions, all of them at break-neck speeds. We got along well enough; we just didn't have that much in common. Once upon a time her father had been wealthy, but his empire started to unravel and he fell on much tougher times than he had ever expected. When he made his hard landing it was at a level that would have looked good to most people, but to him it looked like the slime pit beneath rock-bottom. He gathered what was left of his hopes and dreams and put them all on Cynthia. She was determined to live up to them and that didn't leave much time for me."

"No boys in the family, huh?"

"No. She had a younger sister, as I recall. Her people were all back east. By the time I met her she was out of law school and four or five years into an associate's job. She didn't have much time for family reunions. I never really met any of the members of her family. I talked on the phone once or twice to her mother."

"Where did you meet?"

"In court, actually. I do some work for an insurance company and her firm was representing us. I was giving her information and evidence."

"And goo-goo eyes."

I hadn't heard that expression in awhile. "No," I said, "not initially. It was all strictly business."

"Don't bullshit me, Grant. You're a fast-mover. What did you do, offer her a peppermint stick?"

She was smiling. Noticeably.

"No, nothing like that. We had to meet, so we met over breakfast and lunch. After awhile we moved on to dinner."

"And late-night snacks," Craig said.

"Yes. And late-night snacks."

Now the smile was saying *Naughty, naughty*, but the tone of voice was saying, *You're as innocent as a sheltered schoolgirl at the Convent of the Sacred Heart.*

"So you just stopped seeing one another?"

"Yes. We had a farewell dinner and that was it."

"I figured you for the roses and rituals type. I like a man who stays in character. Very sweet." The eyes were saying *What a chump. It cost you 140 bucks and you didn't even get a farewell bounce.* I thought about saying something but let it go.

"So tell me about the *person*," she said.

"I don't really know what to say, beyond the obvious pieties," I said. "Why don't you ask me questions."

"OK. How dark was her dark side?"

"What makes you think she had one?"

"Everybody does. I told you—don't bullshit me."

"If she did, I didn't see it," I said. "I can't imagine her with some double life that finally caught up with her, if that's what you mean—rough trade and leather, dating spankers and piercers, that sort of thing. Besides . . . ."

She didn't let me finish. "Let me ask you something else—how solid was her marriage?"

"I don't know. I assume it was fine. Remember—I hadn't seen her for over seven years. Her husband certainly resents the hell out of me for not getting to her before the killer did. When we talked, his emotions seemed honest enough. Let me put it this way—until

I see something to change my mind I'll keep working on the assumption that she mattered to him. You can never *really* tell, of course."

"She may have mattered to *him* a lot more than he mattered to her."

"That's always a possibility."

"How emotional was she?"

"She was a lawyer. She could turn it off and on."

She sipped her coffee, stared at me, and shook her head. "I can't figure this," she said.

"Can't figure what?"

"I can't figure out what you saw in her. Here you are, sitting in a bowling alley, throwing back longnecks of Coors. Probably sneaking some scooters on the side too. I can't imagine the lady lawyer hanging out with your sort. Or vice-versa. She sounds like an ice princess in a tweed suit."

"The bowling alley was your idea," I said, "and what makes you think I don't like ice princesses in tweed suits? Throw in a 9 mm automatic and I could get real interested."

She gave me the hint of a smile. "Plus the tits," she said. "Don't forget them."

"And let's not forget the tidy office either," I said, as the smile started to break through.

EIGHT

"OK," she said. "We've got a career-driven Girl Scout in a stable marriage with kids, cottage, picket fence, and a collie that could stunt-double for Lassie. We've got no history of deviance, not even any evidence of extracurricular slap-and-tickle. She's a litigator who handles white collars and she's active in her church. She carries white gloves in her purse, makes contributions to her alumni association, buys magazine subscriptions from the kids going door to door, probably drinks herbal tea, and doesn't even shake hands good-night until at least the third date. What do you bet she drives a Country Squire with a Lisa Simpson doll suction-cupped to the rear window?"

"Alum*nae* association," I said. "And she drove a Volvo wagon."

"Jesus, Grant, you amaze me. You actually dated a woman who drove a *Volvo*. What did you eat for your kissoff dinner—sprouts, seeds, and Boston lettuce?"

She didn't wait for me to answer.

"This is a woman whose idea of intimacy is letting somebody else play her recorder without wiping off the mouthpiece. She'd never get into trouble on her own. The whole thing spells *random violence* in gold neon letters, and you know what? I don't believe a single word of it."

I was watching her finger at the edge of her coffee cup. Most people would trace circles nervously. She just held it there, then slowly took a sip. She was wound tight but she tried not to show it.

"Why don't you think it was random?" I asked.

"Because there's far too much work invested in it—the care taken in the 'surgery,' if that's what you want to call it, the burial, the long drive, the blood-free body, the fact that she was clothed when the Mexican kids found her. Especially the blood-free body. I keep coming back to that . . . add it all up and tell me what you get."

"*Planning*. Something twisted, something we don't understand at this point, but something the killer obviously *did* understand. He understood it well. We've got to get into *his* head if we're ever going to understand it in anything like the same way that he did. And no way is this going to be a cakewalk. Nothing's going to jump out at us. We're not going to get a magic call. We're not going to find an eyeball witness and we're definitely not going to find a file drawer full of precedents and parallels. This one's going to be unique."

She didn't answer.

"Right?" I said.

"Maybe not," she answered.

NINE

"You think this'll be easy?"

"I don't know yet," she answered. "It could be a lot simpler than it looks."

"Where do we start then?"

"Look, Grant, I'm not even sure I want to work with you," she said. Suddenly I wondered what happened to the smiles and jokes.

"You don't even know me," I answered.

"The hell I don't."

"How could you?" I asked.

"I do my homework," she said.

"Wait a minute, who's bullshitting who?"

"Who's bullshitting anybody? You make an appointment to see me. I do some checking and find out who you are. I got a friend at the *Times*; he runs a check through the newspaper morgues; I find out you're a smart guy and maybe even something of a triple-A league hero. Then I meet you and you're gargling Listermint. What cop or PI does that, except a drunk? I can't work with a drunk, Grant. So I'm a little guarded. I hold back for awhile. The longer you talk the smarter you sound. I'm thinking maybe you're sobering up."

"So what else did you find out about me?"

"That you're a fortysomething retired Army light colonel who caught some shrapnel in Vietnam. Your right leg's never been the same since. You came here a few years back, put a PI ad in the phone book, took on some rough stuff at first, and then settled in with a steady-ticket insurance company. How much more do you want to hear?"

"How much more do you know?"

She started right in as if I had clicked the tape machine start button. "You've been dating a lady doc, a surgeon as I remember. That's from a friend at the LAPD, by the way. The *Times* isn't onto your love life yet, though it would make a good story. First a lady lawyer, now a lady doc. 'What's Grant's problem? Enquiring minds want to know.' He's got a thing for professional women—maybe they're a little out of his reach?"

I let that go. It wasn't the first time it had been said to me.

"Not that I'm trying to hurt your feelings or anything," she said. "I'm just making an observation."

"Your information's out of date," I said.

"Yes, why's that?"

"I just had an operation on my leg. It's still sore, but this time it looks as if they might have done some good."

"Really? What are you going to do to impress the professional women now that you can't get their sympathy with that limp?"

"Good question," I said. "Got any ideas?"

"Sure. For starters, stop feeling so goddamned sorry for yourself."

"What makes you think I feel sorry for myself?"

"All men do," she said, smiling again. "That's *generic* advice."

TEN

"Not to belabor the point, but I broke up with the lady doc," I said.

"And that's why you've been drinking your breakfast—because of her?"

"You're the one who said I appear to be sober. I think you even used the word *smart*."

"Army guys always learn how to mask it. It's part of the Basic Officer Course."

"You know a lot about the Army, don't you?"

"I know a lot about guys who drink," she said. "What happened with the doc?"

"I said something that made her angry."

"You did? What was that?"

"I just made a comment," I said, "the kind of thing anyone might say. For some reason it hit her hard."

"It must have been good," she said. "Tell me."

"It wasn't that much. All I said was that when you're dating you talk about love and romance. When you marry you talk about drapes and lawn services and driveway dressings."

"She figured you were trying to back out of marrying her."

"Not necessarily. It was just an observation. Not something about her in particular, just something about marriage. It was something I wouldn't have wanted to see happen—not if we *had* decided to get married."

"But she took it personally."

"Yes, as a matter of fact, but why should she? She's not some Southern belle with a hoop skirt, bonnet, and airhead drawl. She's a practicing surgeon. She spends her days rooting around in lungs and spleens and bowels. She wears gloves that are splattered with blood and she watches med students and interns faint and gag and puke all over themselves. It's not like I was dishing out a dose of reality that she couldn't handle. It was a simple sociological observation."

"And it was *true*," Craig said.

"That's right," I said. "That's *exactly* what I said."

"Of course you said it. I'd have been disappointed if you hadn't."

"So what does that mean? That all men are alike?"

"You're sweet," she said, with a smile that could have done as much damage as one of Laura's scalpels. She took another sip of her coffee and looked at me, waiting for a response.

"I mean it. What are you saying?"

"Look," she said. "We can make this long or we can make it short. If we make it long it's only going to hurt more. Sometimes people look for an occasion to say something they've been wanting to say for a long time but couldn't."

"You're saying that she wanted to split from me, but was looking for the right moment. The overreaction to the comment about drapes and driveways was her way of solving her problem. It was there. It was convenient. She didn't really believe what she was saying; she was just taking the opportunity when it presented itself."

"You really *are* sweet," she said. "That's why I love men. So needy. So frail. You *have* to believe that what you said was true, don't you? Sure, she wanted to split; that happens all the time. It's serious but not fatal. Fatal would be . . . ."

"My being *wrong*?"

"Like I said . . . sweet. And I bet you think I'm being . . . ."

She pulled out her pen, wrote something on the back of the cocktail napkin that came with her ginger ale, and held it to her chest so I couldn't read it.

"As long as you've asked, I think the word is *patronizing*."

She handed me the napkin. She had lettered the word CONDESCENDING in capitals. "Close enough for government work," she said. "How about a drink?"

"I'll pass," I said.

"I *do* like you," she said. "A little cut and you recover right away. You thought the drink offer was a test and you knew you'd rather be right, even it meant you had to be sober."

"And you're saying that all men are like that?"

"No. Most of them would take the drink. Pity for her that she let you get away. There really aren't enough good ones to go around, you know. To be honest, though, I don't think it was just the class thing. It was also the age difference."

"The age difference wasn't that great. She was thirty-s*even*."

"Thirty-eight, actually. I thought you were a historian, Grant."

"I am, of sorts. And she *was* thirty-seven."

"I know she was," Craig said. "That was a bluff. The age difference mattered to *you* though. That's perfectly obvious. She must have picked up on it."

"How old are you?"

"How old do you think?"

"No answering of questions with questions," I said. "I've told you the truth. That's the deal. Now it's your turn."

"I'll tell you," she said, "but I'd just like to hear your guess."

"Thirty-seven," I said.

"Vengeful too," she said, as her eyebrows rose and her smile turned at the corners. "I didn't expect *that* from you. I'm thirty-four."

"I actually figured thirty with points off for lack of sleep," I said.

"I knew you were lying. Men don't really know how to do it. Besides, the real question isn't the years; it's whether or not the years really matter."

"The years always matter," I said, "but they don't have to stop you."

I was waiting for an answer but it came with the eyes. She was staring at me as if she could see all the way inside and whatever it was she saw there seemed to interest her.

ELEVEN

"All right," I said. "We've picked over Cynthia Bladen's corpse and you've sliced and carved me. I think it's time now for me to hear something about you and I don't want it to be that you've got to get back to work."

"I *am* at work," she said, "what did you think this was?"

"I'm not sure."

"What do you want to know? I told you my age. You know what I do for a living."

"What's your first name, for starters."

"Diana."

"Perfect."

"Why?"

"The huntress."

"You think I'm a hunter?"

"A hunt*ress*."

"I don't have the luxury of caring about the way other people end nouns," she said. "Your ex-squeeze, the doc—she's the type who would care about that. Cynthia Bladen would have cared about it. I get called so many ugly things in the course of the day that I'm happy if every now and then one or two of them isn't vulgar or obscene."

"I doubt you take it that easily," I said. "I see you as the type who would skip the soapy mouthwash and go straight for the kidney punches and groin kicks—give them something that will help them remember. Maybe even persuade them to mend their ways."

"I won't say that it hasn't happened," she said.

"I bet not," I said. "Finally we're making some progress. How long have you been doing this?"

"Eight years, two as a lieutenant."

"You moved up damned fast."

"Fast enough to make a lot of other people angry."

"You know what we say in the Army, of course."

"Fuck 'em if they can't take a joke?" she answered.

"No. We say that exceptions can always be made for exceptional people."

"That was a trap," she said.

"Yes, well, I thought it was about time I had a turn. Where were you before San Berdoo?"

"It's not a very pretty story."

"Who would have thought otherwise?" I said, and signaled the waitress. It took about fifteen seconds for the various parts of her body to move together with sufficient coordination to get her up on her feet. She put her cigarette in the ashtray, sighed, and walked toward us. Craig asked for another refill on the coffee and I said I'd switch from ice water to ginger ale. That seemed to make the waitress happy. Fifteen percent of ninety cents is better than nothing.

"You sure you want to hear this?" she asked.

"Of course. It's your turn," I said.

"All right. I was born in Paramus, New Jersey, but grew up in northern Virginia. My father was getting tired of commuting into Manhattan and decided to put his name on the lists of several local headhunting firms. One of them got him a serious promotion and in turn took back what must have been a very nice fee. We moved to the Washington area, to a place just inside the Fairfax County line. He worked for a Beltway bandit firm, doing engineering work. He computed trajectories on missiles . . . that kind of thing. He was the guy who was responsible for developing the definition of *throw-weight* that both the Russian and the American arms negotiators could actually agree on. Very important, I suppose, but his work was always a snorer to the rest of the family. Whenever he started talking about the technical details of what it was that he did we conked out instantly.

"Anyway, there wasn't a whole lot that he was allowed to talk about outside of the office, and the two of us were never as close as we should have been. I got into other things—and not exactly the kind you'd see in the junior high yearbook. My parents sent me off to a military prep school that had recently gone co-ed. Very with-it for those days. It was called the Lynchburg Academy—near Appomattox actually, a few miles east off of 460."

"I've been down there," I said. "Not often, but once or twice when I was stationed in Washington."

"It's pretty enough," she said. "I got passing grades, did some fencing and got into small-bore rifle. My father was pleased and wanted me to go to West Point. He actually got as far as persuading a senator to promise me an appointment, but I disappointed both of them by refusing to go unless the Army would guarantee me the chance to join a combat branch and do some real soldiering. That ended it instantly, of course. The Army doesn't play that guarantee shit and I don't play the sidelines."

"So where did you go?"

"I don't like to even mention the name," she said. "I hated every day of it. After I graduated I tried some jobs but none of them worked out. I lasted one semester as a high school phys ed instructor. The principal (a married man with thinning hair, bad grammar, and a closet full of leisure suits), asked me if I'd like to go out for a drink with him some time. While I was thinking of a suitably direct response he tried to force his hand inside my tee shirt."

"What did you do, drop-kick him into the gym risers?"

"No, I actually broke his wrist and then three fingers. I figured if I kicked or kneed him he'd walk funny for awhile but then get over it. I wanted him to carry the memory longer and have to answer a lot of questions about it."

"And you were fired."

"Of course. I could have brought charges against him, but it was his word against mine and I already had enough demerits to prejudice the case against me. I moved on to a job running a gas station in Ballston; it's a suburb—two metro stops or so from downtown Washington."

"I know where it is," I said. "Where the Thai and Vietnamese restaurants are. Where the yuppies are settling."

"Yeah, exactly. It was a Texaco station. I was supervising three Iranians and two Iraqi ex-Army types. I guess Saddam would have considered them defectors. As far as I was concerned they all still acted like they were on active duty. I spent most of my time trying to separate the five of them. We also had constant theft problems—I could never figure out who was guilty, the employees or the customers. It started with the 12-packs of Sprite and Diet Coke and moved on to the cigarettes and evergreen air fresheners. We had one guy who was actually sort of fun. At the end of each island we had a can of de-gas freshener. It fit in this bracket and after you pumped gas or checked your oil you could spray some on your hands and it took away the gas smell or at least masked it with some heavy perfume odor. Anyway, this one guy kept driving in and stealing the damned things. I chased him once or twice but he was really quick. I asked one of the Iranians why anybody would do that and he told me that the guy was probably using the de-gas as a cologne. He told me that a lot of people did that. Anyway, I got tired of constantly filling out police reports and insurance claims and looked for something else to do."

"This sounds like a pretty checkered career," I said.

"No debate there," she said. "At least I could show 'progressive responsibility' on my resume. My next job was supervising a marina in Selby Bay, Maryland. I lasted one season and about half of one winter. I had these four drunks with time shares on a 48-foot Hatteras they couldn't really afford. Two of them (*Roy* and *Lou*) came on to me one day and I told them to get lost. They weren't in the habit of taking no for an answer, so I threw them off the pier and into the Bay. The water temperature was about 40 degrees, maybe 39. For some reason it made them angry. They brought in a lawyer and the owner immediately settled with them by agreeing to fire me."

"Is that why you got into police work—to start righting some of these wrongs?"

"In a way," she said. "Actually, I had this job while I was in college, one of the few I ever enjoyed, and after I threw the dickheads into the Bay and was looking around for something new it suddenly hit me. I could go back to police work."

"You worked as a cop while you were in college?"

"No, not exactly," she said. "I worked for this woman who was a photographer. Her name was Reynolds. Actually her name was Alexa Anne Reynolds and she had two separate operations going. As A. A. Reynolds she did kiddie photography. In good times she worked for Bachrach and Olan Mills, in tight times she worked for Sears and K-Mart. She had another set of business cards though, with the title Lexa Reynolds, Investigations. Actually, what she did was take pictures for divorce lawyers, PIs, and congressional staffers."

"I can see a certain commonality in that group," I said.

"Right. She was in Old Town Alexandria, near the marina and the restaurants, just below National Airport, and close to the Wilson bridge and the roadhouses and massage parlors of southern Maryland. You talk about the importance of *location* . . . she'd catch all the sinners—going in and out of town, going in and out of other peoples' boats, going in and out of the wrong apartments, going in and out of upscale restaurants with the wrong people, and sometimes just going in and out."

"And you were her assistant."

"Bingo. Actually I lived there too. She had space above her studio and darkroom that she gave rent-free to college students. They took turns working for her in exchange for their rooms. They answered phones, set up appointments, filed negatives, contact prints, invoices, whatever. There were five of us, four with cutesy names: Jason, Gina, Gemma, and Jordan. Lexa could never remember their names, so she called them by their hair color: 'Red,' 'Sandy,' 'Brownie,' and 'Brownie II.'

"What did she call you, Blackie?"

"She called me Diana."

"She remembered your name. You must have made an impression."

"I went out with her on cases; I didn't do the office scut work. Huddling in a small car on a stake-out or lying together in a high stand of beach grass while your subject is drinking martinis and the local mosquitoes are carving out territory on your legs and neck tends to bring people together. At the time I didn't think it was all that great, but a couple years later it started to look different. One night Lexa and I were grinding away with our motor drives and we got within one frame of catching Teddy Kennedy in a picture that would have made even his Cambridge constituents blush. If we had only been shooting at 1/500th of a second . . ."

I held up my glass as if to toast her. "Sometimes life is little more than a succession of missed opportunities."

"Right," she said. "Anyway, I remembered how much fun it was, even when you just came close, so I came out here to San Berdoo and took the police exam."

"Why here?"

"I wanted to do serious crime; I figured I'd go where the work was."

"You could have stayed in Washington or gone to Miami."

"I know. I thought about that, but I wanted to keep the sun and ditch the humidity. The sun was a must. You get a clearer look at the sin and when the bad guys go down you see everything they're leaving in their faces and eyes. So what if you're living in some shithole and get sent to jail; that may be the best place in town to spend the night. It isn't here. Here you see the wiseasses strutting down the boulevards and twirling their sunglasses—then you watch their expressions after you've spread them across the fender of your cruiser and tightened the cuffs."

"And you enjoy that."

"You bet your . . . yes, I enjoy that."

"On this case you might really have the chance to put away someone deserving."

"I know," she said. "You could help . . . if you're up for the small cars and the high grass."

I didn't respond to that.

"There's only one thing," she said.

"What's that?"

"How do you feel about cases where you're personally involved with the victim?"

"They're the only kind you should take. The emotional stakes give you the edge."

"But they bring the greatest pain," she said.

"Yes," I said, "but to whom?"

TWELVE

At some point in our conversation, I wasn't sure just when, I started to look at Diana Craig as intently as I had been listening to her.

Her hair was black and thick. She wore it short and tight but the natural curl added some body and some style. The army would have called it *serviceable*, but it was more than that. Her brown eyes were clear, polished marble, not like a floor in a bank or office building, but more like the prize stones ten-year-old boys carried in their pockets and showed to jealous friends. She had a small nose and a well-formed mouth, neither trendy-full nor thin-lipped and shrill. If you tried to stick a collagen needle into her lip she'd probably bite it off.

She wore very little makeup. I couldn't tell whether her cheeks were tinted with blush or if the peach-pink color was the result of sun and exercise. Her fingers were manicured but not daubed with colored polish. She wore very little jewelry: a gold ring with modest filigree, a simple gold necklace, and small gold post earrings.

I don't know why, but when I look at a woman's crossed legs I always tend to notice whether or not her knees turn white when they're bent. Diana Craig's didn't.

Her posture was good: businesslike but not stiff. I liked the way she carried herself, telegraphing self-assurance and balancing three or four pounds of gun, holster, clip, and cartridges as easily as she carried soft, full breasts and a set of hips that looked as if they would be more at home on a stretch of Laguna Beach than planted in a wooden chair behind a desk covered with forms, paperclips, and stacks of pictures of people who enjoyed doing bodily harm to their fellow man. Or fellow woman.

"So how long do we go on with this psychobabble?" she asked.

"You don't like to *share*? Is that what you're saying?"

"No, I just don't like to talk about myself."

"That's too bad, because I want to ask you one more question," I said.

She frowned. "Remember," she said, "just because I said I wouldn't lie didn't mean I'd answer everything you wanted to ask."

"I understand that," I said. "This is an easy one."

"Go ahead," she said, already bored.

"It's an obvious question: I was wondering whether or not you had ever been married."

"Did I mention marriage when I answered your question about what I did before I came to San Berdoo?"

"No."

"You think I'm holding out on you?"

"I didn't say that."

"I haven't been married," she said. "You have though, haven't you?"

"How can you tell?"

"It's all in the way you talk to a woman."

"What do you mean?"

"Never mind."

"Come on."

"No. I never give away anything I might need later. How long were you married?"

"Twelve years. Before I came to L.A."

"Why did you split?"

"She died. I didn't have a choice."

Most people would have come back with an immediate "Oh, I'm so sorry," accompanied by red cheeks and embarrassed eyes. Diana Craig held her bemused look and sipped her coffee. "What happened to her?" she finally said.

"She was a casualty of the war."

"Is that different from being a casualty in the war?"

"Yes," I said.

"Are you going to tell me the story or just sit there and make me ask again?"

It wasn't something I usually talked about. "I was in the field in Vietnam. She was back in Washington. She needed to reach me because of a family emergency, but she couldn't get through. The Army kept dodging her calls, telling her that I was fine but that the operation in which I was involved was highly classified. She was down on the mall, trying to call the Pentagon for the eighth or ninth time. A mugger went for her purse; she started to resist, and he stabbed her. That was the reconstruction anyway. A simple enough event. Happened all the time there."

She finished off the coffee and slid the cup and saucer out of her way. Then she paused and stared at me for what must have been a full minute. "So tell me, Grant," she said, "you lost your wife, you lost your lady lawyer, and you lost your lady doc. Now somebody's gone and killed the lady lawyer before you could even see her again. The past was pretty bad to begin with, but now somebody's going back and carving out pieces of it. Carving out things you remember and then destroying them. What do you say? Does that make you angry enough to help me catch this piece of shit?"

I didn't respond right away. She had slid her hand to the spoon resting on her napkin and was grasping it tightly. I could see the ridges in her knuckles redden.

She focused on me harder and changed her tone to something just this side of ugly. "Maybe even take a seat and watch the governor's people strap this asshole down on the gurney, see him jump when they put the big needle in, watch them turn the little knob and start the poison flowing? I don't know about you, but I don't like to sit back and watch creeps and defectives keep doing these kinds of things to women. I think it's gone on long enough. I used to just lock them up and turn them over to the lawyers. Most of the time nothing ever happened. Now I want to make sure they don't get out and start in again. I want to be in the front row. I want to be right up against the glass where I can see how much they enjoy being on the receiving end. What about you? Would you like to join me?"

I paused and stared at her before speaking. "It's a date," I said.

THIRTEEN

THREE MONTHS AGO I did a small job for a company called Arcadia Shade and Shutter. They had a penny-ante embezzler named Roy Coehlo who was shuffling invoices and merchandise. The boss was a widow named Helen Calder. She asked me to place a complicated order and then change it a couple of times—to make it easy for Coehlo to diddle with the paper trail and take back a piece for himself. Then she asked me to check out his accounting and to be prepared to testify against him if and when the case went to court.

It was a quickie. People like him fall apart faster than a Ford Pinto. The only surprise in all of it was the retail value of Helen Calder's merchandise. I knew you had to hand over your first-born and three pints of blood in order to buy drapes, but thus far in my adult life I had been spared the details of the wonderful world of shades, shutters, and vertical blinds. Helen Calder was already in financial straits because of the hit caused by Roy Coehlo's rip-offs, but the current Southern California economy had made the situation even worse. After we sent Roy away she gave me a hot cup of coffee and a warm thank you. Then she asked me if I'd be willing to consider taking out my fee in trade.

I said, "What the hell, why not?" I'd been watching L.A. noir movies all my life and lately I'd been wondering how I could actually function as a PI without having slatted shadows fall across my office walls. I hadn't yet worked my way up to the bottle of rye in the corner desk drawer, but with the help of Roy Coehlo and Helen Calder I finally got venetian blinds. And none of that cream-colored tin shit. Mine are real oak, the kind that would normally cost slightly more than two months' rent. Per window.

I was twisting the rod that controlled the set behind my desk, lightening and darkening the room and thinking about Diana Craig and Cynthia Bladen. I find that it's best to play with the blinds in early morning or late afternoon. The sun is most interesting then. It also helps if you have important things to do and are looking for a solid excuse to avoid doing them. That's when you log the best time on the control stick.

Not that there was much that I could do. I had already talked to Donald Bladen and there were no other plausible suspects. Diana Craig was operating the power levers, searching for anything that could reasonably be considered suspicious in Cynthia's private and professional life and hoping that luck might rear its rarely seen head and offer us some physical evidence that hadn't yet been turned.

I took my hand off the blinds rod for a second and called Frank White.

Frank is an LAPD robbery/homicide lieutenant. Tall and black, with the neck, arms, and chest of a Russian weight-lifter, Frank generally greets breakers of the law with all the warmth and understanding of a Raiders' free safety making contact with an interloping wide receiver.

I asked him about Diana Craig.

"I know her," he said. "A San Berdoo legend. She's been assigned the Bladen case, hasn't she?"

"Were you the one who told her all about me?"

"Would I do something like that?" Frank asked.

"Of course you would," I said.

"No comment," he answered, laughing.

"What's the local book on her?" I asked.

"Craig? Smart as hell and even more aggressive. She set a record for promotion to lieutenant. It wasn't in the works long—more like a battlefield promotion."

"Tell me about it," I said.

"Easier for me to describe than for her to do," he said. "Nasty shit from the beginning—a busted drug deal involving rival gangs and double-crosses all around. Everybody trying to screw everybody else, with an automatic pistol in each hand, knives in their pockets, a couple of Army surplus M60 machine guns in their arsenals (among other things), and, needless to say, no regard for any of the civilians in the area. One of the son-of-a-bitches even had a functioning flamethrower. This was your basic contemporary urban war."

"What happened?" I asked.

"The San Berdoo cops encircled the battlefield—a pair of facing warehouses. The deal was supposed to go down in the side street between them, but each side set up in advance inside the buildings. As soon as the war started, the available cops moved in and surrounded the buildings, but there was too much firepower on either side to make any kind of successful charge. Also, the mayor didn't want the buildings blown up because of the civilians in the surrounding neighborhood."

"One Philadelphia is enough," I said.

"Right. Anyway, Craig went up on the roof of one of the buildings and started dropping concussion grenades and tear-gas canisters down the chimneys and vent shafts. Needless to say, this pissed off the occupants, who came up on the roof looking for revenge. Craig picked them off one at a time with her automatic. I should say her automatics; she was carrying two at the time."

"John Wayne lives, and just when you need him most."

"That's right," Frank said.

"What about the other building?"

"That was trickier. The other gang must have seen and heard what was happening to their playmates and decided to head for the basement. They found a rear door that opened onto a loading dock a floor below street level. Their leader—this dick called Chico—looked out and saw a set of squad cars. He started yelling and threatening to spray a local apartment building with his M60 if anybody tried to stop him and his friends from leaving the scene unharmed.

"By now Craig was back down from the roof. She told the uniforms to let Chico pass and even offered him a squad car if he'd promise not to shoot into the apartment windows. She then directed one of the uniforms to drive his car up to the steps leading to the loading dock and turn his vehicle over to the punks. Chico took the keys, said something obscene to Craig and laughed; then he slapped the driver of the black-and-white on the side of his face with the butt of an automatic pistol as he got out of the car. Then he stepped over him and got into the car with his three friends. They slammed the doors and Craig immediately jumped off of the loading dock and onto the roof of the car. They started firing through the roof but she was already off of it, pumping 9 mm rounds through a side window. It was a calculated risk, but it paid off. Chico was the only one who survived. He came out of the car cursing, flailing, and gurgling blood. She clothes-lined him in the throat with her fist and arm and he hit the pavement like a dazed professional wrestler."

"She sounds like your kind of officer, Frank."

"Right. Plus she's got hips that would stop traffic and the kind of chest that the plastic surgeons promise but seldom deliver. Not that I usually make offensive sexist observations like that. I'm simply reporting Jerry Dailey's judgment." (Jerry is Frank's med tech: one-third polyester, one-third state-of-the-art forensic science, and one-third hyperventilating libido.)

"Jerry's a filthy sexist pig," I said, " . . . with acute powers of observation."

"Among his other strengths," Frank added. "So I take it you approve of our Lieutenant Craig?"

"I do like her," I said. "Have you had a lot of dealings with her on the case?"

"Just preliminary stuff so far. She faxed me a request a few minutes ago. I was working on it when you called. She wants me to check and see how many recent homicides we've had that involved breast mutilation, recent being defined as anything in the last five years."

"We talked about it, but couldn't come up with a damned thing. The killer looks like a psycho with mother problems, but manifesting it like a kid in a basement with a science kit. There's obviously more involved here than simple sex and anger, but what, I don't know."

"A real Mr. Wizard, huh? Remember that guy, Jack? He's back again. I was trying to get CNN on cable Saturday morning and there he was—lifting all this heavy shit with a little string and some pulleys, then tossing sodium into water and listening for the bang. He also had his old tried-and-true specialty—dipping a rod into a glass of acid and asking his poor little ga-ga sidekick if he wanted to taste it. And, you know, it never fails to work. The kid looks at him like he's out of his mind. Taste *acid?* Screw that, Science-Man. Watch my tongue dissolve and my lips shrivel up and my chin disappear? No freaking way.

"And you know what, Jack?—the old boy hasn't aged a day. How do those guys do it? I mean, he was rolling up his sleeves and grinning into the camera ten years before I got thrown out of high school Physics class for blowing up old man Harrison's Wilson Cloud Chamber."

"It's the television, Frank. It makes you look fatter and the added weight evens out all the wrinkles."

"Who told you that?"

"Mr. Wizard, Frank. Didn't I tell you? I'm a fan."

"Jesus," he said. "I'm *defenseless.*"

"You know what?" I said, changing the tone.

"What, Jack?"

"So was Cynthia Bladen."

"I know. Terrible. And so damned weird. We get plenty of mutilations, of course. That's nothing new. It's the tidy workmanship that nobody can figure out. We'll keep checking. You never know what might turn up. A look into these files is always like a fresh tour of hell."

———

"So how's Marie?" I asked, changing the subject. "Have you seen her lately?" Marie is Frank's ex. She anchors the weekend news and does special projects for Channel 7. After several years apart they had started dating again.

"*Lately* is a relative term with Marie. I talked to her a week and a half ago. We went out once last month. She took two calls during dinner and passed on the rest of the evening."

"What's wrong with these modern women? They don't know good men when they see them."

"Still nothing from Laura?"

"No, I'm not going to hear from her. That's not Laura's style and I know if I called her I'd be wasting my time. Besides, I think I'll try for Lieutenant Craig. If she doesn't want me she'll probably maim or kill me, so I won't have any problems in the future anyway."

"You think she's interested in men?"

"Why not?"

"No reason. She just doesn't seem like the type."

"She managed to sit with me for an hour and a half today without showing any visible signs of discomfort."

"Remember, she's *tough*."

"And armed. But don't lose any sleep over us. Right now all the lieutenant and I are trying to do is find Cynthia Bladen's killer."

"That's more than enough," he answered, and hung up.

I pushed up my sleeve and looked at the date on my watch. Then I looked at the sweep second hand as it clicked and turned inexorably. The farther you get from the original evidence the farther you are from catching the killer: Rule One at the police academy. The hand kept moving. I pulled down my sleeve. Then I reached up and started twisting the blinds rod; that didn't help either.

FOURTEEN

Betwixt and between is where I usually live. The women I've dated since my wife's death prefer it. Laura liked the fact that my service automatic still operated and that from time to time I might even need it. She liked to hear stories about the number of useful things I could do with a two-bladed pocket knife and the even more interesting things I had once had to do with two blocks of wood and a piece of piano wire. She liked Army-talk and cop-talk, us and them-talk, crime and punishment-talk. Cynthia liked it too, as long as the real thing was kept at a proper distance.

What they both really wanted was a movie detective who could go in and out of character without ever forgetting how to tie a black tie or order white burgundy. They wanted something real, but they didn't want to look it in the eye. Maybe that's what all women want. The capability of violence without its expression. The cave man on-call, but with passable taste in china and crystal and a long memory for birthday and anniversary dates.

It's all straightforward in theory. It's just not easy to put together in practice.

And I understood it all, though Laura never cared for my explanation. "Look," I told her once, "I'll tell you why things are the way they are." We were sitting in The Raymond restaurant, a charming cottage that was once attached to a now-demolished hotel. It was the week before we split. The Raymond sits east of Fair Oaks Avenue, betwixt and between Pasadena and South Pasadena. I was eating lamb and drinking something red and expensive. She was eating something leafy, pointing at me with her fork and staring skeptically.

"Here's the problem," I said, "or at least the situation. It's really very simple."

The crease lines around her eyes and mouth deepened. She was ready to doubt every word.

"The thing is, we all take *civilization* for granted. We look around and we see modern highways and airports and bridges. We see telephones and Toyotas, bath tubs, jacuzzis, and nylon; we see a word-processed menu at The Raymond and we sit on comfortable chairs, ordering rack of lamb and arugula. We drive to the ocean and we see people lying in the sand; we see sailboats cruising north and south and 777's circling LAX. We see clothing, furniture, food, jewelry, art . . . from all over the world. And we don't even have to watch some harried caravan master carting the stuff halfway across the desert while he's picking and scratching at his beard and getting blisters on his behind. All these wonderful things come in trucks and they're all unloaded in the alleys behind golden streets and marble-faced shops. You don't even have to think about them until the clerk presents them to you.

"We see libraries and museums, galleries and theatres . . . ."

"Jack," she said, interrupting me, "will you please get to the point."

"The point is that we're really never more than a step away from the cave. It looks like miles but it's only a few inches."

"Meaning?"

Her tone was 99% impatient skepticism, but I thought I detected the slightest tinge of interest.

"Look, we're part nature, part nurture. Everybody agrees on that. And the nurture's very important. Parents, schools, friends, books, the streets . . . *Important*. But compared to nature? It's next to nothing. You know why?"

"Why?" she said. It wasn't a question dripping with anticipation.

"Look at the genes," I said. "The code is all related to our experience. But what experience? You have to look at a time-chart. We tend to think that we descended from the great apes, went through this little hunter-gatherer phase, started using our heads, developed agriculture, moved into villages and towns and developed language, and then, after about a week and a half, we had the Greeks, the Romans, the Middle Ages, the Renaissance, the Reformation, the Enlightenment, the Romantic movement, a couple of nasty world wars, Korea, Vietnam, Operation Desert Shield/Storm, Osama bin Laden, and finally this candle-lit dinner." I paused for a second, hoping she was still with me, and then I started again.

"That's not the way it really is, Laura."

"How is it then?" she asked.

"The hunter-gatherer period is the whole damned thing. Everything else is an afterthought. Ninety-nine percent of human experience consists of barbarism—men and women wearing greasy animal skins, eating raw meat and a lot of live stuff that crawls. *That's* where the genetic code comes from; that's what we really are. Now we may have made a few improvements, but the bottom line is life in the wild. That's why we're still afraid of heights and why we're still afraid of tight places. We didn't have elevators then and we didn't have Yale locks. If we fell we died; if we were cornered we were eaten."

"What have you been reading now, Jack?"

"Please, hear me out," I said. "Think about this—all day long we're surrounded by things that could destroy us: nuclear weapons, semi's hurtling across freeways at 80 miles an hour, cities built on fault lines, buildings filled with glass and cement that can cut and crush us; gas lines underground, ready to burst into flames, reservoirs in the mountains that can split and wash us away; AIDS, gangs, terrorists, and tax auditors. Do you know what *really* scares us, what scares us viscerally? Do you know what fear it is that we're all born with? The fear of snakes. Snakes? When was the last time you even saw a snake? What odds would you give a snake if you were armed with a .45 automatic? What odds would you give a snake if you were armed with a '54 Buick Roadmaster?"

"What's the point, Jack?"

"The point is that the hunters and gatherers didn't have guns and Buicks. They didn't have the UCLA Medical Center. They didn't have Laura Weeks, M.D. They hadn't even seen a Western movie with tourniquets and knife cuts and good guys sucking venom from their buddies' arms. One bite and you were history. You could hide in small spaces from some animals and you could climb up a tree to avoid others, but that slithering son-of-a-bitch could always get to you."

"OK," she said. "We've got old fears we haven't been able to shake because they're embedded in our genetic code. That doesn't mean we have to be barbarians."

"We're not barbarians. We just think and act like them sometimes."

"Then what's the difference between us and them?" she asked.

"The difference is that we can indulge in civilized behavior but the real motivations, the real fears, the real drives are all still there. Think about this . . . ."

She took a deep drink of her wine, preparing for the long haul.

"The name of the game is *survival*. That's all—*survival*. That means two things—living as long as you can and spreading your personal gene pool as far as you can. Now, consider the very different positions of men and women in this regard . . . ."

She looked at me with the same expression she must have used on her medical school professors—superficially serious and attentive, but, deep down, bored to tears.

I started in again anyway.

"In the average lifetime the average woman has approximately 400 eggs. That's all. Just 400. If one of them is not fertilized she has to wait another month and try all over again. We're talking *investment* here; we're talking limited margin of error. Plus, once the egg is fertilized and she gives birth there's work to be done. That's why women check out potential mates so carefully. That's why they go slowly. That's why they think and estimate and evaluate. They want health and intelligence and virility, a good gene pool. They also want somebody who'll hang around when the work starts."

"And the man is different," she said.

"That's right," I said, pleased that her attention was engaged. "The man is built to stay on the move. He's got millions of sperm, nearly always at the ready. He doesn't go through that checklist process that the woman does. He sees beauty or intelligence or something else that seizes his attention and he's ready to start expanding his gene pool. It's his way of surviving and no matter how civilized we get, those essential facts of life will be crucial to the human equation. Hunters and gatherers banded into families because of the efficiencies involved in the division of labor. Men went out hunting, women stayed home and searched for edible plants. From the dawn of time men have provided the protein and women have provided the carbohydrates."

"Jesus, Jack . . . ."

"It's true, Laura. It really is true. And no matter how sophisticated we get or how extreme our circumstances, we still organize ourselves into structures that mirror nuclear families. Lesbian women do it in SoHo and convicted felons do it in San Quentin. And I'm not just talking about men taking on women's roles in homosexual relationships; I'm talking about the pseudo-adoption of children, the extension of the family to include nephews, cousins, etcetera."

"My God, Jack, you're really into this stuff."

"It explains a lot," I said. "You know what our trouble is? We fight with lawyers instead of punching each other in the nose. You hit somebody in the nose and you get sued for ten million dollars. It's not normal. It's not natural. A little healthy physical violence *is*. What we're doing is collectively repressing on the grand scale. We call it civilization but what it's giving us is cancer and heart attacks and strokes instead of a simple bloody nose."

"That's probably true," she said.

"It *is* true," I said.

"So what's your point—that a certain amount of violence is natural and wholesome? That men should spread their love around the countryside while women stay home and grow carrots? That the forces of the gene pool are so powerful that we'll never really move past the fears and superstitions of cave men? That we should give up law and let grown men get in a ring with oversized gloves and swing at one another like sixth graders?"

"That's not what I'm saying, Laura."

"God, next you're going to want to go away for the weekend with some mens' group and put berry juice on your face and beat a tomtom."

"I don't want to do that," I said.

"Why don't you just take me home?" she answered.

FIFTEEN

"Stop feeling so goddamned sorry for yourself." Generic advice from Diana Craig, SBPD. "And also stop trying to be the one who always has to be right." Subsidiary advice from Diana Craig, SBPD. I thought about that for a second. If I didn't have to worry about always being right and if I could also stop feeling so goddamned sorry for myself, then I could let myself be happy even though I may be wrong. Ergo, if drinking was wrong I could do it anyway since there was no reason why I always had to try to be right. Chop-logic from Jack Grant, the world's unacknowledged master. Whatever else it might be it was certainly grounds for celebration. Unfortunately, Frank was working and Cynthia and Laura were gone, so I would have to do it alone.

I closed the venetian blinds, walked out to the kitchen, and found a grimy bottle of store-brand scotch with at least eight ounces left. How appropriate, I thought—a generic drink. I splashed all of what was left of the scotch over three ice cubes in a highball glass and got out a yellow legal pad and a freshly sharpened pencil.

I wrote Cynthia's name across the top of the first sheet and then drew her body as best I could. I drew a rectangle across the top of her exposed left breast, took a sip of the scotch, and drew a man's face next to her on the page. It was large, half the size of her body, and it was looking at her, dead and mutilated.

I took a drink as a small reward for my drawing talent. The picture wasn't bad and I hadn't even invested any tuition money in one of those Draw-the-Pirate correspondence courses.

I took another drink, gave him some hair, shaded in the sides of his nose, and drew narrow eyes. Then I stared into them, looking for answers.

It wasn't the sort of investigative procedure they would have taught at Quantico or the LAPD academy but we had tried their way already and hadn't gotten very far.

I took another drink, chewed on one of the ice cubes, and added detail to the neck, eyebrows, and ears.

"What are you thinking of, you piece-of-shit son-of-a-bitch?" I was talking to myself out loud now and alternating my questions with drinks of scotch. "What's so bad about your own life that you had to do that to her? What did your mother do to you? How about your wife or your girlfriend? Where did you learn to cut that way? How did a piece of filth like you ever meet a person like Cynthia Bladen? How did you get to her before I did? Why couldn't you wait? Why did you have to kill her? What else did you do to her that we don't know about?"

I took another drink and started to ask another question when I heard a knock at the door. I put down the glass and the lead pencil, walked across the room, and took the doorknob in my hand. I looked through the peephole and saw Diana Craig.

SIXTEEN

"Just what I needed," I said, as I opened the door, "a pleasant surprise."

"What are you drinking tonight, Grant, fuel oil?"

"Scotch, as a matter of fact. Would you like some?"

She just shook her head.

"Come on in, sit down."

"We've turned something," she said. "Are you sober enough to hear about it?"

"Of course," I answered.

She sat down on the couch behind my coffee table, put her purse next to her, and reached into the pocket of her jacket. As she did, her jacket opened enough to expose the 9 mm. I wondered if she slept with it too. "Sit down," she said. "Stop all that Galahad crap and let's get to work."

"Are you sure I can't get you something?"

"Just sit down," she said.

I sat across from her in a wing chair. She put a plastic evidence bag on the table between us. It contained something round and metallic.

"Go ahead, pick it up," she said. "It's not going to explode."

"It's a Saint Christopher medal," I said. "Where did you find it?"

"A few feet from the spot where they found the victim's body. Actually, four and a half feet from the position of the victim's head."

"It couldn't have been Cynthia's medal," I said. "She wasn't Catholic and it's not the kind of thing she would have worn. For one thing, it's too big. I take it it wasn't laying on the surface or you would have found it earlier. Was it buried?"

"Not really. We found it under a couple inches of loose dirt and pine needles. We figure that when the killer dug the grave he put the dirt in a pile. Then he planted the body, took the dirt, and covered it back up. All logical and obvious. However, when you dig a hole like that you don't ever get up all the original dirt to throw back in the hole. Of course, it doesn't really matter because the hole is now filled with whatever you wanted to bury. Still, if you're burying something like a human body you don't want to make it obvious that you've been digging there, so you cover up the grave with leaves and needles and try to scatter whatever's left of the dirt pile."

"So you figure the medal came off and the killer didn't notice it. He stepped on it or accidentally shoved it deeper with the blade of the shovel. He covered up the spot and discovered later that the medal was missing."

"That's what we figure," she said. "Good to know that you're at least half sober. Do you always do this, Grant—drink and sleuth at the same time?"

"Not always," I said. "But try to forget me for the moment. Let's get back to the medal. It *is* very plausible that the killer could have lost it without noticing the fact. When you're moving a body around, digging holes, and worrying about being discovered, your heart is pumping and you're sweating. Your shirt is sticking to you, your hands and arms hurt, and you're dirty and uncomfortable. The farthest thing from your mind is your Saint Christopher medal. You could easily lose it and not notice the fact until it's too late. Besides, there are so many of them in circulation that you wouldn't worry that you'd handed the cops a unique piece of evidence. What's one more loose medal in the great outdoors? Unless, of course, there were fingerprints on it."

She sat looking at me, waiting for me to continue.

"Well?" I asked. "Were there?"

"No," she said, "no fingerprints. There was something else, though."

"Are you going to tell me?"

"Of course I'm going to tell you," she said. "Why do you think I signed out the evidence and drove for an hour and a half to Pasadena?"

"What did you find?"

"Blood," she said. "Type B."

"B for Bladen?"

"You mean you didn't even know her blood type? What kind of a lover are you, Grant?"

She didn't wait for me to answer that. "Her blood type *was* B. So is a lot of other peoples' but other people weren't found with their throats cut next to a lake above San Berdoo. We figure this belonged to the killer. There was a significant amount of blood on it—on the back where he wouldn't have noticed it. It wasn't from some guy who nicked himself shaving. Whoever was wearing this medal took a bath in type B blood."

"And he wiped off the front of the medal but forgot the back. After he killed and mutilated her he sponged himself off, looked in the mirror, saw that everything looked OK, and put her body in the car for a drive in the country."

"That's what we figure."

"I just have one question," I said.

"What's that?"

"Why didn't you call before you drove here? I could have fixed a casserole."

"I didn't want to give you the chance to clean up and put away the bottle first."

"How about some dinner anyway?"

She frowned, staring at me as if she had just bitten into something that had already turned.

SEVENTEEN

"What did you have in mind?" she asked.

"What do you like?"

"Pizza with weird toppings."

"I know just the place."

"I hope it has a liquor license," she said. "I wouldn't want you to have to go without."

"Don't worry," I said.

I took her to a place on Colorado called Amalfi. They do standard pizza plus the duck sausage and pineapple bit. She ordered a personal pizza with four kinds of mushrooms.

"Did you know," I asked, "that in hunter and gatherer societies the women stayed home and hunted for herbs and berries in the neighborhood while the men left and went looking for meat?"

"It makes sense," she answered. "They had to be near the kids. Who knows—that may be why women still do salads and men do steaks. I know, the general belief is that women are always watching their weight, but maybe it goes back to something else."

I couldn't suppress the smile. "Give me the best wine you've got," I said to the waiter. "Something big. A Barolo or Barbaresco."

"What are you celebrating?" Craig asked.

"Rationality."

"Don't tell me I said something that made you think you were right again."

"Is it so important that I always be wrong?" I asked.

"No. Every now and then the percentage has to come up on your side."

"Thanks a lot," I said.

The wine was there in three minutes. They love to sell expensive wine. The faster they get it to you the faster you might need a second bottle.

She tasted it and said it was very good.

"The trouble is," I said, "most Americans just drink Italian table wines and Chiantis, maybe an occasional Valpolicella or Soave. You've got to get into the really good stuff to see what the Italians can do."

"Don't get too excited," she said, "this is all right but it's no Gaja. It's got nice fruit but there's nothing memorable on the finish. It's all nose. Now, nose is nice but I like something a little more chewy. I want some structure."

I just stared.

"Oh no," she said, "did I spoil your treat? I'm sorry. You've got to remember—I used to shadow the rich and famous. I watched what they did and I watched what they drank. Washington's the wine capital of the world. Poor thing, you probably thought you were the only person in Southern California who carried a gun and still knew that Mountain Burgundy is not a type of grape. Look at it this way—you don't have to feel alone anymore."

"I had a thought about the medal," I said.

"What?"

"St. Christopher was bogus. The church disavowed all knowledge of his actions years ago."

"So?"

"So, right after the church issued the press release, some people went out and started buying medals, just to be contrary."

"So what are you saying—the killer is some sort of wiseass?"

"Maybe. Maybe he was making some kind of political statement, a rap on the church or something. Catholics aren't supposed to carry those anymore. If you follow the pope you're supposed to turn your medal back in or put it in a desk drawer or something."

"I don't know," she said. "There are some people more conservative than the pope. I've got an uncle who still eats fish on Friday. My aunt says to him, 'Lou, the pope doesn't eat fish on Friday, he eats veal.' My uncle answers, 'When the pope's in this house he eats fish.' There are still a lot of those kind of people around. They're uptight. They're repressed. They're the kind who make good suspects."

"Maybe it's a prop," I said. "Maybe he just wants to look religious."

"Maybe," she answered.

I took a drink of the wine, wondering where our pizza was. "I have to say, I'm very impressed," I said.

"What? You didn't think I knew anything about Catholics?"

"No, of course not."

"Well, what then?"

"Look, for years now I've dated highly educated women, super-achievers . . . ."

"Yes, dear," she said, patting my hand, "we know about your problem."

"No, listen. They all knew about Catholics and about repression . . . and they knew about a lot of other things too . . . ."

"But they didn't agree with you about those women in the animal skins making up those salads, did they?"

"No."

"And you don't know why, do you?"

"No, I don't."

She took a sip of the wine, swished it around in her mouth, and gargled it lightly. "It's not getting any better, is it? Still, the gesture was very sweet."

"You didn't finish your thought," I said. "Why didn't the other women agree with me about the hunters and gatherers?"

"That's obvious. Because they were too insecure."

EIGHTEEN

"What religion is Donald Bladen?" she asked.

"You suspect him?"

"I always suspect husbands. The best violence is always family violence."

"He's a Jewish Republican. Brandeis, class of '64. Stanford Business School, class of '70."

"So you *have* been doing something else besides nursing your scotch."

"That's right," I said. "Tell me, why do you think family violence is the best?"

"You mean you don't know? All that talk about hunters and gatherers, raw mastodon meat and salads and you don't know?"

"Let's just say I'd like to hear your reasons."

"Let's just say you don't know and be honest about it."

"OK, fair enough. Why?"

She finished off the wine and signaled the waiter. "My friend is still thirsty," she said. "Bring us some coffee and some Anisette; put the Anisette on the side."

"Yes, madame," he said.

"Are they supposed to say *madame* in an Italian restaurant?" she asked.

"With all the job-jumping done by waiters," I said, "they get used to using a *generic* form of address."

She smiled. "OK, you want to talk about violence. Think about Bambi."

"Bambi? The deer?"

"Yes. Remember how all the little creatures in the forest laughed at him when he first tried to stand up."

"Yes. He had long legs and they kept giving out on him."

"But eventually he was able to walk."

"Sure. And run and jump too."

"How old were you when you first started walking?"

"I don't know. Probably older than my mother claims. I was a hell of a lot older than Bambi."

"Precisely," she said. "Think about it. Humans are really something special—neurologically speaking—but it's not evident until after they've grown up, and that takes too damned long. They're born too soon, but that's because it's helpful to walk upright and to walk upright you can only have a certain size pelvis and that means that your baby's head can't be so big that it won't fit through down there. So they're all born too soon. They're dependent on their mothers for years. They can't walk, talk, feed themselves, clean themselves, or, most important of all, defend themselves. They have to rely on their mothers. That means they develop feelings of love but also feelings of resentment. Who likes to be dependent on somebody else? That's why a large part of the world keeps yelling 'Yankee Go Home'. Anyway, just when kids think they're starting to figure out what's going on in life they accidentally stumble into their mothers' bedrooms and find some slobbering animal climbing all over the most important person in the world. And what's worse, their mothers seem to be enjoying it. And what's worse still, the creatures the mothers seem to be enjoying turn out to be none other than their fathers. The ones who bring them presents. The ones who dress up like Santa Claus at Christmas. The ones who barbecue the steaks and carve the Thanksgiving turkey. Who would have thought it?"

"Straight Freud," I said. "I knew that."

"But do you know what they call it?"

"The Oedipus complex."

"No, no, no. The situation, not the little boy's feelings."

"What?" I asked.

"The primal scene."

"So that's what creates the violence—the love of the mother and the resentment of the father?"

"No, no. There's plenty of love and resentment to go around. Man is an equal opportunity lover and hater. And we learn all those good things within the family. If we learn the lessons deeply enough or if we're haunted by some particularly traumatic episode, it can all come back later in some brutal and violent form."

"What did you study in college—psychology?"

"I don't talk about my college, remember?"

"Make an exception," I said. "I admitted I didn't know about . . . what did you call it—the primal scene? That should be worth something."

"I studied English."

"And that's the stuff you learned?"

"Sure. What do you think they do in English class these days, talk about books?"

"Let's get back to Cynthia Bladen. You think maybe Donald found her in bed with some heavy-breathing animal? Maybe she seemed to be enjoying it? And maybe he was unhappy that the animal wasn't her husband?"

"Possibly. Maybe she found *him* in bed with some heavy-breathing animal. Female-type. Maybe she saw him doing something that he'd never done with her. Maybe she saw him doing something that she hadn't dreamt of in her wildest fantasies. Maybe she was getting ready to call Mr. Katz and ask him to file some papers down at the Courthouse. Maybe she was threatening to tell the Domestic Relations judge about Donnie's proclivities. Maybe talk about them in public too. See whether or not he couldn't find it in his heart to do a little better by her than the usual 50-50 California split."

"Only one problem," I said.

"What's that?"

"The mutilation."

"Where's the problem? Maybe the boyfriend was doing things with Cynthia's nipple that Donald didn't like. Donald lost his temper. He took out a little revenge. That would explain the neatness."

"What do you mean?"

"A nice Jewish boy, toilet trained at 9 or 10 months; a Republican—he'd cut in straight lines, just the way he first learned to use his crayons and kiddie scissors.

"Another thought," she said, "maybe the boyfriend was a piercer or Cynthia got into piercing to turn him on. Maybe . . . ."

I was shaking my head.

"What's the matter?"

"I can't imagine Cynthia ever doing anything like that."

She put her hand on my shoulder. "Jackie, Jackie," she said, "when are you going to learn? Mommies do all kinds of things."

NINETEEN

"But we don't have anything firm," I said.

"Unfortunately, that's true. I certainly don't have anything. The LAPD doesn't have anything and neither does the Bureau."

"How hard have you pressed them?"

"As hard as I could. They're looking. They're just not finding anything. Listen, you want anything else here? I've got to get back and check phone messages and emails and faxes. Thanks for dinner. You see, I'll even let you pay without giving it a second thought."

"An old-fashioned girl," I said.

"And you didn't think there were any of them left."

"But carrying 9 mm automatics?"

She smiled. "A lot more effective than knitting needles, don't you think?"

―――

For the next two days we tried to see Donald Bladen. I needed to brief him on the case and Craig wanted to talk to him about his wife. She wanted to ask his permission to search the house without a warrant—see what kind of response it might bring.

We couldn't reach him. He had a short business trip to San Francisco (or claimed he did) and his secretary seemed to be stalling when we asked her about a date later in the week. In the meantime, Craig had to clean up some work on another homicide case and I had to do a quick job for Cliff Henderson, my contact at Valley Mutual.

Cliff had called me earlier that week and told me about a problem with a major client. "Look, Jack," he said, "we insure all the Ticketron outlets in Southern California. You don't even want to think about the premiums they pay. It's not so much the liability as it is the potential for adverse publicity. People don't die from forged tickets, but they sure make a lot of noise about it. Ticketron's reputation has to be cleaner than the mind of a Mother Superior."

"What's the deal, Cliff?"

"Very simple, Jack. This guy from San Dimas bought some tickets at an outlet in South Pas. The clerk told him the gig was practically sold out and that there was nothing left but shitty seats. He also told the guy that this was his lucky day, that he just happened to have two choice seats. The guy bit and the clerk scalped the tickets. The mark got to the Coliseum and it was only half-filled. He went back and confronted the guy and was told that there had been a computer error. The guy apologized profusely, rooted around in his pockets, and offered to give him everything he had: six dollars and seventy-three cents. The mark said forget it and walked out. Then later he thought better of it and called Ticketron to complain about their computer screw-up."

"And there was no computer screw-up."

"Of course not. And you've got to realize—this is the sort of thing that could really damage Ticketron's image. What tripped up the kid was the fact that the gig turned out to be a bomb. He was counting on all the seats filling up later. When they didn't, the mark got wise. There's no way of telling how many times the clerk was lucky in the past. This was the first complaint on him."

"Why don't you give me his name and some vital statistics?"

"Sure. His name's Norman Boulenc. Norman's about 5'9", 135; he looks like a speed freak—stringy hair half-way down to his ass, a patchy moustache, and a tendency to pick at his nose and ears and everything else within reach."

"Sounds like a handsome boy. I take it the guy from San Dimas remembered him vividly."

"He sure did. Unfortunately, old Norman's been laying low for the last week or two. The agency sent one of their own people to the store, but Norman read him faster than a summer beach novel. I told the suits at Ticketron it's time to send in the first team."

"Thanks, Cliff, I always appreciate your support."

———

One of the interesting things about Southern California is that you're allowed to scalp tickets through a service, as long as you don't do it on the grounds of the event. However, you can't scalp at a Ticketron outlet. All the patron is supposed to pay there is the face price plus the fee and tax.

Norman had an easy scam—print out a few choice seats the moment an event was announced and pay for them with cash, to keep the register clean. Then wait until the marks came in and offer them an upgrade at stratospheric prices. All they could say was no and Norman got paid his usual salary anyway. If they bit he was suddenly the happy proprietor of his own prospering ticket service, one that didn't have to rent space or worry about overhead or OSHA or social security or workman's comp, licensing fees or any other damned thing—except for the law. Money straight off the top. Tax-free and in serious quantities.

―――

The Ticketron outlet was part of a record store called Waxworks. I looked at my pencilled note and checked my map; the store was on Mission, a block and a half from the South Pas City Hall. I didn't want to spook Norman, so I did my best to look the part for my meeting with him. I searched through my cupboard and dug out a polyester beige sport coat with imitation leather trim on the pockets and lapels. The coat went nicely with a yellow plaid bow tie, a wrinkled white shirt, and a set of dark polyester pants and Thom McCann wingtips. There were also some nice fabric pulls just to the side of the right front pants pocket that had been inflicted by the ring of keys I suspended from the belt loop above.

I wet my hair and combed it straight back, slipped on a pair of glasses, and drove to the store. The clerks didn't wear badges, but I didn't have any trouble identifying Norman. He was sitting next to the Ticketron computer, picking at something on the side of his nose and poring over a Wolverine comic book. I noticed that he folded each page over after he read it. He was clutching the comic and running his eyes up and down the pages as if it was his millionaire uncle's newly probated last will and testament.

"Excuse me . . ." I said.

"Yeah? What do ya need?" he asked, putting down the comic but keeping it close at hand.

"I need some tickets," I said. "They're for my nephew Donnie . . . sort of a birthday present. He and one of his friends really want to go to this concert and I thought I'd surprise him."

"Which concert?" he said, still obviously worrying about the progress of the Wolverine's adventures, but thinking he might have something nibbling at the end of his line that might make the interruption worthwhile.

I got out a folded slip of paper from my jacket pocket and opened it methodically. "I don't quite know how to pronounce this," I said, "it's something like S-P-A-S . . . ."

"The Spastik Colons. Right, yeah. They're playing at Universal. *Very* big show. Let's take a look. By the way, did you notice who's opening for them?" His tone suggested that I should be overcome with enthusiasm.

He tapped in a code on his computer as I said, "As a matter of fact, I didn't."

"Would you believe the Vertical Smiles? Chick group. Very new, retro-punk. Oh, oh . . . ." He tapped at the keyboard again, harder this time, as if he was trying to get a better answer to his question. Then he repeated the process twice and finally dropped his arms to his sides. For a moment he just sat there, staring at the computer screen in anger and frustration. "Damn . . . this is not good news. Here, let me show you."

He flipped open a ring binder filled with outlines of local venues encased in yellowed plastic sheets. "This is Universal. All I have left are . . . (aiming the point of a well-chewed wooden pencil) these two here. That's the second last row and with an obstructed view. You see, they usually hang the speakers right . . . *here* (pointing again). All you could see from these seats is the back of the lead singer's head . . . when he's on *this* side of the stage."

"Oh no . . ." I said, plaintively.

"Wait a sec. Let me try something," he said, tapping the keyboard again. "Wait a minute . . . wait a minute . . . oh no, that won't work. Your nephew and his buddy—they'd want to sit together, wouldn't they?"

"Of course."

"I could give you one seat in the top row with a side view and one on the top row on the other side with an obstructed view. It's one row down from the other two that are together, but the view's still obstructed."

"Darn it," I said. "Donnie's really going to be disappointed."

"Big show," Norman said, sympathetically. "Wait a minute. What am I thinking of? I had a guy trade me two seats for the Colons this morning. Wait a sec."

He went in the back and came out with two tickets. Their face price was $28.50. "These are really good," he said. "I traded him my tickets for the X reunion show. Oh, wait. I can't do this . . . ."

"What's the problem?"

"Never mind, I'm sorry, this was a mistake."

"What?"

"Well, you see, I got the X tickets from a service. They were fifty-five bucks each. I couldn't sell you the Colons tickets for face price. My girlfriend would kill me. I mean, I'm sorry about your nephew and everything, but, like, I just couldn't do that. Besides I really want to see the show and, you know, like a hundred and ten bucks is serious money. I'm sorry I even brought these out. I don't know what I was thinking of . . . ."

"How much would you take for them?"

"I couldn't . . . well . . . (picking at the other side of his nose now) . . . maybe . . . a hundred and a quarter? I could sure use the cash and I'd hate to see your nephew disappointed. I mean . . . I've seen the Colons before and I can always see them again."

I tried to look nervous and indecisive. Do I push the button, drop the nuclear bombs and obliterate the hemisphere or do I say Nah and go have lunch with the vice president? "Oh, what the heck," I said, "the kid only has one sixteenth birthday, right? I'll take them."

I reached into my wallet. All I had was forty-three dollars, which I spread out on the counter, one wrinkled bill at a time. "I guess I can't do MasterCard on this. How about a check?" I asked eagerly. "Will you take a check?"

Now Norman looked nervous and indecisive. Only this time he wasn't acting. He squirmed some more, ran his left hand through his hair and picked at his nose with his right index finger. "Sure, why not," he said. "You look like a standup guy. I'm sure I can trust you."

"Of course," I said. "I pride myself on that. *My* word is my bond." And *your* ass, I added silently, is Valley Mutual's.

TWENTY

I sent the Norman Boulenc file (actually Norman Tracey Boulenc) off to Valley Mutual and returned to the Bladen case. We still couldn't raise husband Donald, so we decided to try a quick toss of Cynthia's office.

Briggs and Billings was a Bunker Hill law firm with a roll of partners, associates, assistants, clerks, secretaries, interns, and gofers twice as long as the list of my high school graduating class. Housed in a marble tower designed to dwarf both the Library and Civic Center and renowned as an organization capable of hugging a headline harder than a Kodiak bear in heat, I figured B & B must have lost a lot of corporate sleep over the fact that they were never featured in the L.A. Law credit montage. The firm sat on the eighteenth floor of their eighteen-story building and when the elevators parted I felt the distinct need to blink twice in order to make certain we hadn't gone directly past 18 and moved on to the celestial regions.

The grayish pink carpet was softer than a goose-down comforter and as inviting as a chilled glass of pink champagne. There were fresh cut flowers everywhere (birds of paradise, cymbidiums, anthuriums) and inch-thick walls of etched and bevelled glass separating the legal assistants from the secretaries and other lesser mortals. I took it all in and then went into the mens' room to wash my hands and straighten my tie. The room was floor-to-ceiling black marble with matching sinks and gold fixtures, the sort of plumbing I would have expected in the stateroom heads of one of Onassis' honeymoon yachts.

Frank White and Diana Craig were meeting me there. I sat back on a gray leather couch, checked out the newest edition of *Architectural Digest* on the glass coffee table with Art Deco antelope heads for legs, and waited. From time to time I looked up to watch the passing scene: women in flowered, silk dresses and soft leather pumps, men in $3500 suits with Italian ties and matched suspenders, trays with ice buckets and bottles of sparkling water, crystal decanters and bud vases, mirrors that spanned walls, opening up the already cavernous space, Miro prints to the east, Rauschenberg to the west, and in between the happiest-faced Giacometti bust I had ever seen; clerks with European accents and hair fashionably askew, and the occasional scent of twelve-dollar cigars and understated perfume. Invisible price tags were floating through the air and the lowest ones were all in six figures. I figured you'd pay at least $450 an hour to take a piss at Briggs and Billings, more if you wanted to wash your hands afterwards. I couldn't imagine what it might cost if you wanted legal advice too. There was one other thing I couldn't imagine—what Cynthia Bladen could have been doing there.

Not that Cynthia was ever immune to the desire for fine things, but her thoughts always seemed to be on her work, rather than on her workplace. This firm's digs looked like a materialist's nirvana, the heavenly playpen where they'd send the professionally self-indulgent who'd barely escaped the down elevator. Except that hell to the B & B lawyers would be a bad table at Chinois or an off-year bottle of *Cheval Blanc*.

Frank and Diana Craig arrived together, still absorbed in a conversation about the parking lot attendant downstairs. He stands about 5'4" and sports a bright blue and white uniform with gold buttons and dueling fourrageres, the kind of outfit you might see on an admiral in a third-world navy. He stops all of the incoming traffic with an extended, white-gloved palm and an expression that would scare pets and small children. When I apologized for not saluting him and drove on he said something under his breath that I probably deserved.

Before Diana and I could exchange pleasantries or Frank and I trade crudities, Bart Briggs suddenly appeared. Technically, Barton Randolph Briggs, II. It was either the closed-circuit television system or a receptionist operating a hidden button who gave us away. Whichever, it was close to magic. Bart appeared from behind a fitted door that I had mistaken for a fixed sheet of walnut paneling. He floated toward us, his hand extended, the gold metalwork on his suspenders and belt buckle beaming like the sun off the helmets of the palace guard of a B-movie emperor.

"Bart Briggs," he said and we all paused a moment for the trumpets to sound in the wings. "Let's go in here where we'll be more comfortable."

He shepherded us through a different panel and into a conference room with a pre-Ayatollah Persian rug the size of my mother and father's backyard. "What can I get you," he asked, "espresso, cappuccino, mineral water?"

"Lemon Perrier over ice," Craig said, "unless the bottle's been opened and recapped."

Good for you, I thought to myself, don't let this dick intimidate you—go right for the chobes. But instead of a head jerk Bart threw her a sympathetic smile, as if to say, "I know just what you mean. I wouldn't wash my dog's ass in Perrier that had been recapped." The two of them understood one another.

Frank and I said that would be all right for us too. Bart opened another panel and revealed the unexpected presence of a bar slightly larger than that in the Sheraton Miramar. The place was like a corporate haunted house, filled with sealed rooms and secret passages. Bart pushed the lower lefthand corner of the bar mirror and it opened to reveal four shelves of bottled water. He removed several bottles of lemon Perrier, produced a tray of glasses and crystal ice bucket from a shelf beneath the counter, and suddenly we were in business.

"Well," he said, "where do we start? Cynthia is a terrible loss to us. Terrible. I suppose you know that this firm was started by my grandfather. We think of ourselves more as a family than a business. A large family, but a family nonetheless. I feel as if . . . as if I've lost a sister."

It wasn't said in the tones you might expect from the halls of the National Organization of Women. The word *hollow* was the first that came to mind. Bart continued.

"Cynthia did so *many* things for us . . . and all of them *so* well. Most of our work is for corporate clients, of course. Cynthia helped us with the . . . earthier portions of the law. Civil litigation, union matters, occasionally even a bit of criminal work—generally involving the relative of a corporate client . . . ."

(In other words, she did all the dirty work.)

"I can't tell you how much we miss her, *really*."

(It was becoming clear—somebody else would have to pick up a lot of pieces now.)

"I must say that the *dedication* which Cynthia exhibited is all too rare in our society these days."

(She was pulling more than her own weight and Bart's combined, and Bart's—given the dimensions of his belly and wallet—was not inconsiderable.)

"Donald, I know, is devastated."

(But let's be honest—who really gives a rat's ass about Donald? Did I tell you about her *dedication*?)

"We've left her office just as it was. You're welcome to go through everything there."

"Thank you," Frank said. "We will certainly respect the confidentiality of her casework documents, unless of course we find something that bears directly on our criminal investigation."

"Do whatever you need to do," Bart said. "All we want to do is help you to find Cynthia's murderer."

(In other words, we've gone over every scrap of paper in the room and shredded everything that could have posed a problem.

Feel free to sift through the pile of pony shit. Just don't expect to see any silver saddles or hear the sound of hooves.)

———

Cynthia's office was all deep grays and dark lavenders: rugs, drapes, chairs, couch cushions and couch pillows, even down to the desk blotter and scissors and letter opener sheath. The book shelves, desk, and other furnishings were matched, in dark walnut. The set was nice, even if it jostled a little with the scattered purple accoutrements. Frank said it couldn't have cost more than a year's pay for two or three secretaries.

"OK, fellow grad student," I said to Frank, "Let's check this place out."

"What do you mean, fellow grad student?" Craig asked.

"Jack had a teacher once in school," Frank said. "Liked to give advice, especially to nervous graduate students. Told them if they ever wanted to graduate they'd have to start reading more carefully. 'Have you ever noticed the manner in which one dog inspects another the first time they meet? Well, that is the way *you* must go over the pages of your books.'"

"And Jackie did and he graduated," Craig said.

"That's right," Frank said, amused at her calling me Jackie.

There were no books in Cynthia's office except for the California Code and a dictionary, which sat on a credenza behind her desk. The firm's full collection of law books was, presumably, in their library, and though Bart hadn't taken us on a personal tour yet, there was no doubt that they had one, probably big enough to play tennis in if you ever got tired of reading. If she had checked out some books for her current casework someone had taken them all back before we got there.

The shelves contained little more than plants, figurines, gimcracks, and an occasional memento or two. Frank went over each of them carefully and took notes on the items with inscriptions.

I checked diplomas and photographs on the walls but there was nothing out of the ordinary: a picture of Cynthia and Donald at a marina, standing in front of a blue-trimmed, white motor yacht, a picture of Cynthia's family taken at a reunion that must have been held at least ten years earlier, and, on the corner of the desk, a light-and-shadow professional photograph of Donald that probably cost something well into three figures. He wasn't really smiling. He was projecting that dreamy glow of a forties film star or bemused Spanish toreador. Very retro, Norman Boulenc would have said. It was an interesting picture. After the single occasion when I had seen Donald Bladen I had trouble imagining him sitting still and holding an expression without frowning, crying, picking, poking, or running his hand through his hair.

Craig was checking Cynthia's desk.

"Anything in there?" Frank asked.

"What do you think, Jackie?" she answered.

"Bare as a chimp's ass," I said. "That would at least be consistent."

"Doesn't he have a way with words?" she answered, opening and closing drawers and shining a pocket flashlight into dark corners.

"There's nothing," she said. "Some paperclips, pencil stubs, a gum eraser, some empty hanging-file folders, a pocket calendar, and that's it. There's nothing else. *Nada*. Normally you'd expect some parking change, some tampons, an extra yogurt spoon—something human. There's nothing here at all and I haven't found any hidden panels or drawer safes. And no nippy bottle, Jackie. Sorry."

"That leaves the computer," I said, letting the *Jackie* slide a third time. "Unless we want to sift through the dust on the window sill or feel around under the rim of the waste basket."

"Jerry's team dusted for prints as soon as the body was found," Frank said. "There was no reason to believe that she had been abducted from her office, but we checked anyway. You never know; there's always the off chance that you might get lucky. We found just about what we expected to find: her prints, those of other lawyers, and those of some of the cleaning people. There are two that we haven't identified, but they were on the desk, just opposite the couch, probably clients."

Her computer was on a table to the right of her desk. I sat down in the chair, reached, and pushed the power button. It was a Mac G4. The desktop image came into focus and the icons appeared in neat rows. I double-clicked the mouse to open up the individual files.

"A mouseketeer, huh Jackie?" Craig said. "None of that big blue with all those keystrokes for you."

"Lieutenant, why don't you put a lid on the adolescent bullshit?" I said.

Frank smiled and turned away. I was looking at Craig and she was holding her expression, but when Frank turned she gave me the slightest wink.

I turned back to the computer screen. Cynthia had a word processing package icon on the desktop, some other standard software from Apple, and a thing called FormMaker. It was a package for lawyers: boilerplate for wills, warranty deeds, and other common documents.

"Takes all the work out," Frank said. "I bet the son-of-a-bitch bills you too."

"Not enough memory for numbers that big," Craig said.

There was just one other icon: a package called RoloList. It was actually a name, address, and phone list that appeared on the screen as a succession of rolodex cards. Next to the image was a scroll box. When you clicked on the directional arrows the cards appeared to flip and you could read through the entries in the file. The scroll box also contained the letters of the alphabet. You could click on any one letter and the screen skipped to the cards with the names beginning with that letter.

"Welcome to the electronic age," I said, picking up the phone on Cynthia's desk and hitting the button for her secretary. The voice came on instantly. "Yes, may I help you?"

"Yes," I said. "Would you mind getting us a blank disk from the supply closet?"

"For Mrs. Bladen's computer?" she asked.

"Yes."

"I have some right here," she said. "I'll be there in just a moment."

A minute later she knocked, entered the room, and offered me a package of ten disks.

"I just need one. Thank you very much."

"Certainly," she said, and disappeared.

"What service," Frank said. "What do you think Bart would do to her if she refused to cooperate with us—cut off her Evian water?"

"Lame," Craig said. It wasn't up to her nastiness standard. Frank looked at me and smiled. He always did like to be teased by women.

I inserted the disk, waited for the blank icon to come up, dragged the RoloList icon over the disk icon, and waited for the computer to transfer the information. Then I ejected the disk, slipped it into my pocket, and turned off the computer.

"I wonder if there are any juicy notes next to *your* name in that file," Craig said. "I notice you didn't check. Why not?"

"Because I'm not a suspect," I said.

"I don't really suspect you of murder," Craig said, "but there are a lot of other things on which I'd like to reserve judgment." This time the tone was warmer.

TWENTY-ONE

We took the elevator to Parking Level B, which was color-coded in purple. Frank commented on the consistency of the building's design features, then offered a comment on the color purple which would have been considered mildly homophobic if not militantly heterosexist in West Hollywood.

Craig turned unexpectedly polite, telling Frank how much she had enjoyed seeing him and working with him again. She then said that she and I would be leaving together since I had treated her to dinner earlier in the week and the least she could do was reciprocate now.

Frank smiled knowingly and as we turned to leave, Craig took my right hand in hers and walked me to my car. "We can get mine later," she said, gazing at me warmly and giving my hand a squeeze.

I opened the passenger-side door for her, closed it after she sat down, and walked around to the driver's side. Frank drove by in his

Supra ($3400 a year to insure—the favorite of the L.A. car thieves) and threw me a fraternity-brother look that spoke volumes.

I got in the car and turned to Craig. She had the expression of a corporation president whose eyes had just devoured a stack of favorable balance sheets. I reached to take her by the hand and she looked at me as if I was offering her a poisonous snake.

"So what does this mean?" I asked.

"What does what mean?"

"Thirty seconds ago you're holding my hand and talking about taking me to dinner. You're staring at me with saucer eyes and putting out more pheromones than a lonely elk. Now you're playing instant ice princess; I could have mistaken you for part of the upholstery."

"You don't like my technique?" she asked. "It sure got White's mind off of that disk in your pocket. Now we can check it out without having the whole damned LAPD looking over our shoulders. This is *my* case, Jack. I want their help. I sure as hell don't want their interference."

"And so you use and abuse me."

"I didn't say I changed my mind about buying dinner, did I?"

"It's going to cost you," I said.

"Bullshit. You're too old for that," she said. "You'll play along until the moment of truth, then suddenly revert and slip your credit card to the waiter."

"You think so?"

"I know so. I know you."

"How?"

"Trust me," she said, taking my hand in hers again. "I do. By the way, nice hand. Strong but soft."

"Thank you," I said. "I built it up by reaching for my credit card after dinners with modern women."

"Believe me, Jack, you wouldn't really want a modern woman."

"Why not?"

"Too much risk of infection," she said. "Turn left when you leave the garage and head north toward the Hollywood. I know a little place you'll like. Some place not so modern."

———

"Get off at Melrose," she said, "and head west."

"I wouldn't want to head east," I said. "My Spanish isn't that good and you're not getting off buying me a burrito from a restaurant in a converted garage."

"Very funny," she said. "Just keep driving."

We passed Paramount and some of the old Hollywood eateries, now surrounded by Art Deco antique stores, period clothing and costume shops, and the occasional auto alarm and leopard-skin upholstery installer. "I like Emilio's," I said, "but I guess we're not going there."

"Just drive," she said.

"It was Frank Sinatra's favorite restaurant . . . and I *still* like it."

She didn't respond.

We were making good time. The traffic was unusually light for Hollywood. Except for the fact that I was passed by a speeding Honda Civic driven by a guy wearing a Nixon mask and a purple Lincoln pimpmobile with eight occupants, I could have momentarily forgotten where I was. The pimpmobile was something special, with its color-matched wheel covers, continental kit and accordion-like pipes. Two of the girls in the back seat were sitting on their coworkers' laps, trying to put on makeup. It must have been hard without a spray can and putty knife. The one closest to the window gave me an open-mouthed grin and a tongue wag. I smiled back politely.

I watched the signs go by, block by block: Vine, Lillian, Cahuenga, Cole, Wilcox, Hudson, Seward . . . when I got to Las Palmas I turned to the lieutenant for enlightenment. She raised her right index finger and pointed straight ahead. She didn't even bother to say "Drive."

At Highland she told me to take a right and cross Santa Monica. "We're going to stop just below Sunset. Wherever you can find a place to park, do it."

"That's a long way from Musso and Frank," I offered.

"We're not going there. Look—there's a place. The guy in the Datsun's just pulling out."

I parked on the east side of the street, turned off the ignition, and looked around. I didn't see anything but a pawn shop with bars thick enough to contain King Kong and a record store with fluorescent paint all over the windows advertising the newest album by the Vertical Smiles. "Look at that," I said. "They've got the new album by the Smiles. Chick group. Very retro."

Craig looked at me, seriously at first, and then broke into a smile. "Let's go," she said.

Next to the record store was a steel door with a heavy-duty lock. Craig inserted a key, turned it, and hit the door with her left shoulder. "Come on in," she said, leading me up a narrow stairway to a small apartment above the store. "My sister owns the building and the record shop. She comes up here sometimes during the day to have some coffee and get off her feet. I use it whenever I'm in L.A."

The place was simple in the extreme: a worn couch that opened into a hideaway bed, a long Formica coffee table with pitted brass legs, two maroon overstuffed chairs, a floor lamp, and a brick-and-board bookshelf with a 12" Sharp television and a Panasonic portable radio. Off to the side was a bathroom with a shower—apparently a recent addition—and in a distant corner a makeshift kitchenette with a sink, hot plate, and office-model refrigerator. It wasn't the sort that Bart Briggs would have entrusted with his lemon Perrier, more the kind you see in the corner of a service station bay with some greasy wrenches on top and a rag hanging from the door handle. Behind the door to the apartment was a desk-size table with a fold-up chair. The table and the collection of material piled on it were covered with a torn white sheet. I was imagining stacks of old *National Geographics* from the shape of the piles, but Craig pulled off the sheet and revealed a computer, printer, and two stacks of hardware and software manuals.

"*Voilà*," she said. "Hand me the disk."

"Terrific," I said. "I knew you'd find a way to get out of buying dinner."

"Such dedication," she said, "I'm really inspired. Your girlfriend's dead and mutilated and you're wondering whether to go for the soup or skip straight to the salad course."

"I always go for the soup," I answered.

"Not tonight, big boy. I've got some cheese, some crackers, maybe an olive or two, and—don't worry—a nice bottle of wine. But first you've got to earn it."

She turned on the power switch and I handed her the disk. She popped it into the slot and waited for the icon to appear on the screen.

"Another Macintosh mouseketeer, I see."

She just glanced and smiled, then double-clicked on the icon and waited for the computerized rolodex to appear on the screen. When the image appeared she paused, turned to me, and said, "I'm sorry for being so thoughtless. I bet you'd like something to drink while you wait."

"I can get it," I said, and walked over to the refrigerator. I opened the door and found five cans of Lipton ice tea. "Would you like one of these?" I asked. "Sure," she said; I handed it to her and she set it beside the computer keyboard without opening it. I scooted one of the armchairs beside her fold-up chair and sat down next to her.

"All right, Mrs. Bladen, just what is it that you've been up to?" she asked, and scrolled through the first set of entries.

Adelman, Jeanine, 617-4720
Aguilar, Miguel, 382-2601
Ammerman, Jules, 394-8774
Atlas Car Repair, 318-1542
Avalon, James, (626) 304-2792
AWA Caterers, 971-1965
Bawman, Carl, 434-2108
Biehl, Loretta, 341-1654
Big Three Restaurant, 491-3489
Blattner, Roland, 683-1947
Bowman Builders, 644-3606

Brownell, Louis, 491-3987
Brownstein, Marilyn, (626) 348-3982
Bruckmann, Ernst, 748-2728

She took her hand off of the mouse, scooted her chair back, and opened her can of ice tea. "*This* will keep you awake," she said, "not like beer and wine and all those things that you like."

I didn't respond. She stared at the screen intently. Then she clicked the mouse and scrolled forward, an entry at a time, but much more rapidly.

"I don't see anything very interesting, do you?" she asked.

"No. I assume the people are all friends and clients. I don't see any names of millionaire playboys or professional killers. That doesn't mean she wasn't involved with them in ways that she'd want to keep hidden from Donald, but, as you say, on the face of it there's nothing striking. It wouldn't be hard to check. Where's your phone?"

"Here." She reached down on the floor behind the computer's surge protector and pulled out a pink Princess phone with a twisted, yellowed, plastic cord.

"Antique time," I said, and punched in seven numbers. The phone rang and a male voice answered.

"Jeanine Adelman please."

"You got the wrong number," the voice said impatiently.

"Interesting," I said, punching in a second set of numbers. Instead of a ring I got the three-tone signal and the robotic female voice: "The number you have reached, *382-2601*, is not in service. Please check the listing and dial again."

"A wrong number and a number not in service."

"Try Ammerman," Craig said. I did.

"Parkway Limousine," a male voice said.

"Excuse me, is there a Jules Ammerman employed by your organization?"

"Julie Hanrahan?"

"No, *Jules Ammerman*."

"Sorry, no."

"Not there," I said. "Call the car repair," Craig said.

I did and I got the robotic voice. "The number you have reached, *673-1542*, is not in service. Please—" I hung up.

There was no James Avalon, no AWA Caterers, no Carl Bawman, no Loretta Biehl, and no Big Three Restaurant. Roland Blattner's number was not in service; the Bowman Builders' number was for an escort service; Louis Brownell was not at the "Thompson Residence," when the very drunken Mr. Thompson belched into the receiver, and Marilyn Brownstein and Ernst Bruckmann might have been out on the town with one another locked in a sweaty embrace but neither of them had a phone in service with the numbers in Cynthia Bladen's list.

"Bingo," Craig said.

TWENTY-TWO

"You should have heard the guy belch at me," I said. "I'm used to having the phone slammed down, but that was a new twist."

"You shouldn't call at dinnertime. Speaking of which . . . ." She got up and walked over to the refrigerator.

"So what do you make of the list of phony numbers?"

"It's obviously something that was rigged—either by Cynthia Bladen herself or by someone trying to mislead whoever was assigned to investigate her death. It's a ringer. It's bogus. That means it's got to be there for a reason."

"Unless some clown was simply playing with her computer."

"Did you see anything obvious—joke names, for example, or phone exchanges that aren't used in this area?"

"No, none that I can think of."

"Neither did I. Don't you think if somebody was just doodling they'd doodle at random?"

"Probably. So what are you saying?"

"It's got to be a message of some sort."

"The patented voice from the grave." I was surprised at myself the moment I said it. Technically she was still in a refrigerated drawer; I already had her buried.

"Yes," Craig said. "Either that or a false lead from the killer."

"You think the killer could have access to Cynthia's computer?"

"I think a lot of people could have access to her computer."

"You're right. With all those damned sliding doors and secret passageways it would be easy. Plus you've got the night crew, the possibility of a phony technician coming in, or a temp secretary—a piece of cake."

"This is just what we needed," Craig said. "Why don't we celebrate it with some wine?"

"You're certainly loosening up fast," I said. "I thought you'd work straight through until the killer was arrested, jailed, tried, convicted, and working on a second or third appeal."

She walked over and put her hand under my chin, turning my face and eyes toward hers. "Didn't I tell you—solving murders turns me on," she said. "It also gives me an appetite."

"Then what are we waiting for?" I asked.

———

Dinner was a tin of English water biscuits, a large wedge of blue cheese, some mixed Greek olives, and a bottle of Santa Cruz Mountain Zinfandel. We sat together on the Salvation Army couch, our meal spread across the brown Formica coffee table.

"This is really progress," she said.

"What—the possible break in the case or your sitting next to me on this romantic couch, dining by reflected neon?"

"Both, of course. Plus the fact that you're suddenly more interested in food than in Cynthia. That shows you're putting the past behind you. Or at least you're putting something in front of you besides 90-proof Scotch."

"I have to give you some of the credit," I said. "Even though you enjoy trying to make me out as some kind of a lush, you *have* helped me."

"With what—my shrewd detective work or my animal presence?"

"Both, of course. Plus the fact that you were willing to take the risk and bring me home with you. Not everybody would."

"Pure pragmatism," she said. "Home is where the Macintosh is and you were the one carrying the diskette."

"Somehow I think you would have been capable of getting it away from me if you had wanted to."

"Probably," she said, taking a sip of her wine.

A few moments later she took another sip, put her glass on the table, turned to me, put her right hand on the side of my face, and kissed me. I was more than a little surprised and my expression must have reflected the fact.

She followed the kiss with a pat and said, "Sorry, I just couldn't stand to see you squirming there, thinking should I or shouldn't I?"

"So you did it to break the tension?"

"Yes."

"It didn't work," I said, putting my arm around her waist and pulling her close for a second kiss. A longer one this time.

"My, my," she said. "We *are* forgetting about the past."

It was the first time I had ever touched a woman's waist and back and brushed against the grip of an automatic pistol in the process. She continued to sit close but she reached back with her right hand, slipped out the automatic, and placed it on the coffee table. Then she leaned forward, pressing her breasts against my chest, and reached farther. This time she pulled a thin leather case out of the back of her skirt and put it on the table next to the pistol. It looked like a nail file case, but slightly larger.

"My gravity knife," she said.

"Oh," I said, unable to think of anything else.

"Don't worry," she said, moving closer. "I don't have any other weapons."

"I wouldn't say that," I answered, as the phone suddenly rang.

TWENTY-THREE

Diana got up slowly, walked over to the computer table, and picked up the phone.

"Hello," she said, "Yes, this is she . . . Frank? Thank God you called. Grant just had a half a glass of wine and he's climbing all over me."

I stared at her in disbelief. She put her hand over the phone. "Insurance. Nobody ever believes the truth."

"Yes . . ." she said. "Really? Just a second . . ." She picked up a pad and pencil and started jotting down notes. She wrote silently for nearly five minutes. "How long ago, Frank?" (More notes.) "Anything else?" She waited for Frank's answer, then wrote something down. "Thanks a lot," she said. "What—Jack? . . . of course I was kidding. He's still weeping over his old girlfriends. Right . . . thanks again."

She hung up. "I thought you always told the truth," I said.

"I only promised to tell *you* the truth, nobody else."

"How do I know you're not lying to me too?"

"You don't. That's the deal—I stand behind you and promise I'll catch you. It comes down to whether or not you're ready to let go and fall. Are you?"

"It depends on where you want me to land," I said. "What did Frank want?"

"One of his people turned something. The chunky guy named Jerry . . . the one who wears the light blue leisure suits with the stained cuffs and the cans of sardines in the pockets . . . ."

"Jerry Dailey."

"Right. One of his people was sorting through printouts and files and came up with a case roughly similar to Cynthia Bladen's. It was an older woman (Diana paused to check her notes) . . . Margaret Watermann. They found her body in the Mojave, near a narrow river bed after a flash flood. What was left was pretty far gone but you could still tell certain things: her throat had been cut and her navel and surrounding tissue were removed."

"Her *navel*?"

"Yes. There was also no sign of blood on her clothing and no blood found in the immediate vicinity of the burial site."

"Wait, back up a second. How big was the wound?"

She checked her notes. "Something like eight inches by four inches—a large area. I don't know why the killer cut so much, but the area included the navel. Another link with mother. Jesus, talk about cutting the cord . . . ."

"Interesting."

"Yes. Frank's people should have come up with this earlier, but the case fell into bureaucratic limbo. The body was found by an off-duty policeman from Kingman, Arizona, just adjacent to the California border. Somebody from Needles was sent to check it out. At first they thought she might be a tourist visiting Lake Havasu."

"London Bridge-ville."

"Right. There isn't a damn thing else worth visiting in that area and it was a long way from Los Angeles. If somebody wanted to kill her and dump her body in the desert there's a hell of a lot of desert that's closer to home. So the Arizona police were brought in first thing. It turned out later that Mrs. Watermann wasn't a tourist at all. And she didn't come from the Mojave, unless oceanfront property in Newport Beach is your idea of a desert. What she was was an heiress and the owner of a cosmetics supply company that does eight figures' worth of business annually in Southern California alone."

"How long ago did they find her?"

"Four weeks. They figure she was dead at least a week when the Arizona cop found her. He was hiking through this river bed, whistling and twirling his walking stick and suddenly there she was, or rather what was left of her."

"Any suspects?"

"A load, but no hard evidence yet to connect any of them to the murder."

"The first jackals out to feed are usually the ones with a taste for money."

"Right. The Orange County cops have a list of suspicious employees in her company, some nasty industrial rivals, and three pissant kids who might have been getting bored waiting for mom to kick off so that they could have their turn at wasting the family fortune."

"How old was she?"

"Fifty-three."

"Hell of a time to die," I said, "and a hell of a way to do it. Anything else?"

"I got the name of the lieutenant in Orange County who's handling it. Frank said he'd tell him to expect a call from me."

"No, I meant were there any other similar cases?"

"Not really. There was a black hooker named Mona Nevelson who worked the Navy and Marine trade in San Diego, but her killer's M. O. was different. She was stabbed and there were cuts on several parts of her body, but none on her throat. Her body was found in the back seat of an abandoned car, not buried miles from town in a shallow grave. They also found blood everywhere—on the victim, her clothes, the window, the seat, the floor, you name it."

"At least we've got a second case," I said. "We've got a pattern. However small, it's still a pattern. What do you want to do—check with the guy in Orange County or start work on deciphering the phone list?"

"I was thinking about rejoining you on the couch, but since you want to get back to work, I suppose we can," she said.

"I didn't mean right away," I said, trying to recover. "I meant later."

"You're lying, Jack," she said. "I told you before—men don't know how to do it. So why do you even try?"

"OK, so I'm damned if I do and damned if I don't. You start getting into the case, you grab my attention, you tell me about a whole new lead, and I respond to it. That doesn't mean I want to work now rather than curl up with you; it just means you were quick enough and sharp enough to sidetrack me from what we were doing. Correction: *momentarily* sidetrack me."

"Bullshit," she said. "Good bullshit maybe, or at least better-than-average bullshit, but bullshit nonetheless. All in all I'd score it as a quick recovery under difficult circumstances."

"But not good enough . . . ."

"I didn't say that. Maybe you deserve a *little* slack."

She walked over, sat back down beside me, and met me halfway with a kiss. While I held the kiss she slipped the tail of her blouse out of her skirt and reached behind her. I wondered what she was reaching for this time.

She unhooked her bra and pulled away from me. "Ever see this done?" she asked, reaching up her sleeve and pulling out the bra.

"No," I said, "I wonder if Houdini could have done it. I don't think they ever put him in a bra."

She smiled and slipped off her blouse. I looked at her for a long moment, then held her and kissed her on her mouth, neck, and whatever else I could reach. She pulled back slowly, then came forward and kissed me again. She lay against me for several minutes and then kissed me a third time. And a fourth. Then she slipped her blouse back on and buttoned it.

"What was that?" I asked. "You're not the sort to stop and not follow through."

"That was intimacy," she said. "The place between friendship and love."

"If that's where intimacy is, then where is romance?" I asked, not trying to press her but interested in what she might say.

"On the drugstore racks for $3.95," she answered. "Go home and get some sleep. Pick me up at seven for breakfast."

I walked out into the night air and looked up and down Highland, forgetting for a second exactly where I had parked my car. Two retro Madonnabes in black bras and lace panty girdles walked by, snapping their gum and playing with their costume-jewelry necklaces. I turned, walked toward my car, and stood at the curb, turning my ignition key over in my hand and wondering what those last few minutes with Diana were all about.

Maybe she wanted to show me that while Cynthia was slashed and dead she was still alive and whole.

Maybe she wanted to give me something to take home and think about, something to hold my attention and block out all the distractions.

Maybe she just felt like taking off her blouse and seeing what would happen.

I got in the car, rolled down the window, turned on the ignition, and turned away from the curb. I was driving by instinct, not really concentrating. I put my elbow out the window and rested my hand against the top of the window frame. Fifteen minutes later I realized I was nervously tapping the roof of the car with my fingertips. I felt warm so I turned on the fan and angled the plastic directional slats at my face. As I drove along Los Feliz toward the Golden State, I was still trying to figure out what had happened.

TWENTY-FOUR

My mailbox was stuffed with bills and junk mail, but there was also a small padded mailer wedged in the slot. The return address was Laura's. I opened it up and found a blue striped tie and a pair of cufflinks I must have left at her apartment. There was no note.

I walked into my apartment, saw that I had left all of the lights on when I left, and walked over to my makeshift desk. My telephone answering machine light was blinking. I hit the button, adjusted the volume, and began to take off my tie and shirt.

(Click) Hello Mr. Grant. My name is Ron Russell and I'm calling to invite you to contact me for all of your investment needs, at (626) 304-9999. Remember, your financial future begins today.

(Click) Chack? Thees ees Reeck. I left your core wecks in your laundry locker. Thenksomuch. I owe you won, Buddy.

(Click) Jack Grant? This is Larry Dean; I'm your local class rep and I'm calling on behalf of the Alumni Association to see if you're coming to our reception next week for President Cheedle. We haven't

received your RSVP card. Please call me at (626) 843-6219. Remember, space is limited. Hope to see you there!

(Click) Jack? Frank. Jerry's turned something. I'll try to reach you at Craig's. If I don't, call me as soon as you get back.

The machine beeped three times, announcing the fact that it had done its job and was through for the night; then it began to whirr as it rewound its tape. I threw my clothes in the laundry basket in my bathroom cupboard, put on my blue robe, and walked out to the kitchen.

I twisted the top from a bottle of Rolling Rock, took a long drink, and looked around for something to go with it. I found a piece of cheese in some plastic wrap and the remains of a bag of pretzels. Standing at the counter next to the sink, I unfolded the sheet of paper on which I had written the phone numbers from the list in Cynthia's computer. I opened the drawer beneath the phone, took out a notepad, and started playing with the numbers, wondering whether or not Cynthia could have been using a simple substitution code.

I worked intently for six or seven minutes until the beer, cheese, and pretzel crumbs ran out. Then, as I put down the empty bottle and tried to refocus my attention, I realized that I was more interested in Diana Craig than I was in numbers, codes, suspects, and hidden messages.

I gave it my best shot anyway. There was one last Rolling Rock and I took it and the notes to my desk—actually a discarded table from the apartment complex's laundry room, which I had refinished one day in a fit of nervous energy. The pine top was stained to resemble oak; I still hadn't figured out how to disguise the pitted chrome legs.

I tried to determine which numbers were repeating at levels of frequency that might be associated with specific letters, but every time I made a pass at it I kept coming up with words like *asgsga* and *bmegsb*. It didn't take me long to realize that if I wanted to find Cynthia's killer some time before the Second Coming I would need help.

It was eleven-thirty—seven and a half hours before I had to meet Diana. I turned on the television and started cycling through the cable channels. The AWA wrestlers were shouting at one another on channel 26, promising a spectacle of dismemberment for anyone willing to come to the Amphitheatre Saturday night and fork over twenty-eight bucks.

Being a WWF man myself, I clicked them off in mid-scream and tried channel 27, the citizens' access channel, where six feminists were seated in a circle, talking about seizing control of their own lives and bodies. One of them—a woman named Elaine—was brandishing a gynecologist's speculum as if it was a broadsword and threatening to challenge male hegemony in the Examining Room. Unfortunately, she ran out of airtime before she could do anything interesting with it. I made a mental note to try them again in a week: channel 27 was finally starting to show real promise.

The next segment was a lecture by a scientist named Adjani who kept referring to himself as *Professor*. I remembered his name from the papers. He was a postdoc at UCLA whose grant had run out at about the same time as his mental capacities. He first accused the University of being part of a federal plot to stop him from revealing the true secrets of the universe—all of which seemed to come down to the untapped medicinal potential of unripened kiwi fruit. As he got further into it, however, he started worrying that all of those little black seeds he was eating might take root in his stomach and start to sprout. At that point he accused the University administration and the Department of Pharmacology of plotting to kill him. I wondered where he got the money to buy TV time. Tonight he was lecturing on colon disorders and saying a lot of scary things about the cumulative effects of a steady diet of avocados.

My attention span snapped after four and a half minutes and I reached for the remote control. Channel 30 had Italian soccer, channel 31 was running a Three Stooges short, and channel 32 was broadcasting the highlights of a high school football game between San Dimas and West Covina. VH1 had Prince (I refuse to say "the artist formerly known as . . ."), resplendent in purple spandex, 3-day beard, and tightly-curled chest hair, but I thought the pink paisley guitar with the anatomically correct sound hole was a little over the top and hit the channel selector again.

Charles Bronson was killing people on channel 37 and Pat Robertson was saving them on channel 38. I thought it was nice the way these things tend to balance out. Channels 39 through 42 were all running commercials, but channel 43 had "Sherlock Holmes in Washington," and I settled in for the duration.

―――

The phone woke me at 3:45. I was still in the chair and the television screen was a blank glow. I was instantly covered with perspiration, the result of equal doses of fear and anger. As I reached for the phone I realized that the fear was winning.

TWENTY-FIVE

It wasn't a garbled voice with a foreign accent apologizing for reaching the wrong number. It was Frank: "Craig's been shot; we're on our way there."

The call was patched from his cruiser; I could hear traffic and street noise in the background.

"How bad?" I said.

"She's alive; that's all we know," he answered. I thanked him, threw on the first clothes I could find and ran down the steps of my apartment to my car. The street lights were still on as I made a sharp turn and sped toward California Boulevard and the parkway and freeway beyond.

———

When I got within a block of Highland I could see that it was completely blocked; the bouncing police cruiser beams looked like a combination of power surges and short-circuited northern lights. I found a place on Romaine a block and a half away and ran toward the flashes and reflections. There was a circle of police vehicles and ambulances and as I approached I was stopped by a young patrolman with a long black club and a short, serious face.

"Let him through," a voice said. It was Jerry Dailey's. The guy stepped back without saying anything.

"How is she, Jerry?" I asked.

"She'll make it," he said, laughing. "I can't say the same for the other guy."

"What's so funny?" I asked.

"She took a single slug in her left shoulder. It made a nice hole but it still went straight through. The other guy . . . ."

I left before he could finish and ran toward the nearest ambulance. The doors were still open but the body inside was covered with a gray sheet. There was a red circle of fresh blood over the chest; it was glistening in the strobing roof lights. I ran to the second ambulance, twenty or thirty yards away. The paramedics were locking the gurney in place and the driver was getting ready to close the doors.

"Leave it open," I said, "I'm going with her."

"Who the hell are you?" the driver asked, closing the door on the left.

"Bruce Wayne," I answered. "Open the damned door so the lieutenant can breathe."

Not the brightest thing I ever said, since she was surrounded by oxygen tanks, but Diana heard it and seemed to appreciate it. She arched her head to look at me, then fell back and said, "Bruce. Thanks for coming."

"What happened?" I asked.

"Beats the hell out of me," she said, coughing and then clearing her throat. "Somebody tried to shoot me and I shot back."

I got in the ambulance, sat down in the jump seat, and took her by the hand.

"I *knew* you'd do that," she said.

"Do you want me not to?"

"Of course not," she said.

The driver started to close the right ambulance door and then suddenly opened it again. Jerry Dailey was there.

"Sorry if I'm intruding," he said, smirking.

"What is it, Jerry?" I asked.

"I just wanted to congratulate the lieutenant," he said. "We're gonna take pictures of the asshole who tried to clip her and put it on the wall at the Academy range. What a shot group. It was poetry, Jack, poetry. On his best day, even Frank's uncle, Charles White couldn't do it. I'm talking prone position, I'm talking sandbags, I'm talking tripods, I'm talking point-blank range. You should see the son-of-a-bitch. Five rounds that would fit inside a circle the size of a tiddlywink. Two of them were on top of two others, all mashed together. They're comparing the lieutenant to fucking Robin Hood. And right square in the center of the heart. It was surgical, Jack, *surgical*. By the way, don't squeeze that hand too hard; that's a precision instrument."

"Any make on him yet?" Diana asked. Her force was stronger now.

"Not yet," Dailey said. "A Latin homeboy traveling light. No I.D., just guns and money. We'll keep checking. I took his fingerprints. He was very cooperative, by the way. What do they say—cold hands, warm heart?—not this one."

"Thanks, Jerry," I said, in a dismissing tone.

"I'll let you two alone," he answered, smirking again.

The ambulance drove to the Kaiser Hospital in east Hollywood. The emergency room was nearly empty—too late at night for the heavy traffic, too early in the morning for the next round. The residents and interns were drinking coffee and hitting on the nurses; the orderlies were checking out the time on the wall clock every few seconds and going through the motions of cleaning up.

"Gunshot wound," one of the paramedics said, but the docs just looked at one another and continued sipping their coffee. I expected one to say 'Flip you for it?' but no one did. One highly dedicated healer put down his cup, whispered something to a nurse sitting at a computer terminal, and ambled over. "Put him in number one," he said.

"*Her*," I said. "And I don't want you to touch her unless you're the best of what's available."

He looked right through me, said he was the senior resident, and went back for a final sip of coffee. Then he joined us in a makeshift area created by a sheet-curtain.

"Are you her husband?" he said.

"He's my witness," Diana said. "Don't screw anything up."

The doc pulled back the sheet. Diana's blouse and bra had been cut away and a makeshift bandage taped over the wound. Her pistol and holster were still in place.

"You can't bring that in here," the doc said.

"I wouldn't try to take it away from her if I were you," I said. "Just fix her shoulder."

He looked right through me again. I wondered where they learn how to do that. Then he cut off the bandage and I saw the wound for the first time. It was blood-red and blue; the round had punched straight through, but not without taking a lot of skin and muscle and blood along the way. The resident gave her two injections. "These will cut the pain and help prevent infection," he said. "We'll get you something to take when that wears off." Then he swabbed the wound, checked for fragments and collateral damage, put in the sutures, and put on a fresh bandage.

"Thanks," she said. He looked at me for a response and I looked right through him. "We'll keep you here for a day and see how you do," he said.

"Forget it," she said. "If I need you again I'll come back."

He shrugged, wrote the prescription, and handed it to me without comment. I told Diana I'd be right back and went around to the front of the building and down to the ground level to the hospital pharmacy to fill it. When I got back they had rolled her into an empty room off the main hallway. "How are you doing?" I asked.

She reached up with her good arm, slid her hand around my neck, and pulled me down to kiss her.

TWENTY-SIX

THE GLOW FROM THE Pasadena street lights was wrapped in morning mist and the accompanying moist smog felt like flecks of greasy dust against the skin. I could taste it too: a mixture of carbon and metal, pooling at the back of my throat. I was still driving with my arm out the window and still tapping my fingers against the roof. Diana didn't seem to mind. She was slumped in her seat with her back to the door. Her eyes were open, but she was drifting, probably because of the painkillers.

I drove up to my apartment building on the common peoples' portion of Oak Knoll Avenue and flipped my turn signal through force of habit. I don't know why I bothered to, since I was the only one on the street. At least I thought I was. Then I saw something and another automatic response tripped in the back of my head. In front of my building, leaning into the curb, was a dark blue van with a ladder tied to brackets on the roof and a splatter of paint and drywall spackle across the bumper. I could see the glow of a cigarette at the corner of the driver's window. Contractors come early in L.A. in order to beat the traffic, but they don't come at 6:07.

I turned into the driveway just before mine, backed around methodically, and headed south. I looked in my rear-vision mirror and saw the dust and leaves scatter behind the van's exhaust pipe as the driver turned on the ignition.

"What's going on?" Diana asked.

"Welcoming party," I said.

She started to reach for her gun and then winced.

"You don't need that yet," I said. "They've got to stay with me first."

I turned left on California and headed east. "You sure attract a crowd," I said, turning toward her and smiling.

"How do you know they're after me? It's probably somebody trying to collect on one of your bar bills."

"They're probably after both of us," I said. "They came at you earlier and now they've found out who I am and where I live."

"I know," she said, letting the reality sink in. "I'm sorry about the smartass comment."

"Forget it," I said, reaching over and patting her leg. "I'd hate to see you go out of character." She covered my hand with hers for a second.

I pulled into the Pavilions lot, eased through as if I might park, and then exited on the west side, turning north onto Hudson. The van was still with me but holding back. I turned east on Del Mar and south on Lake, slipped through the tiered parking garage between Macy's and Borders and was suddenly back on Hudson. I went around the block again but this time turned north on Lake rather than south and then turned east on Cordova.

Between Lake and Mentor is a wide and fashionable alley called Shopper's Lane. It runs the length of the commercial section of Lake Street and provides a north-south passage through the parking lots that adjoin it. Above Cordova the pedestrian traffic increases because of a short row of restaurants on the east side of the Lane. Between Cordova and the restaurants is a parking garage and beyond the restaurants a connecting street that takes you back out to Mentor and back around to Cordova. I was at least a block ahead of the van when I turned onto Shopper's Lane and I quickly turned right, into the parking garage.

I grabbed my ticket from the dispenser, accelerated, and drove up the ramp; then I turned sharply, trying not to let the tires squeal, and parked behind a concrete block retaining wall. I popped open the glove compartment and took out my automatic and two back-up clips.

"Get down," I said.

"No way," she said, starting to open the door.

I ran across the open lanes and stood behind a pillar, ready to open up on anybody stupid enough to drive into an empty parking garage.

I looked over and saw Diana close the door behind her and hurry as best she could to the back of my car. She was steadying herself against the fender with the heel of her automatic.

I brought my own automatic up to eye-level, leaned against the pillar, and waited.

TWENTY-SEVEN

I WAITED FOR TEN minutes before I signaled Diana to get back in the car. I rolled up my window and told her I thought it was safe to leave now.

"Not bad work," she said. "This town is all driveways and parking lots and connecting alleys. You could have been exiting in any one of four directions or you could have been circling back on them, driving right up their tailpipe."

"That's right," I said. "I could have been."

"But instead you led them into Box Canyon and waited. You were ready to pick them off one at a time."

"That's right, ma'am. I don't think it's mannerly for outlaws to come after a woman, especially when she's wounded. Besides, I had the angle and my shooting iron manages to get off a few more rounds than Colonel Colt's."

"So does mine," she said, changing the tone. "Why did you tell me to get down?"

"Because I wanted you to get out of the car and cover the driver's side so we could catch them in a crossfire. I knew you wouldn't dream of taking orders from me, especially not when you had a hole in your shoulder and something to prove. I figured the best way to protect you was to bring you into it and the best way to bring you in was to tell you to stay on the sidelines."

"You're lying again," she said, "but the lies are still high quality. You're damned fast on your feet for a former cripple."

"It's nice to be appreciated," I said.

"Where do we go now?"

"Obviously not to my apartment. I know a place."

I drove to the newest incarnation of the Huntington Hotel, this version guarded by the Ritz-Carlton lion. I took the back streets of San Marino, just to be sure we didn't have company.

"This place is on the same street as my apartment," I said, "but the rents are noticeably steeper at this end."

"I can't afford this and I won't let you pay," she said, as we turned into the grounds of the hotel.

"I do some work for them from time to time. That won't be a problem," I said.

"Part-time house dick?"

"Something like that."

I pulled into the valet parking garage and immediately attracted a crowd of people with white gloves and black uniforms. When they got close enough to recognize me they pointed to the far end of the garage, opposite the ramp that led to the second level. Diana and I parked, walked along the back of the main building, and entered the valet parking office where the keys are stored. I picked up the house phone and called the assistant manager. Three minutes later the inside door opened and a blonde woman with a nametag that read *Caroline* handed me a plastic Ving card. She spoke matter-of-factly: "Room 128, in the lanais."

"Thanks," I said. We followed her into the east wing of the main floor of the hotel, avoiding the lobby and circling past the central gardens and fountains.

"This room is in a separate building, in an older section of the hotel," I said. We walked to the west end of the building, crossed the picture bridge over the hot tub and Japanese garden, and walked into a smaller, private building with individual porches overlooking the pool.

I slipped the key card in and out of the lock, opened the door, and extended my hand. "Your room, lieutenant. You're on the end of the building, so you've got plenty of exits if you need them—hallway, stairwell, and porch lanai. The porch is cement. Sprinkle some sugar and salt out there and you'll be sure to hear uninvited visitors. I think you'll be a lot happier here than in the hospital. What can I get you?"

"Where do you think you're going?"

"I'm going to catch the outlaws."

"Not just yet," she said, closing the door and bolting it.

TWENTY-EIGHT

"I can't stay here," I said. "You'll talk me into things that will take my mind off the case. I'll lose my focus."

"You probably don't have much else *to* lose," she said.

I didn't comment. "Come here," she said, taking my hand and pulling me down beside her on the king-size bed. "Tell me. What are you going to do?"

"First, I'm going to try to find out if the guy you shot was an old friend from San Berdoo."

"What then?"

"I'm going to try to find an expert on ciphers and start working on Cynthia's phone list."

"So you think the one who shot at me may be part of some gang payback."

"It *looks* like that. The guy was Hispanic, according to Jerry, and if he was part of the group you chopped up in San Berdoo he and his remaining fraternity brothers would have plenty of motive."

"That was a long time ago."

"Maybe he's been a house guest of the state and just got out," I said.

"Maybe, maybe not. It could all be smoke and mirrors," she said. "They could be luring us down the wrong street, watching us piss away our time and getting farther and farther from the evidence of who killed Cynthia Bladen."

"*And* the woman from Orange County."

"Right. Margaret Watermann."

"Very plausible. While we run around in the desert smog chasing ghosts and gangbangers the real killer or contractor escapes attention, the one who hired the guy in Hollywood," I added.

"Right," Diana said. "So what are you going to do if you can't identify the shooter *or* find a cipher expert?"

"I'll come back here and try to talk my way into that king-size bed."

"Actions speak louder than words. Why do you have to *talk*?"

"Because you're still armed, and discretion is the better part of valor."

"So you're afraid of me then."

"No, just discreet."

"Good," she said. "I like a discreet man. So what should I do—hope you succeed or hope you fail?"

"If I succeed I'll be back too."

"Then I can't lose," she said.

"That depends on what you consider winning," I said.

She just smiled and kissed me good-bye.

I went back to the main building of the hotel and called Frank. I got one of his sergeants, a woman named Drew. "He's with Dailey," she said. "Do you want me to get him?"

"No, just tell him I'm on my way," I said.

I slipped through the back streets west of Oak Knoll, turned left on Glenarm, and headed for the freeway and the rush-hour traffic awaiting me. I found it two miles above the Golden State interchange: an unending triple-strand bracelet of colored metal, twisting through the Arroyo on its way through town, down toward the Pacific.

As we crept closer to the freeway interchanges I watched the turn signals start to flash as the hopeful looked for better, faster lanes. It's always a vain hope, of course, but the Angelenos are a tolerant breed and they generally wave each other on. Nobody really changes position anyway and the exercise helps to pass the time.

Forty minutes later I walked into Frank's office. He was running a spoon around the inside of a cup.

"What is that?" I asked. "Yoplait?"

"I don't know what the hell it is," he said. "It was the only thing left in the machine. The side of the cup says it's *belle et bon*."

"I wouldn't eat it if I were you."

"I'm not," he said, "I'm just sort of moving it around and trying to figure out whether the lumps are supposed to be there or not."

"Any make on the would-be hitter?"

"You mean DC-10?"

"Why do you call him that?"

"Jerry's nickname," Frank said. "The guy was very high and very well endowed. Proved that the founding fathers were wrong: all men are *not* created equal. He was so wired it's a wonder his feet were on the ground when Craig shot him."

"What was he doing?" I asked.

"Speed."

"And there was a lot in his system?"

"Enough to break the sound barrier," Frank said.

"That doesn't sound like a pro. At least not the kind of pro I'd want to hire."

"He could be in from San Berdoo, trying to settle old debts, but those debts are pretty old by now."

"That's what Diana said. No print record? We thought he might have just gotten out and was making up for lost time."

"No. Nothing anywhere."

"Did he have anything interesting on his stomach?" I asked.

"I asked Jerry," Frank answered. "Just some half-digested capsules and a puddle of stomach juice. You sure you don't want some of this stuff?" He held up the cup and spoon and pointed it in my direction.

"Thanks, but no," I said. "Any scars or identifying marks—anything at all to go on?"

"A tattoo of a naked woman inside a heart."

"Identifiable work?" I asked.

"No. Pin and ballpoint."

"Jesus," I said. "On a part of his body where a lot of people could have seen it?"

"Depends," Frank said.

"On what?"

"On how many people had the pleasure of examining the right cheek of what seemed to Jerry to be a particularly hairy ass."

"Odd place for a tattoo," I said.

"Maybe he was ahead of the fashion curve."

"Must have been a close friend who did the work."

"Or somebody who liked a broad canvas," Frank said.

TWENTY-NINE

I LEFT FRANK TO sort through whatever he could turn on the late but not lamented Mr. DC-10 and drove to UCLA to see a man about a cipher.

His name was Ralph Isley and his putative field was medieval history, but he was one of those people who know everything except how to stay in touch with the real world and how to stay out of trouble. He had called me in December of 1998 (I think about it as late fall since I learned not to talk about *winter* out here). His wife was bedding down with the paperboy and Ralph Isley had to hire me because it was clear that she and her newsprint-stained lover were conspiring to kill him.

At least that's what *he* thought was happening. In fact, the man who owned the paper route and drove the van from whence the Isley paper was unceremoniously thrown each morning was sixty-seven years old and safely at home in Azusa scratching his new by-pass scar. Mrs. Isley was actually meeting with a man of the same name (John Todd) and, regrettably, leaving notes to be mailed to him in the corner of the 8 x 10 corkboard above her kitchen telephone.

She was trying to surprise Ralph with a special Christmas present—a personalized calendar with his favorite pictures actually printed on each monthly page: Ralph at the British Library; Ralph at the Uffizi Gallery; Ralph in his apron, puttering in his makeshift root cellar; Ralph in Bayeux; Ralph in New Haven looking over the tops of his glasses, delivering a conference paper; Ralph in Prague, smiling in the rain; Ralph in his tattersall shirt spreading lab-bunny droppings on the ground around his yellow roses; Ralph in Alanya, Turkey; young Ralph in Sandusky, Ohio, standing next to his mother and Aunt Rose; Ralph resplendent in his tweeds, the day his monograph on Juliana of Norwich won the Goutchley prize; Ralph with his Cairn terrier Robbie, asleep in his lap; and Ralph in his study, chewing on an unlit, straight-grain, bent-billiard pipe—last year's Christmas gift from Nora.

John Todd the paperman was resting in his rumpus room watching the Wheel of Fortune turn, while John Todd the printer was dragging his feet; Christmas was fast approaching, and Nora Isley was writing frantic notes to herself and to the man Ralph would have called Todd *secundus*. Time is running out. I can't wait any longer. If you can't do this I'll get somebody who can. You promised me you would. He has to be surprised. I can't wait another year. And so on. When Ralph came across the notes he put two and two together, came up with six and a half, and called me.

When I presented my report and my bill and waited for him to flush with shame or cry out in rage or relief, he simply said, "Thank you for your work," wrote me a check, and returned to a pile of notes scrawled in green ink on faded onionskin. The twelfth century was beckoning and he had more important things to do than worry about a simple mistake. I tried to soften it by telling him I had done all I could to make sure that his wife wouldn't suspect she was being investigated, but he brushed the fact aside, saying that she was used to him by now and still loved him anyway.

I asked him what he was working on and his eyes glimmered with interest. What followed was a thirty-five-minute disquisition on a cache of manuscripts in the Mercian dialect that had been found in a lead box in an outbuilding of an estate near Aberdeen by a wayward Scotsman looking for a pitchfork and bean sack. Trying to appear interested, I asked him about the later history of the manuscripts and he ticked off every owner and editor through whose hands the documents had passed. One was a WWI major-turned collector named Rively and when I asked for more details about him Ralph gave me everything but his neck size, including the dimensions of the walnut cabinet (inherited from Rively's great Aunt Charlotte) in which the manuscripts were eventually housed. He also gave me the academic pedigree of the Huntington Library Director and the corporate pedigree of his sidekick development officer who later convinced the major's heirs and assigns that a more comfortable resting place for the family treasure would be in Pasadena, where they would cuddle the manuscripts in their very own hot little hands.

When I called Ralph today after finishing with Frank he had no idea who I was. I said something about his wife and about the manuscripts in Mercian and about our talk and he promptly recapitulated my part of the conversation word for word.

I found a parking place and his building, knocked on his office door, and waited for a response. "Come in," he said, and I tried to open the door. It was wedged. "Push," he said. I did and it opened wide enough for me to slip through. The floor was covered with boxes and papers and he had apparently shoved some of them against the door so that he could reach those in the corner beyond.

I reminded him who I was and he just stared. "I want to ask you something," I said. "I need help and I figured if anyone could answer my question you could."

"Well sit down," he said, "sit down." He reached for his Christmas pipe—a little worse for wear now—and stuffed the bowl with some special blend in a clear plastic pouch with a tobacconist's logo and zip-strip in matching red. The tobacco itself was nearly black and smelled like something designed to drive away children and small animals. He turned on the industrial-strength fan above the window behind his desk. "Special ventilation system; I had to negotiate with the Chancellor," he said. Then he lit the pipe and the fire reflected in his eyes. The smoke was dense, but the fan pulled it very efficiently, sparing visitors any possible discomfort. It also pulled the hairs on the back of his neck into a nearly horizontal position. "Well, what can I do?" he said, engaged.

"I need help with a cipher."

"What kind?" he asked.

"I'm not sure. We have a series of numbers that look like phone numbers, but aren't."

"Clem Greene."

"I beg your pardon . . . ." I said.

"Quentin C. Greene. Actually Quentin Clemmer Greene. Nicknamed *Clem*. From Mississippi originally. He doesn't look at all like a Clem. That's probably why the name stuck. He's here in town."

"And he's an expert on ciphers?"

"*The* expert, with the possible exception of Win Hamer. Actually Winston Bradley Hamer III."

"Do you know either one of them?"

"Personally?"

"Yes."

"Of course not. But I know *of* them."

"Tell me what you know," I said.

He looked at his watch. "Perhaps I should just give you the essentials," he said.

"I'd appreciate that."

"Clem Greene and Win Hamer go back a long, long way. They were at Choate together and then, in the late thirties and early forties, at Yale. Norman Holmes Pearson recruited the two of them into the OSS. He was head of X-2, the counterintelligence branch at OSS/London. The Ryder Street group."

"Responsible for cracking Axis codes."

"Among other things. Greene and Hamer were Pearson's prize pupils. Greene had the edge in schoolwork, Hamer in athletics, though in each case it was a close call. Alan Turing once said that Clem Greene had the finest intelligence he'd ever encountered in a man who'd chosen literature over science. Win Hamer never forgave him."

"Greene?"

"No, Turing. But Greene too."

"So they were rivals," I said.

"Friendly rivals, they would say."

"There is no such thing," I responded.

Ralph assumed a professorial tone. "Very good, Jack." I felt as if I had just received extra credit on my midterm.

"And does Hamer live in Los Angeles too?"

"Oh yes. Clem and Win have a monthly lunch at the Jonathan Club. They talk over old times and play one-upsmanship games. I'm surprised you weren't aware of them. Didn't you see the picture in the *Times* last summer?"

"Which picture?"

"The picture of Clem Greene receiving the Society of Britain medal. It was presented by the British Ambassador; he made a special trip to California just for the event. I'm surprised you don't remember it. The mayor was there and some other prominent locals. Clem was at center stage. Win was standing behind him wearing a forced smile. He looked as if he'd like to be putting an ice pick into Clem's neck."

"So you think Greene is the one I should contact."

"Oh yes, if he'll see you. If he won't, call Hamer. They're both very good."

"Any ideas on how to approach him?"

"Offer him money."

"But you said he's a member of the Jonathan Club. He shouldn't need any money."

"He doesn't. Clem Greene is an only child from the richest family in Biloxi; he also married the heiress to a Pittsburgh steel fortune. He simply likes to have more."

"I'll see what I can do," I said.

Ralph smiled without speaking, tamped down the ashes in his pipe, and returned to his papers.

THIRTY

WITH THE RICH AND famous I usually start with a *Who's Who* entry, figuring they'll offer up information there that they won't put in the phone book, but when I looked in the white pages on the off chance that his name just might be there it actually was, along with his address and phone number. If you want to make money you have to advertise.

I knew his area of the Palisades. He and his neighbors sit on a high bluff overlooking the Pacific. The air is cool and fresh and the ground is more secure than that at Malibu. Fewer fires; fewer mud slides; fewer tourists; fewer teenagers in 4 x 4's. Except for the fact that I was $6,000,000 and some change short I could have moved in any time. When I called and told him I wanted to 'employ his expertise' he agreed to meet me for drinks later that afternoon. He suggested the Miramar bar at 4:00.

I got there early and asked the woman at the door to watch for a man named Greene looking for a man named Grant. It turned out to be unnecessary. When Quentin Clemmer Greene walked through the door his name could have been emblazoned in a neon halo encircling his close-cropped head.

He was about 5'8" with gray-black hair and thick, matching eyebrows. He wore a brown tweed jacket with flannel slacks and a sweater vest over a checked shirt and brown wool tie. His complexion was red and weathered but he looked healthy for a man in his eighties who chain-smoked British cigarettes through a yellowed ivory filter. I particularly liked his haircut. You can always tell the difference between a $12 job and a $75 job—the $75 job looks like your hair was never cut; it just stopped growing when it reached a state of perfection.

The introductions were cool and formal.

"Mr. Grant."

"Mr. Greene."

"Please, sit down."

"Thank you."

The waitress approached and asked what we would like.

"I'd like a Gibson," he said.

I ordered a fino sherry and sipped it with a straight face.

"So, Mr. Grant, tell me about your project," he said, tasting his Gibson and pronouncing it "quite acceptable."

"I represent a client whose wife has been found murdered."

"So you're a detective then?" he asked.

"Yes, quite," I said. He seemed to like the *quite*.

"Go on."

"So far we've found nothing of note, with a single exception." I figured he'd like the *single* too.

"And what was that?"

"A list of phone numbers in a computer file. The numbers were fabricated."

"How do you know that?"

"They were attached to names but the numbers were not the numbers of the individuals listed. Some were not even in service."

"But the exchanges were plausible."

"Yes. We theorize that the victim had to use correct exchanges in order to avoid arousing the suspicions of anyone searching through her computer files. Only the last four numbers, we believe, are part of the code."

"You say *we*. Is that the royal *we*, Mr. Grant?"

"No. I'm working on the case with a police lieutenant."

"And why is he not here?"

"*She* was shot."

"She? Very interesting. Presumably she was shot for a reason."

"Presumably."

"The likeliest being that your theories are accurate."

"Yes."

"And that would mean that you are in danger as well."

"Quite," I said.

He paused to take two long puffs of his cigarette. "Forensic work fascinates me," he said, "as I'm sure it does you. I don't have time for enough of it, regrettably. Did I happen to mention my fee?"

"No, I don't believe you did," I said, "but I wouldn't be concerned about that if I were you."

"Oh? And why not?"

"Because a person with your skills should be able to accomplish the decipherment in a matter of moments." (*Accomplish* the *decipherment?*) "I must tell you," I said, "that I sought the advice of a man whose judgment I know to be impeccable. This man informed me that there are only two individuals in America capable of doing this work and that both of them reside in Southern California. The second is a man by the name of Hamer. In the opinion of my informant, you are (I don't know any other way of saying this) the better man. Hamer is quite good, actually *very* good I'm told, but I was instructed to approach you first."

"Cigarette?" he asked, opening a sterling, monogrammed case. It was an antique. I wondered if he had picked it up during the war.

"No thank you," I said.

He put out his current cigarette, finished his Gibson, signaled the waitress for a refill, and put a fresh cigarette in his holder. He lit it, exhaled, and smiled knowingly.

"Mr. Grant, I am a straightforward man, as you are. I do not believe in false modesty. Indeed, I find it rather banal. Your informant was quite accurate. Winston Hamer is an able man. I say that as one who has numbered him among my particular circle of friends for many years. He *could* decipher your set of numbers. I am quite sure of that. On the other hand, we do not honor the truth when we twist it in the name of good manners. Winston Hamer is still the finest player of polo in the state of California over the age of fifty and he is approaching his eighty-third birthday. He is a skilled golfer and a man whose ground strokes are just this side of a tennis professional's. He has a hunter's eye, a surgeon's hand, and a wine steward's palate (by the way you really should try one of these Gibsons), but in the area of cryptanalysis . . . ."

"He is *not* the better man."

"Quite."

"Then you'll help me."

"It's rather a duty, is it not, what with the fallen lieutenant?"

"So I thought," I said.

"Burke was quite wrong, you know. The age of chivalry is not dead."

The waitress approached. "I'll try one of your Gibsons," I said.

"There you are," Greene said.

———

We chatted for a few more minutes. I asked him about his experiences in the war. He parried the question and spoke instead about gin. "Short for *Geneva*, you know. The juniper berries are crucial, of course, but insufficient. There must be body, but also a certain smoothness. You must feel it on the tongue but it dare not weigh too heavily. Americans bruise their gin and then they freeze it. They don't really want to *taste* their drinks, you know."

"Certainly not their beer," I said.

"But who would want to taste that?" he said, smiling, and puffing on his cigarette. "Every beer in the world is superior to American beer. Don't you agree?"

"I particularly prefer Indian beer."

"Yes, quite. Kingfisher?"

"Or Golden Eagle."

"Yes, in those lovely large bottles."

"The greatest crime," I said, running my fingertip around the circle of the martini glass, "is perpetrated against fine Chardonnay."

"Exactly," he said. "It should never be chilled. I won't tolerate it above cellar temperature. Would you?"

"No, but I seldom drink American Chardonnay. Once one has become accustomed to Puligny-Montrachet it's so difficult to drink anything else."

"In white wine, of course."

"Yes, of course," I said.

"You are quite an interesting man, Mr. Grant. Have you always been a detective?"

"No, for many years I worked for the government, but I'm not at liberty to discuss my activities on their behalf."

"Yes, yes," he said, his eyes widening. "And what of the lieutenant? Is she equally interesting?"

"Much more so," I said.

"I should like to meet her."

"I'm sure she would enjoy meeting you," I said, tightening my teeth and holding my expression.

"Now, where are the numbers?" he asked.

"Right here," I said, taking a copy of the list from my jacket pocket.

"How can I reach you when I've finished?"

"Try the two numbers at the bottom of the column, the ones in pencil."

"Very droll," he said. "I shan't confuse them with the others."

"I look forward to hearing from you. I trust it won't be long."

"I have an engagement this evening, but I'll have a look first thing tomorrow," he said.

"Thank you," I said.

"Don't mention it," he said, shaking my hand, looking to his left and right, and then disappearing from the bar.

I hurried to the lobby phones and called Diana. I was anxious to tell her of my meeting with Greene. The switchboard connected me with her room and the phone rang. It rang again and again—eight times without an answer. For a second I thought she might be in the bathroom, but there is a phone in the bathroom, and two phones in the main room. I let it ring four more times. Then I ran to my car.

THIRTY-ONE

I WAS JUST PASSING the giant fig tree on the south side of the Miramar when I thought I should call Frank. He could get there faster and deploy a small army in a matter of minutes. But then I thought better of it, got my car from the lot, and pulled out onto Wilshire.

If someone had already gotten to her I was too late anyway. If there was some foulup or misunderstanding there was no reason to draw attention to her by calling out the LAPD and any collateral cavalry from Pasadena.

I caught the 405 from Santa Monica Boulevard, headed north to pick up the Ventura, and then drove due east to the San Gabriel Valley. I got off at Lake, took Lake into Oak Knoll, but then stopped just short of the hotel's entrance and turned right on Wentworth, parking behind the hotel's lanais. I cut across the lawn and through the flower beds, smiled at an angry groundskeeper, caught the edge of the picture bridge and turned left into the building proper.

I was walking quickly but I slowed as I approached Diana's room. Standing to the right of her door with my automatic in my hand I knocked gently. There was no response. I knocked again. Suddenly I heard the chain lock slide off its catch and saw the door's bar handle turn.

I came through the door with my arm braced and my gun aimed at chest level. The second my foot hit the carpet the barrel of an automatic hit my face between my nose and right cheek. I moved my eye as quickly as I could and found myself staring into Diana's.

"Room Service?" I said.

She closed the door, locked, and bolted it. "Room Service?" she answered. "You're lucky you're still standing there and not splattered across the front of the door or holding your groin and doing a dance to the pain gods."

"Where were you?"

"I was right behind the door after the first knock," she said. "I looked out through the peephole and saw a hand with a gun in it about to knock again and got ready to respond in kind."

"No," I said, "I mean earlier. I called you about forty minutes ago and there was no answer."

"I was here."

"Why didn't you pick up the phone?"

"Oh, come to think of it I wasn't here."

"Where were you?"

"I went down the hall for a second, to get some ice."

"You went down the hall?"

"Yes, daddy, wasn't I allowed to?"

"I don't think it was a very good idea," I said.

"Well, my arm hurt like hell and my knee felt worse. I fell on it, remember. Since I couldn't sleep I decided to do something about the pain. Ice was safer than a trip to the drugstore. Besides, I had on this one-size-fits-all robe with a gun underneath."

"How do you feel now?"

"Wonderful. Do you think you could go out in the hall with your gun and come in like that one more time?"

"Seriously."

"I feel a little better."

"Good. Let's see what's in the minibar." I found four airline bottles of Chivas and fixed us each a double. "I've made progress," I said.

"You have? Why don't you tell me about it?" she said, sliding back in an armchair and putting her bare feet on the edge of the bed. The robe fell open across her thighs. I saw the bruise on her knee; it was reddish purple. I decided to take another look at her thighs.

I told her all about Greene and about our chat. I told her how I tried to avoid paying him by holding out the possibility that I'd go to his rival, Hamer. "I appealed to the primal male need to maintain dominant relationships," I said.

She smiled. "I bet you were really in your element. By the way, did he pay for the drinks?"

"No, as a matter of fact he didn't."

"That's what I figured. You think he'll have something for us by tomorrow?"

"I certainly hope so."

"So what do we do until then?"

"How about some dinner?"

"Fine."

"And some wine?"

"Sure."

"And some cappucino and cognac?"

"That sounds good," she said. "What about after that?"

"Do I have to plan everything?" I asked.

"I thought you already had," she answered.

THIRTY-TWO

Frank told me once that there were two things you could never trust: room-service veal and the eye-witness testimony of a mother-in-law. I still defer to him on the latter, but the Ritz proved him wrong on the veal. Diana had hers with rice; I had mine with something that started out as a potato but ended up as something much more interesting. We shared a green salad and a bottle of Dehlinger Pinot and then split a tiramisu.

She took the two minibottles of Amaretto from the minibar and poured them into our mini-capuccinos. "That's called a Marlinespike, did you know that?" she asked.

I tasted it. "Great drink," I said. "Terrible name. A Marlinespike should be made of things like rum and bull's blood, not capuccino and Amaretto."

"Bull's blood actually *is* a kind of wine, you know."

"Spanish, right?"

"Yes, but Hungarian too," she said. "See how many interesting things you learn when you come to my bedroom."

Her robe was separating at the top now as well as at the bottom. "Quite a classroom," I said.

"What would you like after your Marlinespike?" she asked.

"That depends. How do you feel?"

"I thought you could tell *me* that."

After I moved our dishes to the center of the table, slid back the braces, collapsed the sides, and rolled it into the hallway, Diana invited me to join her on the bed. "How's the shoulder—seriously?" I asked.

"It's not too bad," she said, her left arm laying at her side. "Just don't expect any bear hugs."

"I don't expect anything. That way I'm always surprised."

"Come here," she said, leaning toward me. I sensed the slightest wince of pain as she tried to turn her body. "Relax," I said, putting my hand on her cheek and kissing her.

"I am relaxed," she said, "but you're not."

"Sure I am."

"No, you're not. You're afraid you're going to hurt me."

"Is that bad?"

"No, it's sweet, but it's also unnecessary."

I kissed her again and then slid my hand around her back, holding her close but being careful not to touch her shoulder.

"Go ahead and undo the clasp," she said. "Don't be so shy."

The next kiss was longer and deeper but as her legs started to move against mine the nightstand phone rang and we both tensed.

"Who knows we're here?" she asked.

"Nobody," I said.

The phone rang again and as I reached for it she took the corner of the sheet in her hand.

"Yes?" I said.

"Mr. Grant, this is Caroline in the assistant manager's office. There's a Lieutenant White trying to reach you. He says he has an important message for you."

"Is he on the line now?"

"Yes."

"Put him through." I waited for a second for the connections to engage.

"Jack?" Frank said.

"Yes."

"I thought you might be hanging around the hotel. Listen, I just got a call from a man named Greene. He's trying to reach you. He called me when he was unable to catch you at home."

"I gave him your number too. Did he say anything specific?"

"No, but he does a hell of a British accent."

"Was he at home when he called, Frank?"

"Yes. He said he'd be there for another half hour."

"Thanks for calling me."

"Breakthrough on the Bladen case?"

"I hope so. I'll get back to you as soon as I know anything."

I found my wallet and Greene's number and got back on the phone. Diana was lying in the corner of the bed, uncovered, watching me. The phone rang twice before he picked it up.

"Quentin Greene," the very proper voice said.

"Mr. Greene, this is Jack Grant. Lieutenant White said you were trying to reach me. I didn't expect to hear from you this soon."

"I didn't expect to call you," he said. "My wife was detained and I had a few moments to work on your problem. I need to see you."

"Right away?"

"No, I must go out now, but first thing in the morning."

"You've solved it?"

"Yes, I believe I have."

"How early can I see you?"

"Come at nine. Come to the house. Do you know where we are?"

"I have the address; I can find you."

"One other thing . . . ."

"What's that, Mr. Greene?"

"Please don't park in front."

"What is it?" Diana asked. I turned to look at her. It took a second for the question to register. I wasn't used to engaging in serious business discussions with women wearing nothing but yellow panties and a shoulder bandage.

"It was the cipher specialist. I gave him the names and numbers from Cynthia's computer. He says he's solved it."

Her eyes were bright, eager. "Are you going to see him now?" she asked. I couldn't tell whether she wanted me to rejoin her on the bed or hurry off to find out what Greene had learned.

"I can't see him until the morning," I said.

"Oh," she said.

"Disappointed?" I asked.

"I was curious to find out what he might have turned."

She must have seen the hesitation in my eyes. She patted the bed beside her and said, "What are you waiting for—a gilded, engraved, and embossed invitation?"

"No, I was just taking in the view."

"You're lying again," she said. "You must think I'm a sucker for it."

"Aren't you?"

"Maybe a little," she said, holding out her hand.

"You feel cold," I told her. "Do you want me to turn on the heat?"

"You can," she said. "I could have covered myself but I didn't want to spoil your view."

"I'm glad you didn't," I said, reaching up and moving the toggle switch on the thermostat to *heat* and turning the fan dial to *high*. "It'll be warm in here in a minute or two and you won't have to cover at all," I said.

I started to say something else but her lips and then her tongue stopped me. I broke the kiss and said, "I like the way you interrupt."

"I won't let it happen again," she answered.

THIRTY-THREE

I HAD NO IDEA what Clem Greene had to tell me but I knew it wasn't enough to get me out of Diana's bed with any measurable degree of enthusiasm. This was work, *our* work perhaps, but work pure and simple. I figured my curiosity would take twenty miles or twenty minutes (whichever came first) to kick in. It took twenty-five. The fact that I could still catch a hint of Diana's scent on me didn't make it any easier.

At 7:45 in the morning there's no easy way to get into or across the basin. I decided to take the Pasadena to the Santa Monica and drive due west to the sea. That way I'd be coming up the coast if I had any time to spare. Better to be sitting next to the Pacific than in Sherman Oaks at the interchange of the San Diego and Ventura freeways. I was on the PCH at 8:25 and when I checked my watch again at 8:30 I decided to pull off to the side and check the morning tide for hints or answers. The clouds were thick and gray and the southbound lanes of the highway were clogged with traffic, all crawling toward Santa Monica. It wasn't the beach you see in the movies.

And it wasn't the beach you see at night, with parked cars wedged at odd angles and prowling singles waving at each other with beer bottles and wine glasses from the decks of shoreside restaurants and bars.

It was the beach they dragged each night with steel-mesh blankets, waking half-buried drunks the hard way, the beach with public restrooms you shouldn't enter without heavy, impermeable boots, a chastity belt and a sidearm, the beach with scavenger birds and lumps of homeless bodies dotting the park and promenades that abut the Santa Monica Pier. It was the beach with bad food and worse people, where you learn to raise your eyes above your normal field of vision and focus on the horizon beyond.

I couldn't hear the water over the sound of the traffic as I balanced my thermos cup on my knee and poured myself a cup of hot coffee. I scanned the morning *Times*, checking my watch every few minutes. The news was mostly deaths and lawsuits with a sprinkling of foreign civil wars and local acts of random violence. At 8:50 I headed for Clem Greene's digs in the Palisades. I left the highway, drove up Chautauqua Boulevard, and worked my way around to Ocampo Drive. The sun didn't shine any brighter there, but the birds of paradise and bougainvillea provided enough color for any sky to envy. I located Greene's house and then drove on, parking on a side street behind a lawn-service pickup. When I walked back I tried to look like a member of the neighborhood, dressed in comfortable clothes, taking a morning constitutional.

Above the sea the air was clear and the mist that drifted across the bluff was free of dust and diesel smell.

Greene's house was Spanish Revival Majestic with rolling lawns and iron gates. The fan palms had been spaced by a landscape architect and the gray-tile circular driveway in the front of the house looked as if it was cleaned and polished each morning by German elves. Any errant weeds were probably banished before being summarily killed.

The Armed Response alarm system sign was prominently displayed and the closed circuit television camera over the gate was scanning the drive that led to the rear of the house like a robotic Weimaraner trained to eat first and ask questions later, if at all.

I walked up to the porch and rang the bell next to the weathered oak door. The chime was nearly as long as the first act of *Aida*. Greene opened the door himself, looked out at the street, and said "Come in." I didn't expect a handshake and chat with assorted musings about the weather, but Greene looked as if he was expecting a platoon of Beirut militiamen.

"Let's go in here," he said, gesturing in an easterly direction. He took me into a library that was a step above the main floor of the house and overlooked the driveway and side yard. I could see the television camera. It was still panning. Greene pulled the drapes and turned on a bank of lights above the walnut table that ran the length of the room. I noticed the switch that he used. It was a rheostatic model but instead of a dial it had a button with a vertical, moving light that traveled from top to bottom on the switch plate as the intensity of the ceiling lights increased. He was facing down his fears with high tech tools.

"Please sit down," he said. "Would you like coffee or tea?"

"Coffee," I said. "Black."

He pressed the top section of a credenza and a panel opened to reveal a warming tray and matched china tea and coffee pots. He placed napkins on the table (I didn't see where they came from) and poured coffee for both of us. Then he returned the panel to its closed position and pushed it gently until he heard the click. I wondered whether secret drawers and passageways were the newest fixation of the Los Angeles rich.

"Now," he said, "I believe we should get started."

"Thank you for getting back to me so quickly," I said.

He didn't respond to that but put his coffee cup on the table next to a leather-bound folder. Then he sat down across from me, opened the folder slowly, and began to speak.

"As you well know, Mr. Grant, there are many types of ciphers, from simple substitution and transposition ciphers to ciphers of considerable complexity. The cipher you gave me to break was quite basic. It is termed the Polybius Checkerboard. Polybius was a Greek writer who proposed an elementary method of substituting two-digit numbers for letters of the alphabet. In the case of your particular cipher the numbers run together, but that poses no great problem.

"Essentially, the Polybius Checkerboard places the letters of the alphabet in a five-row square box. The letters y and z share the twenty-fifth space and in the case of y or z the letter in the cipher is determined by the verbal context in which it appears. This, of course, poses no great problem either."

Since nothing seemed to be posing a problem for him, I wondered why he seemed so tense and apprehensive.

"The vertical and horizontal sides of the checkerboard," he continued, "form, in effect, x and y axes as in a graph. Thus, one can easily indicate a particular letter by identifying its location on the checkerboard. The letter *j*, for example, is in the second row and fifth column; it is represented by the number 25. Your given name would thus be rendered: 25 - 11 - 13 - 31."

"Simple enough," I said. Unless he had rehearsed it he was doing the numbers in his head.

"Yes, quite."

"What message, might I ask, did Mrs. Bladen leave?"

I was trying to move the conversation forward without winding him so tight that he might snap.

He paused before speaking. "That was the murder victim's name—Bladen?"

"Yes. Cynthia Bladen."

"The attorney?"

"Yes," I said.

"She left a list of names," he said. "Here they are."

He took a loose sheet of paper from the left side of the folder and slid it across the table to me. His hand trembled slightly; he seemed to be glad to be rid of it. There were five names in all and they were typed:

Mariani
DiStephano
Brienza
Santos
Alhambra

He sat looking at me, waiting for my response. He still hadn't touched his coffee.

"It seems clear enough," I said. "Albert Mariani, Donato DiStephano, Antonio Brienza, and Arturo Santos are all well-known local criminals. Together they control approximately 80 percent of the organized crime in Southern California. I don't recognize the name *Alhambra*, assuming it's a name. Of course, it's also a place, southwest of San Marino and San Gabriel, but I'm not sure that that's of any significance. There used to be a drug dealer in East L.A. named Joey Alhambra but Joey had an untimely meeting with a small hammer and a long piece of piano wire—I think around 1987 or 88. The others are all alive and more or less well."

He stared at me for several moments before speaking. "You're certainly very sanguine."

"What did you expect? When you're looking for a murderer you don't begin with garden parties or meetings of the Junior League. You look for a group of murderers; now we have such a group; that means that we're making progress."

"They certainly *are* murderers . . . systematic, merciless, and violent murderers," he said. "If they killed Mrs. Bladen they will certainly not hesitate to kill the two of us."

"They certainly will not," I said.

"Well what do you intend to do?" he asked, insistently.

"I intend to find out who was responsible for Mrs. Bladen's death and have him (or them) sentenced to death by lethal injection. Failing that, I intend to kill him (or them) personally."

"That's very bold of you."

"It's my occupation. And Mrs. Bladen was a friend. I'm surprised at you, Mr. Greene."

"Surprised—why?"

"You went up against Hitler and the Axis war machine. Why are you bothered by a little local scum?"

"May I remind you that we had an army of our own, Mr. Grant, and they stood between my tiny unit and Berlin. Besides, it is one thing to deal with a madman, quite another to deal with a rational organization motivated by greed."

"No, it's really not," I said.

"I beg to differ," he said.

"You *may* differ," I answered, "but you would still be wrong."

"And why would I be wrong, Mr. Grant?"

"Because any person who kills has already made one mistake, Mr. Greene. The odds are good that he will make more."

THIRTY-FOUR

WHAT A GREAT LINE, I thought. "*It's my occupation.*" Fortunately Frank wasn't there or he would have cleared whatever was on his stomach at the expense of Mr. Greene's nice walnut table. A rich fantasy life is a great comfort: One Man Against the Mob: the Jack Grant Story—Morgan Creek and Castle Rock have bid the Towne/Coppola script up to a cool 5 mil and the word from CAA is that Scorsese's now ready to commit. Jimmy Gandolfini likes the Tony Brienza part and Bobby D's mulling over the role of Fat Artie Santos. We'll have product for Christmas release and foreign rights that will push the final numbers past Harry Potter's.

———

And the title role of Jack Grant will be played by Maury Povich. Or maybe Phil Donahue with contacts and a dye job. Jesus, I thought, all you need is a studio audience and a microphone and the bullshit would flow like the Nile. I was glad Diana hadn't been there to hear it. I would never have seen the glistening eyes and the yellow panties again.

The traffic was thick on the San Diego, creeping north toward the Valley. It gave me plenty of time to think about what I had said. The weight of the reality became clearer and clearer as I let my head scroll through the resumés of the names on Cynthia's list.

Albert Mariani was strictly old school. None of that surgical slicing. Just a single round to the head, through the right eye preferably and straight on to the brain. Always in a car and always in daylight. Fast. Simple. A calling card for the cops: *this one's ready for planting, boys. Save the detectives' and the coroner's time and the taxpayers' hard-earned green.* The only problem was that Albert didn't do civilians; at least he hadn't done any that *I* knew of.

Donato (Danny Stephens) DiStephano did though. Danny was an equal opportunity executioner and while his techniques varied they were always ugly. In 1986 when Jesus Montalvez tried to move in on Danny's gambling operations in south-central L.A. he was put on a boat, his arms were strapped across a truck axle, his legs were broken, and he was thrown into San Pedro Bay. Opinions varied on the broken legs. Some thought that Danny was worried that Jesus might be able to kick his way back to the surface. Others said that Danny read somewhere that a crucifixion wasn't complete without them.

Tony Brienza started as a street soldier and worked his way up in the Carlucci organization. When he was on the streets he killed with a revolver or an automatic. When he took over the family he started killing with a shotgun. His accountants told him that a shotgun has a higher kill percentage. Whenever he was crossed he preferred a length of steel pipe. He started with the victim's feet and moved toward the head. Slowly.

Fat Artie Santos preferred silent killers: razors, knives, wire. "I don' wanna draw no fuckin' cops," he'd say. "Those motherfuckers somehow always know how to fin' me anyway. So why make it fuckin' easier?" Artie's M.O. was the closest to my case, except that Artie was usually messier. He liked to see pools of blood. He liked to see it on the street and sidewalk and he liked to see it smeared on walls and telephone poles and car upholstery. "Hey, this is fuckin' Hollywood," he'd say. "It should make a fuckin' statement. When they find the bodies I wanna hear the screams from fuckin' Long Beach to fuckin' Malibu. You ain' jus' puttin' some piece a shit away, you're telling the asshole wannabe who wants to replace him to think twice about it."

A nice quartet. And you could get them together even easier than you could have reunited the Beatles. If there was serious money to be made they'd all be there. And you wouldn't have to deal with noisy crowds and roadies and vendors and groupies and agents and publicists. This group didn't want publicity. All they wanted was the gate receipts. And the hearts, lungs, and spleens of anyone who thought about trying to short them.

But who was Alhambra? New kid in the basin? A relative of Joey's? Maybe somebody with a knife. Somebody who liked to cut rectangles of flesh from women's bodies before he buried them in the wilderness or the desert. Somebody much tidier than Fat Artie. Somebody who didn't want to attract attention. Somebody who was happy enough just to kill. And carve out a little warm skin in the process.

I eased into the right lane a full mile before the Ventura interchange. In traffic this thick I always play it safe. For the moment I was surrounded by semi's and pickups. I couldn't see anything on my sides so I looked up, hoping to see some sky.

The canopy of smog over the Valley was thinner than the jungle ceiling of South Vietnam, but not by much. At least there weren't any mortar shells or Chinese grenades dropping through the palm fronds and into the center of our convoy.

I entered the interchange ramp and pointed myself east but I wasn't really going anywhere. The Ventura was worse than the San Diego. The commuters were sipping coffee from wide-bottomed mugs and catching sentences from folded newspapers while the tourists in the rental Tauruses and Sables were looking at their watches and wondering how long the lines at Universal were going to be.

After ten minutes of feathering the brake the traffic loosened enough for me to cruise at a brisk 20 mph. As I came into Studio City and approached the Laurel Canyon exit I was flying at 25. At the Hollywood interchange we stopped again and I rode the brake, easing ahead and trying to stay focused enough to avoid bumping the car in front of me. To pass the time I looked into the rear-vision mirror, even though I knew I'd see nothing but rows of colored metal boxes, with thin-lipped, impatient drivers, receding forever into the distance.

I looked, then blinked, then looked again. Three cars behind me was a large blue van with tinted windshield and a ladder strapped to the roof. Even in the filtered glare of a smoggy morning I could see the glow of a cigarette near the driver's window.

I signaled and moved into the right lane. The van followed. At the Lankershim exit I signaled again. The van was four cars behind me now. I looked in the mirror and saw its right turn signal blink. As I headed south on Lankershim the van was two cars behind me. I turned left, caught Cahuenga, and then turned again, quickly working my way through side streets. Suddenly the van was nowhere in sight. I pulled into the driveway of a deserted house with a large For Sale sign and drove around to the back. I checked my watch, waited for ten minutes, and then drove back onto the street. Still no sign of the van. Then I drove back to Cahuenga and pulled into the covered lot of a small office building.

I called Greene and got his answering machine. "This is Jack Grant," I said. "If you're still there, leave. Leave immediately and don't tell anyone where you're going. You can reach me through the channel you used before."

Then I called Frank and told him what happened.

"I've got some people on the way to check Greene's house," he said. "Are you sure you were being followed?"

"There are a lot of blue vans in Southern California," I said, "but this one also had a ladder on the top. It changed lanes when I changed lanes and it exited when I exited."

"Lankershim's a busy exit," Frank said. "I wouldn't start looking over my shoulder that often this soon. It was probably just a coincidence."

"Why aren't you as suspicious as you used to be?" I asked.

"I still am," he said.

"Only you're suspicious of me now, is that it?"

"I didn't say that. All I said was it could be a coincidence."

"How soon can you be free?" I asked. "We've got a lot to talk about."

THIRTY-FIVE

The Pacific Dining Car is in the demilitarized zone between the developing corridor of mid-Wilshire office buildings and the tightly planted garden of downtown Los Angeles high-rises. A local tradition, it consists of an old train car with some new wings. The food is excellent, the portions are large, the waiters are friendly, the restrooms are clean, the wine list is ample, and the prices are familiar—they're the same as those they used to charge on the trains when your only choices were to pay, to go to sleep hungry, or to try to make a meal out of club-car bar fruit.

I didn't have anything in my stomach but the lingering acid of Clem Greene's coffee and Frank told me he hadn't eaten since lunch the day before. We arrived together, handed our car keys to Tommy Florio, the parking attendant, and asked for a big table in a quiet corner. I ordered juice, eggs, toast, fried potatoes, coffee, and homemade sausage. Frank had the sausage, juice, coffee, toast, and a stack of pancakes.

"Their sausage is the best," he said, "always big and spicy."

"Just like you," I said.

"Yeah, right," he answered.

We downed our juice and asked for refills. "So tell me," he said, "what did you turn?"

"More than I bargained on. I told you that Cynthia left a group of numbers in her computer . . . ."

"Yes, you did."

"Greene deciphered them."

"That's good. What did he find?"

"Five names: Mariani, DiStephano, Brienza, Santos, and Alhambra."

"Jesus," Frank said, "why the hell would she be involved with that group of dirtbags?"

"I don't know," I said. "I don't know that she was. All I know is that their names were in her computer."

"Who's Alhambra?" Frank asked. "Not Joey Alhambra. They planted him years ago."

"I don't know. I thought maybe you'd have some ideas. That's why I volunteered to take out a loan and buy you breakfast here."

"I'll do some checking," he said.

"Thanks. What do you figure that group had in common?"

"Besides greed, an appetite for violence, and the lack of any semblance of human feeling or morality?"

"Yes."

"I don't know. They've worked together in the past when it suited them, especially Danny and Fat Artie. They've all been competitors over the years, but they've always tried to avoid outright war—too bad for business. Instead they stick to their own turf and their own action. Albert had one of Tony Brienza's people blown up a couple years ago, but for some reason or other the two of them made peace fast. Maybe Albert offered up somebody to Tony. Maybe Tony's guy was a rogue, trying to freelance—who knows? I'll take a look at the files and see what we've got that's current."

"I'd appreciate it," I said. "You know, I just can't imagine Cynthia being involved with them. I can't conceive of her caving in or selling out like that. I can't even visualize her in their presence. None of this fits—at least not for me."

"Maybe not," Frank answered, "but I don't have any trouble imagining them burying her in the woods if she got in their way."

"Maybe she found out something they didn't want her to know."

"Maybe."

"I'll see what I can find out," Frank said. "How's the sausage?"

"Terrific."

"Didn't you and Cynthia eat here every now and then?"

"Yes, as a matter of fact we did," I said. I was going to say something else but my thoughts seemed to just trail off.

———

I asked for a refill on the coffee and Frank stood up. "Let me check on what's happening in the Palisades," he said.

He was gone for almost ten minutes. When he returned he noticed that I had gotten him fresh coffee and said thanks.

"What's the word?" I asked. You could never tell from Frank's expression.

"Nothing really," he said. "Our people went to Greene's house, but nobody was home. There was no sign of violence, no sign of a break-in."

"Were there any cars there?"

"No, the driveway and garage were both empty."

"And Clem Greene has a good security system."

"The best," Frank said, "and no alarms were set off. He even has a set of closed-circuit TV cameras."

"I know."

"He and his wife probably went to work."

"He doesn't work," I said. "I don't know about the wife."

"Maybe they went out to play."

"Maybe."

"*He* made the appointment, didn't he?"

"Yes, for 9:00."

"To him that's probably early. He wanted to meet then so he'd have the rest of the day free."

"If they could find me they could find him," I said. "And they wouldn't have picked me up on the 405. They would have picked me up in the Palisades."

"And they would have snatched him first, found out what he knew, and then gone after you."

"That's what I'm figuring."

"Like I said, it could all be a coincidence."

"I hope it is," I said.

"We'll have somebody keep an eye on Greene's house. What are you going to do now?"

"Check on Diana."

"Jack . . . ."

"What?"

"If it wasn't a coincidence you'll want to be careful."

"I know," I said, and signaled the waiter for the check.

THIRTY-SIX

THERE IS NO EASY way to get to Pasadena from downtown except the freeway or the back streets to Huntington Drive. If I *was* being followed the tail would have no trouble staying with me on those routes. It took more time but I cut the chances by taking the Hollywood west, driving through Silver Lake, past Griffith Park, and on to the Ventura in Glendale. The combination of freeways and streets makes it tougher to stay with another car in a fast flow and then disappear when you hit neighborhood side streets. Either way, if I was actually being followed the tail would think I was headed west or north, not northeast.

I didn't see anybody along the way and when I hit the Ventura and started winding through the mountains, past Sycamore Canyon and Scholl Canyon, I took my eye off the rear-vision mirror for a few minutes and thought about Cynthia.

The things you remember are never the things you expect to remember. One night I was supposed to meet her for dinner at 6:00 sharp at a place in Costa Mesa. I was held up on a case and then got stuck on the Santa Ana freeway between Buena Park and Anaheim and arrived an hour and a half late. I expected her to be angry, but she wasn't. She was sitting on a terrace outside the restaurant, poring over a novel called *The Dream Maker*. She was so absorbed in the book that when I arrived she almost seemed disappointed. I asked her if she wanted a drink and she said, "You go ahead, I want to finish this chapter."

Since the book was obviously more interesting to her than I was, I asked her about it. "It's about a couple who keep having the same dreams," she said. "They lie in bed at night, thrash around with nightmares, and wake up in the morning and talk about what happened. Each time that the husband narrates his dream the wife tells him that the dream she had was exactly the same as his. That spooks both of them and they realize that something's going on that can't be explained in any normal way. The wife believes that she's somehow become psychic and that this power is going to destroy their marriage rather than save it. She flips out. The husband's frightened by the dreams and frightened by his wife and he tries to deal with it all by talking—he turns manic, telling his dreams over and over, trying to exorcise the demon inside by bringing it out in the open."

"So what is it," I asked, "a horror novel?"

"No," she said, "it's a mystery. I think the woman's the villain, or rather the villainess. I think she's made it all up and tricked the husband into revealing his dreams and fears and fantasies."

"Why would she want to do that?"

"I don't know yet; I've got another seventy pages to go."

"So it's not about the supernatural."

"No, it's about trust."

I remember saying something lame about my being late and knowing she would wait because she *trusted* me. She came back with something sweet, reassuring, and brief, since she wanted to get back to her chapter rather than make small talk.

Later during dinner I asked her about *her* dreams and she told me about her most recent ones in minute detail. "You must really trust me to tell me all of that," I said.

"I do," she said. "I *do* trust you."

Actually the dreams weren't very interesting—mostly standard anxiety stuff, the sort of thing you'd expect from a young lawyer with a heavy case load, a set of impatient senior partners, and a bad commute. Still, I remember her willingness to describe them for me.

On the few occasions when I said something to Laura Weeks about her dreams she made it clear that she didn't want to talk about them. That only increased my curiosity; perhaps that was why she refused to discuss them.

I hadn't asked Diana yet what went through her head when she slept. She probably had dreams, but I figured she didn't *have* nightmares; she *gave* them.

As I thought more and more about Cynthia I realized that what we had was heavier on trust than on passion. There are times in your life when you need that and Cynthia and I were always able to give it to one another. With her, it was something I never expected to lose. Maybe I hadn't—my name *was* still in her Rolodex.

I kept coming back to my comment to Frank—I couldn't imagine her being involved in anything sordid or illegal. I knew her too well and trusted her too deeply.

The other image I kept returning to was that of a midsummer weekday afternoon. Cynthia and I were on the beach in Montecito—the more private section down by the Biltmore, away from the boulevard, the traffic, and the strip of sprawling Santa Barbara resort hotels. A few locals were walking between the tide line and the steps and stone wall, tossing balls or sticks and running their dogs through the sand and into the warm ocean water. The pelicans were cruising the coast between Montecito and Hope Ranch and the oil platforms were dotting the skyline and breaking the view of the Santa Barbara Channel.

Cynthia was lying on a white blanket, wearing the briefest of pink and white bikinis. Strategic parts of her body were exceeding the limits set by the spandex, but she was paying no attention because she was telling me about a case she had been assigned. I don't remember it now and I couldn't really focus on it then, but it had something to do with a contract between a group of farmers in the central valley and a large trucking company that had gone into receivership before it could cart off the farmers' vegetables and fruit to the southern California markets.

As I watched and tried to listen I kept saying to myself, "This is a very attractive woman who is entirely too dedicated to her work. If I ever need a lawyer I'm calling her first." She kept talking and I kept watching and together we passed a pleasant afternoon. Whenever she asked, "So what do you *think*?" I nodded and hmmmm'd a lot and told her I was sure that her clients were in very good hands. Somehow I remembered clearly what I had also said to her then: "They've found a lawyer they can *trust*."

———

I turned off the freeway and followed the Tournament of Roses Parade route down Colorado Boulevard. Then I turned right on Raymond and started slaloming my way through the back streets of Pasadena. I didn't want to be obvious about it, but I didn't want to be followed either.

I crossed the parkway at Del Mar and headed south on Marengo to the side entrance of a strip mall that stretched along Glenarm. There's a unisex hair salon in the mall called Turning Heads which I use from time to time. All the beauticians are black and they all have names like Danelia; they give the best haircuts in town and they're always amused when a white, male face comes through the door. Their windows are tinted gray and they front on both Glenarm and Marengo, so you get a good view of anyone who might be waiting outside for you. I stuck my head in the door, greeted the woman who usually cuts my hair—Rayletta—and looked out a few windows. Then I walked through the parking lot and into the Thai restaurant that replaced the Japanese restaurant that replaced the Mexican restaurant, picked up a carry-out menu, looked out a few more windows, and went back to my car.

I got to the Ritz in about six minutes, parked in the ramp, and walked around to Diana's room. I knocked on the door, identified myself, and she let me in without wedging the barrel of her automatic between my cheek and eye. Instead she extended her right index figure like a gun barrel and worked it playfully between my ribs.

"That's a warmer welcome than I got last time," I said. I turned toward her, kissed her, and took a long look. She was wearing a red Ritz-Carlton souvenir tee-shirt that was at least a size too small and stretched snugly across her chest and hips.

"Where'd you get that?" I asked.

"From the gift shop. I called and they delivered. It comes in three different colors. What do you think?"

"I like it a lot."

"It's too tight, but you probably like it that way."

"Yes, well . . . we're all entitled to our personal standards. How's your shoulder?"

"It hurts like a son-of-a-bitch. I was trying to cheer myself up with a little shopping."

"Are you still taking your pills?"

"No."

"Then that's why it hurts."

"So, who cares? I'll survive."

"I won't. Not if you dress like that."

She just smiled.

I got some ice from the mini-tray in the mini-freezer in the mini-bar, poured some juice over it, and called Frank. I wanted to know if Greene or his wife had returned home yet. They hadn't. While I talked, Diana sat in the adjoining chair with her feet resting across my lap. I hung up and asked her why she was trying to distract me.

"I'm not just trying; I'm doing it," she said.

"Why? Don't you want me to do my job?"

"What's your job—staring holes through my tee-shirt?"

"Finding Cynthia's killer."

"Oh. Well, I'll say this, you seem to be doing it well."

"Thank you."

She paused for a second before speaking.

"I notice you've switched to juice instead of scotch lately."

"That's because you're distracting me."

"I figured it was because you wanted to stay sober and not miss anything," she said, turning from side to side in the chair, showing off the tee-shirt and its contents.

"My compliments on your ability to distract."

"Maybe that should be my new job."

"Yes? Well, you seem to be doing it well."

Again the smile, but this time with a rub of her right foot against my leg.

———

"So what have you learned?" she asked.

"I'm not sure."

"You're not sure what you have?"

"I know what I have; I don't know how it all fits together."

"So tell me what you have," she said. Her feet were no longer stretched across my legs and rolling against my thigh.

"Cynthia's phone numbers were actually part of a simple cipher. Greene broke it and gave me the message, which was a list of five names: Mariani, DiStephano, Brienza, Santos, and Alhambra."

"Christ, what wonderful company," she said. "Who's Alhambra? Not Joey Alhambra. He's already been killed, planted, and replaced."

"I don't know. It could be the place rather than a person, but that doesn't make any sense. That group doesn't hang out in Alhambra—more like Bel Air, Palos Verdes, or Newport Beach."

"You think your old girlfriend could have been in bed with the mob?"

"No, I can't believe that."

"So what was she trying to say and who was she trying to say it to?"

"I don't know."

"I haven't heard much on Mariani or DiStephano lately. Tony Brienza was in the papers a month or two ago . . . an incident in Beverly Hills, I think."

"Yes. He was at a restaurant and didn't like the food. When he and his entourage got up to leave he said something about needing to make a stop first. Then he went out to the waiting area, walked up to this ornamental fountain behind the maître d', unzipped his fly, took out little Tony, and relieved himself before the assembled patrons. The wife of some big arts donor told him that his act was "in disgusting taste." "Yeah, well, lady," he said, "if you think this is bad, don't order their fuckin' veal." By then the owner had been called. He stormed out from the kitchen, saw that it was Tony Brienza, thought better about calling the police or the lawyers, cringed and groveled for a minute or two, threw in some additional apologies, and told Mr. Brienza that there would be no charge for the dinner. "Give the money to your fuckin' help," Tony said, "they look like they could use it.""

"A real charmer," Diana said. "I haven't heard too much about Fat Artie lately. They suspected that he was involved in the killing of that state legislator, but nobody could prove it."

"The one who was blocking the contracts Artie was involved in."

"Right. The one they found with his nose sliced off and a pair of ice picks in his heart and brain."

"Yes."

"Why would your lawyer friend want to get involved with scum like that? Surely she wasn't representing them."

"I can't believe that she would be. Maybe she found out something about them and they had her killed."

"How would *she* find out about *them*?"

"That's what I've got to figure out," I said, "along with the identity of Alhambra."

"Why don't we go talk to Mortie Gold?"

"Who's Mortie Gold?"

"You don't know Mortie Gold? You've got a real treat coming."

THIRTY-SEVEN

"So who is Mortie Gold?"

"The tailor to the stars . . . and to the scum."

"You think he might know what our gang of five is up to?"

"He might."

"How do I find him?"

"What do you mean *I*? I'm going too," she said.

"I think you should stay here and rest a while longer."

"I feel fine."

"What do you mean you feel fine? You told me that your shoulder hurt like a son-of-a-bitch; how can you investigate a murder case? If you take your medicine you'll be groggy. If you don't take your medicine you'll be in terrible pain. Why don't you just sit tight for a few more days and let your body heal?"

"I appreciate the thought, but let me worry about that," she said. "You're not an expert on my body . . . at least not yet."

"I'm willing to learn," I said.

Again the smile. "Come on," she said, "I'm getting tired of this cage."

"Let me go first," I said. "If anybody's hanging around I'll take care of them. If not, I'll drive back on Wentworth and park behind the building. You can go out the side door at the end of the hall and cut through the garden and eucalyptus trees."

"How will I know when you're there?"

"Give me eight minutes. If I'm not there when you look out, go back to your room and wait for me."

"OK. Just one thing . . . ."

"What's that?"

"If you leave me here and try to find Mortie by yourself you will live to regret it in more ways than you can possibly imagine."

"I figured as much," I said. "I'll see you in eight minutes."

Mortie Gold had a shop on Melrose, surrounded by costume dealers, Art Deco antique stores, and nail parlors with window ads in fluorescent paint. He had been there for thirty years, according to Diana, and had continued to refuse to move. He had worked for Edith Head back in the glory days and when he opened his own shop a lot of the actors and studio types came to him for civilian clothes. Mortie's suits were conservative, but always stylish. He carried Oxxford suits off the rack at $1,650 and up for the middle class; his tailored suits for his favored clientele started at a cool $2,850. He had a selection of Tino Cosma ties at $125 and up for the tourists looking for a souvenir in a Morton Gold bag and a locked case of one-of-a-kind diamond cufflink and stud sets for the Cartier crowd who preferred one-stop shopping. Mortie was strictly old Hollywood with new Rodeo Drive prices.

At least that's how Diana described him and she wasn't far off. He looked like a shrunken version of Willard Scott, with split-lens horn rims, an over-the-shoulder tape measure, and a dead cigar protruding through thick, liver-toned lips. He carried his tailor's chalk in his left hand and turned it over nervously while he talked. His store was done up in red walnut and gold filigree and most of the shoppers checking out his goods looked as if they could pay as fast as he could price.

When we walked in he was busy talking to a kid with a $75 haircut and a nervous expression, a rich boy whose parents probably sent him there. He was wearing tight black slacks, a black mock turtleneck and a long coat with enough fur on it to give heart attacks to a park-full of animal-rights advocates. It wasn't hard to hear what Gold said to the kid; you could have heard it in the middle of the Melrose traffic: "Slip off your coat. Here, . . . Selma . . . Selma! . . . take this coat and lock it up in the back. We're going to be busy for awhile. Step up here young man, let's see those pants."

The boy stepped up on a carpeted platform in front of a three-sided mirror. Gold started sliding his right hand up the kid's leg and grabbing at his crotch. "Look at this, look at this. No material there. What—are they trying to save money or choke you to death? Doesn't that hurt? Doesn't that pinch you? Who sold you this, the Marquis of Sade?"

"I, uh, got them at . . . ."

"Don't tell me, I don't want to know," Gold said, reaching around with his left hand and grabbing at the kid's butt. "So what is this, spandex? You've got no room to breathe in your seat. You try to bend over and you poke out your *tuckus*; you try to sit down and you cut off your *shvontz* and *baitsim*. What kind of choice is that?"

"That's why I want something hand-tailored, Mr. Gold," the boy said, gathering up his courage.

"Hand-tailored? You mean you want something human. These pants I wouldn't put on my worst enemy. These pants I wouldn't put on the German general staff. And the German general staff *liked* these kinds of pants. And the German general staff *wore* these kinds of pants. And their pants had more room in them than *these pants!*"

"I'd like a whole suit, Mr. Gold."

"Young man. Here you can have whatever you want. Here you will get clothing that you can wear. You can stand up in it, you can sit down in it, you can bend over in it, you can jump up and down in it, you can climb trees in it and you can dance in it. Morton Gold will make you look sexy; he will make you look like a *macher*. He will make you look like somebody who has lots of money and who always smells good. Here, stand still."

Gold opened a drawer in a table next to the mirror and took out some forms. Then he started in again, pulling and feeling and this time taking measurements. The numbers looked like chaotic scribbles. "What kind of goods were you interested in?" Gold asked.

"You mean material?"

"Of course I mean material. What do I sell here?"

"Something gray."

"So, you want to bury people? You want to drive a black Cadillac with lilies in the back? You want to smile at strangers all day and act like you're sad?"

"No, I just wanted something conservative."

"You want conservative, vote for Barry Goldwater. You want clothing, you come to Morton Gold."

"Why don't you pick something nice?"

"I will," Gold said. "And shirts? Do you want real shirts or do you want to keep looking like Captain Kirk in his pajamas?"

"I'll need some dress shirts."

"I'll make them up for you. I do the best Egyptian cotton. They start at two hundred and twenty-five dollars."

"I didn't know you could get cloth from Egypt," the boy said.

"And what did they wrap the mummies in, Glad Wrap and twist ties?"

"Yeah, right. I'm sorry. Why don't you make me six of them?"

"I will," he said, taking some final measurements. "So tell me," he said, "what are you going to do when I turn you into Mr. Sexy?"

"I don't know. I guess I'll have to get used to it for awhile."

"Ah *boitshik*," Gold said, slapping the kid on the back, "you go see Selma now and she'll take your credit card. You come see me in six weeks and we'll start dressing you human."

Gold slipped the list of measurements in a separate drawer as Diana and I approached him. His smile had already dropped before he saw her. "No, no-no, no-no, not the *shikseh* lieutenant with all the goddam questions." He put his hand up at the side of his face as if he was shielding himself from flies or mosquitoes, headed past the fitting mirror, and pushed his hand against a piece of walnut paneling, revealing the office beyond it.

"*Oi*," I said, "again with the secret panels." Diana was right behind him. She followed him in and held open the panel for me. "Hello, Mortie," she said, "how's business?"

"Terrible, terrible," he said. "So who is this, another person to torture me?"

"This is a friend of mine," she said. "He likes to ask questions too."

"And does he have a name?"

"Jack Grant," she said.

"Grant? I have a customer named Grant. He owes me money. What size are you—44 Long?"

"It doesn't matter. I can't afford prices like this."

"Prices like what? Have I said anything about prices?"

"Don't try to bribe him, Mortie," she said.

"Bribe? Bribe, lieutenant? You're here ten seconds and already you're accusing me of felonies?"

"I just want to ask you some questions, Mortie," she said.

"I know you. You want me to talk about my customers. You want me to be unethical. You want me to break peoples' trust. You're wasting your time, lieutenant."

"I've got plenty of it," she said. "Ever come across anybody named Alhambra?"

"Alhambra? You mean that place off the freeway with all the poor people?"

"No, Mortie. A person."

"There was Joey Alhambra," Gold said, "but he never bought anything here. Too cheap. Zoot suiter. Thought it was still the forties. I don't deal with people like that."

"Sure you do, Mortie. You just deal with the rich ones. Like Fat Artie Santos."

"Mr. Santos is a valued customer. I don't know anything else about him."

"Have you seen him lately?"

"I see a lot of people, lieutenant."

"Let's play a little game, Mortie. I'll give you four names and you tell me what they're doing these days: Albert Mariani, Donato DiStephano, Tony Brienza, and Fat Artie Santos."

"What do I know? They're businessmen. Sometimes some of them buy suits from me. Sometimes they buy shirts. A lot of people do."

"I thought business was bad, Mortie," she said. "I thought business was bad all around. Business isn't bad for them. When was the last time you made something up for them?"

"Look, lieutenant, my records are my business. You got no warrant I got no answers."

"I've got something much better," Diana said, "I've got Tony Brienza's phone number. I can call him up and tell him Mortie Gold said he was a fat-assed wop who doesn't pay his bills. I've got Fat Artie's number too. Which one should I call first?"

"*Tren zich!*" Gold answered.

"You talk to her that way?" I said. "You're a brave man."

"Fuck you too, fuck you double," he said.

I just smiled and nodded at Diana, as if to say, "Should I take this one or do you want it?"

"Bye-bye, Mortie," she said. "I've got to go make some phone calls. I'll see you around . . . a little bit of you here, a little bit of you there . . . ."

"Don't threaten me, lady."

She came in close and said, "You think that's a threat, you *putz*? I'll give you a real threat—you start answering my questions or you'll be sitting on the street with a tin cup and a cardboard sign, drinking Thunderbird and dodging dog piss."

"All right, all right," he said. "I'm an honest businessman, an artist even, and I have to put up with this."

"You make dirtbags look good, Mortie. I'm not sure that makes you an artist."

"Ask your questions," he said.

"Same question," Diana said. "Tell me about the four pieces of shit. Have you seen any of them lately?"

"I made a suit for Danny and I sold Tony some shirts and ties."

"They came in for them themselves?"

"Tony did."

"Any interesting small talk?"

"No, nothing."

"Mortie," she said, "I just look patient . . . ."

"All right, all right. He said business was good. Very good, and he wanted to celebrate with some new clothes."

"How many shirts and ties did he buy, Mortie?"

"How should I remember that?"

"Mortie, look at me. Do I look like a person who'll put up with your bullshit?"

"He bought a lot."

"What's a lot?"

"Forty-five shirts and forty ties."

"Why not a matched set?"

"All my ties are originals; Tino only makes a few in a single pattern. Tony bought all I had."

"How much did that cost him, Mortie?"

He stared at her angrily before speaking. "Fifteen thousand dollars."

"He makes that in a couple hours," Diana said, "selling women and dope."

"I wouldn't know about that," Gold said.

"I know. You're only a businessman. An artist."

"That's right," he said.

"Take care of yourself," she said. "And why don't you go wash your hands."

We got back in the car. "I liked the line about the tin cup," I said.

"I knew it would work. To him poverty and death are the same thing."

THIRTY-EIGHT

As we drove back to Pasadena I noticed that Diana changed her position in her seat several times. "How's the shoulder?" I asked.

"I think it's getting better," she said. "There's just this dull throb now."

"You liked reaming Mortie," I said. "That's what you needed."

"I wish he had given us more."

"We're in a recession and crime is a growth industry. That's not really big news."

"No, it's not," she said. "When we get back to the hotel, let's check in with Frank and see if he's got anything."

It took us forty minutes to get back and another ten to drive through alleys and parking lots to make certain we weren't being followed. Frank was in a meeting with his captain, a hard case named Loram, but he got back to me fifteen minutes later. I told him about our meeting with Mortie Gold.

"Did you buy anything from him?" he asked.

"Are you kidding?"

"You should have," he said. "A couple silk ties . . . lay some charm on the lieutenant."

"Right."

"We don't have anything at this end, but Jerry Dailey told me he might have something on Alhambra."

"What's he got?"

"He caught me just as I was going in to meet with Loram. When I got out he was gone. He's probably in the lab."

"We'll come there. It'll take us about twenty-five minutes."

"I'll find him and tell him to stick around."

———

I went through my normal routine, picking up Diana on Wentworth, then headed for Glenarm and the entrance to the freeway at the Parkway. We got downtown in a little over twenty minutes, parked, and met Jerry in the hallway outside his lab. There were stains on his pants cuffs and on his shirtsleeves. He was wiping his hands with a grimy paper towel.

"Jesus," he said, "the only thing I hate more than a week-old body is a perforated bowel. Hi Lieutenant, hi Jack. How you doing?"

"Hi Jerry," I said.

He threw the towel in a recycling bin, started picking at his fingernails, and said, "Anybody hungry?"

I looked at Diana. "I'll take some coffee," she said.

"You don't want this coffee," he said. "Let's see what else they have."

He took us to a room marked Snack Bar that was wall-to-wall vending machines and coin changers. The coffee machine said: Coffee: As You Like It. "I hate that," Jerry said. "It insults your sense of taste. You could float a horseshoe in that shit. It's sure as hell not the way *I* like it. How about you, Jack?"

"I'll have something cold. Diana?"

"I'll take a ginger ale."

"Get me a root beer, will you Jack, an A & W," Jerry said.

I returned with the three cans. Jerry was digging around in his pants pockets. He pulled out a crushed bag of bacon rinds and a tin of smoked oysters. He broke off the metal key from the bottom of the tin, put the peel tip into the key slot, and started winding around the sides. "This is an art," he said. "You know why?"

"Yes," I said.

"You do? Why?"

"Because you have to keep the concentric circles of tin lined up at the same time that you're working against gravity. Otherwise the tin peel gets all screwed up and bent up and you can't get the can opened."

"That's right," Jerry said. "What else?"

"When you finally get to the end you have to peel it loose very carefully. Otherwise you can snap it too hard and splatter that slimy shit inside all over yourself."

"That's exactly right. How did you know that?"

"As a professional detective I have highly developed observational skills."

"Right," Jerry said, opening the tin. "Want some?"

"Jesus, Jerry. That smells like squirrel shit soaked in linseed oil."

"I know. Don't you want any?"

"No thanks."

"Lieutenant?" he asked.

"I'll pass," she said. "Tell us about Alhambra."

"OK. You sure you don't want any of this?"

We both shook our heads.

"OK, there was this place near San Luis Obispo on Morro Bay. What it was was a glorified motel, but the name of the place was Fantasy Village. Each room was done up in a different style. There was Conan's Cave . . . Ali Baba's Hideaway . . . Tarzan's Treehouse . . . Bluebeard's Cove . . . Cleopatra's Barge, and King Arthur's Castle. The wife and I used to stop there every now and then. I liked this room called Robin and Marian's Forest. It was sort of like old England; they had these babbling brook sounds and tapes of hoof beats. They had plastic vines all over the place and they gave you these green terry-cloth bathrobes. They served you roast venison and they had these pewter mugs with English ale. The wife really liked it. Except once they screwed up and put us in this damned room called Snow White's Cottage. It was like . . . ."

He paused for a second and looked at Diana.

"It was like, you know . . . for people who want to be watched. They had the damn seven dwarfs hidden all over the place and every time you opened a door or turned on the jacuzzi or sat on the bed, one of their heads popped out and looked at you. They were on springs and the eyes were loose and rolled around a lot. That night I had a couple of beers before dinner and we drank a bottle of wine with the meal. Lorraine went off to change into her green bathrobe and I had a couple of after-dinner drinks from the minibar. Then I stretched out on the bed for a second to rest. I rolled over on my side to reach for the TV remote and all of a sudden one of those damn dwarfs popped out from behind the nightstand. I think it was Dopey. Anyway, he scared the shit out of me. I jumped up in bed and yelled. That scared Lorraine and she came running in from the bathroom to see what happened. She turned on a light and out jumped another of those little son-of-a-bitches. This time it was Grumpy. I reached over and without thinking grabbed hold of his ears and pulled his head loose from his body. That must have set off an alarm because the manager was at the door a minute later. He was madder than hell. He charged me an extra eighty-seven dollars."

Diana was smiling. "What about Alhambra, Jerry?" I asked.

"I'm getting to that," he said. "One of the rooms was called the Alhambra. It was for blacks. You know, there's that castle or palace, whatever, in Spain—from when the Moors were there. The room was really fancy—all silks and stuff, with ornate ceilings and stuffed bodyguards with copper scimitars. They gave you pajamas with bright colors and baggy pants and there was this mechanical guy who fanned you all the time."

"But you didn't stay in that room," Diana said.

"No, the maid showed it to us. It was her favorite."

"And this was on Morro Bay?"

"It used to be," Jerry said. "They tore it down a couple years ago."

———

"So it's not there," I said.

"No, I just said it wasn't," Jerry answered.

"So it probably doesn't have anything to do with our case."

"I didn't say that," Jerry said.

"Well, Cynthia couldn't have been there recently and neither could the mob people."

"No," Jerry said. "You're missing the point, Jack."

"What's the point, Jerry?"

"The point is that you're looking for somebody named Alhambra. What I'm telling you is that it could be a place."

"We thought about that. We didn't think this group would lower themselves to go to a place like Alhambra."

"Look," Jerry said, "maybe there's a hotel called the Alhambra or some business with Alhambra in the title. Maybe there's a company somewhere that's a front. Maybe one of those assholes drives something called an Alhambra. Maybe one of them has a home somewhere called Alhambra. You know, like Tara, or something, but with a lot of gold shit on the ceiling. Hell, I don't know. It was just an idea."

"Thanks, Jerry," Diana said. "We'll check it out."

"OK. How's the shoulder, Lieutenant?"

"You know those commercials where you see the sore muscles and joints with the red pain waves all around them."

"Yeah, sure," Jerry said.

"Multiply it by five or ten."

"Any ooze?"

"No."

"Then you're doing fine. I'll tell you what—I know exactly when the pain will stop."

"When's that?" Diana asked.

"When you find the piece of shit who killed Mrs. Bladen."

THIRTY-NINE

For the next two weeks we drove the streets of Alhambra: Mission and Alhambra Road, Valley and Atlantic Boulevard, Fremont, Grand, Commonwealth, and Woodward Avenue, Main Street, and Huntington Drive. We checked out gas stations and dry cleaners, restaurants and grocery stores, theaters and parks, liquor stores and pharmacies.

We met a man named Jorge Lozano who told us he knew Fat Artie Santos. He also told us he knew the Cardinal Archbishop of Los Angeles, the Queen of England, Boris Yeltsin, and Emiliano Zapata. He was especially proud of his friendship with Yeltsin. "No bullsheet," he said. "An honest man." I asked him if he had ever met the King of Swing or the Duke of Earl and he said he hadn't.

We met people who were angry at the mob and the dope dealers, angry at the mayor, angry at the president, angry at their congressional delegation, angry at the local street gangs, angry at the local businessmen, angry at the police, and angry at all the things they couldn't think of offhand but were still worth being angry about.

We met a lot of people who weren't angry about anything but wanted us to give them any change we could spare.

We met a lot of people who didn't want to answer questions but wanted to sell us anything we might be interested in buying.

We met two people who wanted to know how *they* could get jobs asking questions, and we met three people who volunteered to tell us anything we wanted to hear, assuming that the right price could be negotiated.

We met a woman named Ribiera who knew somebody named Mariani, but the Mariani she knew worked in a foundry in East L.A. and played guitar in a mariachi band. We met a lot of people who knew the Brienzas, but the Brienzas they knew owned an Italian restaurant in San Gabriel that did carryout pizza, salads, and submarine sandwiches. I met a man who knew somebody named Stephens, but his first name was Dwight; Diana met somebody who knew another Stephens but his first name was Duane. A lot of people had heard of Fat Artie Santos, but except for Mr. Lozano no one had claimed to have met him and no one expressed any desire to do so.

We walked about fifty miles, ate a lot of Mexican food, drank a lot of beer and tequila, and learned absolutely nothing, except for the fact that there are far more businesses and other enterprises with *Alhambra* in the title than the average person could possibly imagine.

Diana's shoulder healed, but her captain started to make noises about her lack of progress on the Bladen case. She held him off with a series of notes, faxes, letters, memos, and formal reports.

The cops always love paper. Short of results, nothing else quite covers the ass.

Still, he was losing interest in the case. He said something to her about getting on with the rest of her life. I talked to Donald Bladen and he angrily brushed me off. "The hell with both of them," Diana said. "If we're the only ones who care about this case we'll just break the damned thing by ourselves."

The problem was, neither of us quite knew how.

Then we met Madeleine Riscal.

Frank had found her by accident. She owned the realty firm that had sold him his condo near the Via Marisol. His condo association was hitting him up for fees that were never specified in his purchase agreement and when he called his original agent, Mary Louise Langan, he learned that Mary Louise had left the business and moved back to Kansas City. Madeleine was holding the firm together during tight times and offered to sit down with Frank and see what she could do to help.

After she helped him she helped us. We met with her in her office on Mission in South Pas. She told us that Frank had told her in passing that we were checking out businesses, locations, and anything else we could find with *Alhambra* in the title. It had been no more than another shot in the dark. Madeleine was a local businesswoman and Frank figured it wouldn't cost him anything more to ask than a few seconds of his time.

"You wouldn't have heard about it," she said, "but everybody in the trade has."

"Tell us," I said.

"It's really very simple," she said. "The Alhambra is a resort hotel, or rather it soon will be. Absolutely top of the line. Eight hundred rooms, twelve interconnected pools, two dozen tennis courts, a 36-hole golf complex, skeet shooting, stables, a half-dozen restaurants, two floors of shops and boutiques, a 600-seat movie theater, and a set of gardens that would make the residents of Babylon turn emerald-green with envy."

"And whose project is it?"

"I don't know," she said. "Alhambra Enterprises Inc., whoever that is."

"*Where* is it?" Diana asked.

"Scottsdale."

"That must be quite a piece of ground that they developed."

"Yes, it's quite a piece of ground," Madeleine said. "It sits on the largest parcel of commercial real estate in the southwest. You can take jeep rides into the Sonoran Desert without crossing the lot lines of the complex."

"Who owned it before?" Diana asked.

"I'm really not sure," she said.

"And when is it scheduled for completion?" I asked.

"Here," Madeleine said, opening up a trade magazine with a twelve-page feature on the project, complete with artist's renderings and current construction shots. "It's scheduled to open next fall. You want to take this with you?"

"Thanks," I said. "You've been very helpful."

"You're welcome," she said. "Can I sell you a house or condo while you're here?"

"Not just yet," Diana said, "but we might have some business for you soon. Have you got any units open at San Quentin?"

Madeleine smiled. "What are you thinking of, a nice starter unit overlooking the yard or maybe something a little more upscale with a view of the bay?"

"I was thinking more of something on death row," Diana said.

FORTY

Sky Harbor International Airport was under construction when we arrived, but the contractors had carefully protected both the live and ceramic cactus plants and endless glass shelves of "local crafts" that the gift shops were trying their best to peddle. Everything in sight was either pink, beige, or aqua.

From the windows of the lounges you could see Camelback and the Phoenix Mountain Preserve. The mountains punctuated the landscape, rising like giant misplaced stones, and the skies were mostly blue and mostly clear, though a trace of light smog hovered over the city proper, suspended above the latticework of small buildings and long streets like a thin sheet of fine yellow shroud in the hot desert air.

"L.A. 1947," Diana said, "but without the orange groves."

"Instead they give you cactus."

"Cactus is nice," she said.

"The mob's always loved this town," I said, "but there's not much crime."

"That's because you don't shit where you eat," Diana said.

We worked our way through the boulevard that circles the airport terminals and drove east to the Hohokam Expressway. It looked like a dried-up L.A. riverbed. I had the wheel; Diana had the map. "Turn right on Van Buren," she said, "as long as we're heading in the right direction, let's check out the scenery."

The expressway was lined with cement barriers. "The contractors are working *here*," I said. She pointed and I turned on Van Buren. When she pointed again I turned left onto something called the Papago Parkway. "OK," I said. "I'm on the Papago Parkway in the Papago Park. What am I looking for?"

"The Desert Botanical Gardens," she said. "Look—they're there on the right." I saw a sign and groups of buildings. Mostly I saw saguaros covering the basins and moving up the hillsides like so many extras in a desert *Fantasia*.

"Very nice," I said.

"The arms project from the cactus to balance it," Diana said. "Those things are *very* heavy."

"I know. And if you rustle them the local authorities are pretty unforgiving."

"That's right."

"This is the first break we've had," I said. "How much longer do we have before we have to get back to reality?"

"About six seconds."

I rolled down the window on the rental Taurus and the hot, heavy air was sucked in across our faces.

"Why are you doing that?" she asked.

"I don't know," I said. "When we walked out of the terminal and got the rental car the air was much hotter than I expected. I wondered what it would feel like out here."

"It's hot everywhere. The problem is the damned swimming pools and lawns," Diana said. "If you let the desert alone you don't get this kind of humidity. Not that it's like Washington or New Orleans, but it would be more comfortable if they kept the people out and just let it all alone."

"I didn't know you were so interested in nature," I said.

"I'm not; I just don't like people," she said, showing me her game face.

"You don't?"

"I'll take dogs any time."

"And you don't make any exceptions?"

"I don't make many," she said. She was looking at the map. I couldn't tell whether or not I caught the hint of a smile.

"Where do I turn?"

"On McDowell. Take a right."

I did.

"OK. Now take a left on Scottsdale Road and drive north for about fifteen or twenty minutes."

"Can't you be any more precise than that?" I asked.

"OK. Drive north for about nine and a half inches on the map."

"That's better," I said.

Finally I caught the smile, but it didn't last long.

As we crossed Osborn Road the succession of auto dealerships and pink and cream stucco restaurants gave way to bookshops and art galleries, with an occasional clothing or jewelry store thrown in for the sake of variety. At Indian School Road a man in greasy, shredded clothes suddenly walked into the middle of traffic. I hit the brake hard. Surrounded by loose money and new buildings he walked unconsciously, like a dazed animal in an empty ballroom. He was overdressed for the climate, but the desert is cold at night and he had no safe place to put his clothes but on his own back.

"L.A. 1992," Diana said.

"A private slice of hell, but still better than in the northern plains tundra," I said.

"I'm not sure *he* knows *where* he is," Diana responded. "A lot of times they just keep walking. The cops won't let them spend the day on a bus stop bench discouraging the tourists and the mall security people will put them back on the street before they even have a chance to find a dark corner and start to get comfortable. Lately I've seen them slip into parking garages. Sometimes they even slide under the cars to catch a little rest. The carbon monoxide makes it a lot easier. Tough times, Jack. Even here."

"Especially here," I said. "Whenever you go up fast you come down hard."

"Some people aren't affected. They buy up land and build resorts."

"What are we looking for?" I asked.

"Shea Boulevard. A major east-west thoroughfare, just above McCormick and Gainey Ranch. We've got another ten minutes or so. You won't miss it. Turn right there."

———

There was a light at Shea and Scottsdale, a large commercial cross defined by intersecting strip malls. Just below the southeast corner was a Western clothing store with a giant plastic horse staring out across the highway, looking for business. "Need any chaps?" I asked. "Or how about a riding quirt? I can imagine you swinging one of those."

"Right," she said. "Since you've stopped thinking about scotch all the time I noticed you're thinking about other things instead."

"Think that's a good sign?"

"It's progress," she said.

"My most important product."

"Don't run into the car in front of you," she said, as I turned onto Shea.

———

The noon sun was just above us now and even with the air conditioning at full tilt I could feel the heat from the windows and door frame. We passed some dusty housing developments and a series of modern churches with vaulted roofs and cement parking lots ringed with palms.

"There it is," Diana said, pointing across the desert toward a long roofline with assorted towers and balcony railings. "Turn at the next corner."

The road was called Alhambra Way. The paving, gutters, and large blue street sign were all new. I drove through a barren sheet of gravelly sand and burnt vegetation for three-quarters of a mile and turned right into the tiled circular drive that formed the entrance to the complex. The main structure was completely under roof and farther along than it looked from a distance. The lay-down areas paralleling the buildings were still piled with cement forms, bales of reinforcement wire, plywood sheets, scattered pieces of cut sheetrock, and irregular stacks of mismatched masonry. Cranes and dozers were everywhere and a line of double trailers blocked the remaining portion of the entry drive. Temporary utility poles were draped with wire to power the trailers and their outsized air conditioners were pumping hot air into the sky and drizzling steady lines of water drops into the sand.

"It looks like they're serious about this," I said.

"I'd say they're damned serious," Diana answered. "It looks like the skies opened up and it rained money."

We walked along the hurricane fence that surrounded the construction site, noticed the top course of concertina wire that ran its length, and caught a glimpse of the pools that checkered the ground behind the principal structure. The golf courses were shaped but not yet sodded, and we could see some dozers off in the distance to the east, sculpting traps and water hazards. The slabs for the tennis courts were in but there were no nets or fences yet. We could hear drills and power saws to the north, but a mound of palms in the middle of the golf course obstructed our view. "Probably the stables or the garages for the desert vehicles," Diana said. "This isn't a hotel; it's a private city."

Even though we saw machines and heard power tools, we didn't see any people. They were enclosed in buildings or dozer cabs. There was an empty efficiency about the place that I felt the moment I stepped out of the car. Diana sensed it too. "It's a *thing*," she said, "not a place."

"If they put in money like this you can be damned sure they intend to take out much more."

"They will," she said. "You can count on that."

"Business is sprouting up all along the Arizona and Nevada borders," I said. "California's too damned expensive and it's too damned seamy. Most of the kids in the Phoenix prep schools and military schools are from L.A. You can fly back and forth for a song. People who have seen their kids flipped out or strung out think it's safer and cleaner here. Less temptation. Less time for the boulevards and more time for the books. L.A.'s a platinum sewer where the fun kills. This place is different. Or so they think. It's a step into the past."

"You know what that means for the dealers."

"Sure. This is the future."

"And the money doesn't have to be dirty. For years this town grew. It's only on temporary hold now. As soon as the recession starts to lift it's going to explode."

"And when it does they'll be ready."

"This place is ready now," Diana said. "I can see it coming; anybody could. They'll start by discounting the rooms and edging out the competition. They'll bring in the crowds in heavy numbers and sell them cocktails and jeep rides. All strictly legitimate—they won't even have to *bend* the law. They'll institutionalize the damned thing and set up the turnstiles. And if things get tight somewhere down the road they've got a built-in, recession-proof safety valve. Just think of *one* possibility. Say the clean business slacks off a little. Say they need some cash flow. Dope attracts too much attention, so what do they do? They place a couple of ads in just the right upscale magazines in the Far East. They turn this place into a resort for Asian businessmen who want to break par and get laid. It's isolated here and the place is self-contained. Who's going to complain to the cops? They can charge two hundred and fifty dollars a day to play golf but they can charge a hell of a lot more to play house. Multiply five hundred dollars a trick by eight tricks a night by a hundred girls by three hundred and sixty-five days. Then skim eighty percent. What do you think you get?"

"More than enough," I said.

"You're damned right. And that's only one operation. Think of the size of this place. Think of what you could do."

I turned to each side, taking it all in, and suddenly noticed something. "Look," I said.

Diana turned and stared. "What the hell is he doing?"

"Just what you think he's doing," I said.

No more than fifty yards away was a neatly dressed young man, standing in front of the sculptured stone entrance sign, THE ALHAMBRA. His pants were open and he was moving from side to side, urinating on as many letters as he could hit.

"They haven't even opened and already they've got a dissatisfied customer," I said.

"Come on," Diana said.

"What are you going to do?"

"I'm going to talk to him."

I don't like to walk up to people pissing in public because they tend to see you as a threat or a fresh target, but Diana walked straight toward him. "Nice shot," she said.

He didn't answer, but sprayed the second A, doused the H, and gave the M and B his last few drops. Then he zipped his fly and turned to walk away.

"Just a second," Diana said.

He stopped, turned, and looked at her.

"I want to talk to you," she said.

"What the hell for?" he asked.

"I was just wondering why you were doing that."

"Why not?"

"I asked first," she said.

He turned again and started to walk.

"Tell me, goddamn it," she said.

He turned and spat out the words. "Because the whole thing is an obscene pile of shit."

"It's a damned *big* pile," she said.

"Look," he said, pointing east, beyond the hotel structure.

We both looked.

"At what?" Diana asked.

"Goddamn it, look," he said.

We looked again.

"I don't see anything but desert," Diana said.

"Of course not. That's all you're supposed to see," he said. "Here, look." He extended his arm next to Diana's face and pointed toward the base of a mountain. "Now look closely. What do you see?"

Diana put her left hand over her eyes to shield them from the sun. "Wait a minute," she said. "They're houses. Coming right out of the ground, right there on the side of the mountain. You can barely see them."

"When you're on the mountain behind them you can't see them at all," he said. "They blend right into the landscape. The group of buildings to the left there is Taliesin."

"The Frank Lloyd Wright place," I said.

"Yes," he said. "The whole point was to blend in with the land, not sit on top of it like this ugly piece of shit, blocking the view of the mountains and the sunrise."

"You live around here?" Diana asked.

"Down the road," he said.

"What's your name?" she asked.

"What difference does it make?" he answered.

FORTY-ONE

His name was David. No last name, just David. Diana was able to convince him that we were on his side and I was able to talk him into some lunch. We got in the car and he directed us to a place just south of Shea with a large wooden sign and the words A Fresh Start. I was expecting something green with a lot of yogurt, nuts, and seeds, but the name referred to the conversion of an old Texaco station into a restaurant as well as a new line of work for the proprietor—a man named Haddis—whose pictures were generously sprinkled along the entryway walls, around the broad archway at the front of the dining room, and down the facing corridors leading to the restrooms and the emergency door.

Carl Haddis the restaurant owner facing Carl Haddis the former electrical contractor. Carl Haddis in his Korean War uniform near the 38th Parallel facing Carl Haddis in his size 46L pinstripes in the Arizona Governor's office. Carl Haddis in his kitchen wearing a chef's hat and brandishing a barbecue fork and Carl Haddis at the edge of the old Texaco station, wearing a plastic hard hat and driving a shovel blade into the ground with a polished brown wingtip. Mrs. Haddis the wife (Nell), Mrs. Haddis the mother (Flo), the little Haddises (Pam and Todd), and a mixed assortment of relatives and hangers-on. At the center, beneath the framed, first dollar, the opening day shot: Carl and Nell surrounded by men in loud shirts, all of them smiling and dragging their fingertips across five o'clock-shadowed cheeks while their wives and girlfriends fluffed beehived hair. All of them were holding cigarettes, except for one prosperous man in a wide-lapeled, double-breasted dark suit who was holding a highball glass.

The specialty of the house was a hot sauce that Carl served in soup bowls. I put a little on my roast beef sandwich and though the sauce wasn't hot enough to make my lips numb it was serious enough to mask most of the flavor of the beef. I took a taste of the second half of the sandwich plain and then decided to daub some sauce on that half too.

Diana ordered a barbecued chicken breast and a salad. She passed on the hot sauce. David ordered a salad made of cold chunks of filet on a bed of lettuce with cold potatoes and cold green beans on the side. He drizzled a little hot sauce on the beef, tasted it, and then added some more.

Diana and I were drinking coke; David was drinking iced tea.

"I came here fifteen years ago," he said. "It was a little sleepy but it was nice. You could still *hear* the desert, if you know what I mean."

We both nodded.

"Sometimes it's still OK. A lot of the rich people go up to Flagstaff for the summer and when the temperature gets up into the triple digits everything slows to a quiet, even pace. That's the way I like it. You find yourself some shade, you wait for the winds to come across the basin, and you watch the moving clouds and the changing colors in the sky."

The waiter refilled David's iced tea and brought us fresh cokes.

"The tourists all come for the saguaros, of course, but there's a hell of a lot more in the desert than the saguaros."

"We saw the desert garden on our way in," Diana said. "It looked nice."

"Didn't you stop?"

"We didn't have time," she said.

David shrugged. "You should have made time. Did you know there are more different mammals in the desert than in the rain forest?"

"No, I didn't," Diana said.

"Nobody does. You should have stopped at the garden. They've got this mock-up of an Indian village that's really worth seeing: tents, huts, tools—all authentic. The Indians knew how to pull life out of the desert. They faced it on its own terms." He paused and sampled the fresh tea. "Not like these asshole builders."

"They'd die in the desert," I said. "That's why they have to bring the city with them."

"You're damned right," David said, stabbing a piece of beef with his fork and dipping the corner of it into the puddle of hot sauce.

He was enjoying it, so I asked what I'd been wondering all along. "What do you do for a living, David?"

"A lot of things," he said. "Mostly I just try to buy time. I figure you don't live to work, you work every now and then so you can live. But then people come along and piss all over your life. Sometimes I piss back."

"So who are these people?" Diana asked. "They must have a hell of a lot of money."

"They've got money all right," David said. "You know what I think?"

"What?" Diana answered.

"I think the money's dirty."

"Why do you say that?"

"Because they keep hiding behind signs and titles."

"Who's fronting it?" Diana asked.

"A couple of suits from L.A. They say they represent a large set of investors, but whenever we try to get close they throw lawyers and smoke at us."

"So you're part of some organization?"

"We're not very organized," David said. "A few of us get together. We have meetings. We call up the politicians, tell them what we think. It doesn't do any good. We had a lawyer for a while, but we didn't have enough money to pay him. It wouldn't have made any difference though. He couldn't do shit."

"So most of the locals are behind this," I said.

"Hell yes, they're behind it. They need work. They have to eat."

"Hard to argue with that," Diana said.

"I know," David answered. "It's the damned system that gets me, not just them screwing up the desert."

"What do you mean?" I asked.

"It's always the same."

"What?" Diana asked.

"When people are broke they sell their valuables, but once the land is sold it's gone forever. Why do those bastards always have the money to buy?"

"Because of what they sell," I said.

"What do you mean?"

"You said you think their money's dirty," Diana said.

"So?"

"What do people with dirty money sell?"

"I don't know—dope?"

"Among other things," Diana said. "When times are tough they sell more."

"Then they have the money to buy other things at bargain prices," I said.

"Like land."

"That's right," I said.

"Cocksuckers." He turned to Diana and said, "Sorry."

"That's all right," she said. "I probably would have said something worse."

———

We asked David if we could drop him off somewhere and he said no. I paid the bill and we walked out to the parking lot. I opened the windows and turned on the air conditioning. Diana and I stood there, watching David walk away. His hands were in his pockets and his eyes were on the ground in front of him.

"Inland surfer," she said.

"Yes, and look what they've done to his ocean."

FORTY-TWO

I CALLED FRANK AND told him what we'd seen and heard. I also asked him if Clem Greene had ever turned up.

"No," he said. "The housekeeper told us that Mr. and Mrs. Greene were vacationing in Europe and that she didn't know when they would return. I asked her if she was in contact with Mr. Greene and she said no."

"I don't like the sound of that," I said.

"No. We may never hear from Quentin C. Greene again."

"How did the housekeeper learn that he was in Europe?"

"She said he called her at her home."

"Shit. You don't have her phone tapped, so there's no way of verifying the story."

"No. The phone record *does* show a call from the international terminal at Heathrow Airport," Frank said, "but that doesn't mean anything. Anybody could place a call. She *is* their housekeeper though. We talked to some neighbors and checked her tax records, just to be sure."

"It wouldn't be hard to trick her with an affected British accent. Clem Greene's is pretty generic."

"Or to intimidate her," Frank said. "She's got four small kids and a sick husband. One wave of a baseball bat or a straight razor and they'd have her attention. I figure with Greene we simply sit and wait. We could get Interpol in on it, but I don't see that it would serve any purpose. He's either already dead or somewhere in hiding. Either way he doesn't have anything new to tell us and there's no reason to draw unnecessary attention to him."

"The mob has plenty of contacts in Interpol."

"Sure."

"Thanks for checking."

"Forget it. What are you going to do now?"

"We're going to try to get some more information at this end. We'll probably come back tomorrow."

"Keep an eye on the rear-vision mirror."

"Thanks. I always do," I said.

It took some doing but Diana and I found a branch library in the neighborhood with a film reader that made copies. It mustn't have gotten too much use, because the librarian was anxious to unlock the drawer with the microfilm run of the *Arizona Republic,* find an additional chair for me, and warm up the reader. It was probably a nice break from stamping Judy Blume books and directing patrons to the best-seller rack.

Diana turned the crank and watched the screen and I dropped dimes into the slot and pushed the red plastic PRINT button. The Alhambra project had been front page news for weeks the previous year and we walked through months of daily and Sunday editions to make sure we didn't miss anything.

The pile of copies kept mounting and I asked the librarian if she had a container that would hold the complete stack. "Why, certainly," she said eagerly.

She took a typing paper box out of her desk, removed the remaining sheets, and said, "Will this do?"

"It's fine," I said. "Thank you; that's a big help."

"I'm here to serve the public," she said.

Behind her tinted glasses was an attractive face. "It's not often we get someone who truly uses the library," she said.

"Well, thank you again," I said. I walked back to the station where Diana was working and put the copies in the box.

"You old charmer," she said. "Don't ask for anything else. She might give it to you."

"She was very nice," I said, in an objective, professional tone.

"She wants you bad," Diana answered. "The typing paper box is only the first step."

"How often does somebody like me walk into her life?"

Diana looked around. An acned teenager with his hand in a bag of nacho-flavored Doritos was whispering to another kid who was reading *Lolita* and picking his nose. "Around here?" she said. "Probably not very often."

We satisfied ourselves that we had gotten as much as we were going to and drove off in search of a hotel. The Hyatt at Gainey Ranch looked especially nice, so we drove in. The main building sat behind a central fountain at the end of parallel rows of palms and saguaros. The glass doors enclosing the lobby were opened during the day and the breeze off the desert mingled with the air conditioning. Diana sat down in a pink and gray armchair and kept an eye on the people behind me while I went to the front desk.

"How did you sign the register?" she asked, as I hit the button for the east tower elevator.

"Dr. Grant and niece. How about a bath and some room service?"

"Sounds good."

Everything on the menu seemed to involve tomatillas and blue corn. Diana was taking a shower so I went into the bathroom and asked her what she wanted. "Steak," she said. "They've got to have steak."

"They do, but it's got salsa on it and something on the side that sounds like it might grow wild along the edge of the highway."

"Tell them to bag that and give me some sort of potato. I'll take some coffee too and a bottle of red wine."

"You want a bottle just for yourself?"

She thought about it for a second. "How thirsty are you?"

"I'll get some beer too."

"Fair enough," she said, as she leaned against the side of the shower curtain. I stood there watching, not sure whether the view through the wet curtain was intended for my benefit or a lucky accident.

We looked through the newspaper copies as we ate. Alhambra Enterprises, Inc. was fronted by two men: a local named Roy Hitchcock and an L.A. connection named Charles Sales.

Hitchcock was a developer who specialized in strip malls and parking decks. Sales' role was never specified. He looked familiar, even through sunglasses and a thick moustache, but I couldn't place him.

"*Roy Hitchcock*," Diana said. "It sounds like a made-up cowboy name. Very hip. Very local. *Sales* is perfect too. Top seller of the month, with his picture on the boss' bulletin board in the office coffee room."

"I met somebody like that once," I said. "Years ago. We were thinking about buying a house and we started talking to this realtor named Vern Virnoche. He took us into this room that had a long table and something on the wall that looked like it was made for a kids' version of Wheel of Fortune. It was a round piece of wood with a spinner in the shape of an arrow. The whole thing was a little rough around the edges, with crooked black lines dividing the circle into a pie. Each section had a dollar amount on it with gold-sticker numbers. The highest amount was twenty-five bucks. Vern explained to us that each month the broker let the top salesman have a spin. Whatever the arrow landed on was the salesman's special bonus. I remember that there was one section that was only good for $2."

"A generous son-of-a-bitch," Diana said. "At least he didn't put up a Lose Your Turn section."

"That's right. Anyway, Vern told us the whole saga of the Bonus Board—that's what they called it—and then sat down, smiled at me knowingly, and said, 'I've spun that wheel more than a couple of times.' At that point I think we were supposed to fall at his feet and start reaching for our checkbooks. I didn't do that, but I politely acknowledged his prowess as a salesman." She smiled. "Of course, there was one clear difference between Vern Virnoche and this guy Charlie Sales."

"What was that?"

"Charlie looks like he buys his suits from Mortie Gold. Vern used to get his from Sears. The Kings Road collection, as I remember. A lot of nice browns and blues."

"So you didn't buy a house from him."

"No, but he wasn't bitter. I thought at first he was setting us up to feel guilty—if we didn't buy he couldn't take his free spin—but it was actually too late in the month for him to catch up with the leader, somebody named Laverne. I think what he really wanted was for us to come back a week later and give him a running start in the next cycle."

Diana poured some more wine into my glass. "Thanks," I said, and held up one of the pictures of Charlie Sales to the light. "I've seen this guy before; I know it."

"I think I have too," she said. She looked at the picture, thought for a second, and then walked over to get the phone off of the desk. She had to free up the cord from behind the desk leg, but after she did she carried the phone over and handed it to me. "Here, let your fingers do the walking."

I called Frank at home but got his answering machine. I tried the office but he was gone. I asked the desk sergeant who was still there. He gave me Jerry Dailey.

"Jack, how the hell are you? I was just thinking about you. You know how you like wine? Well I just checked out some guy with a whole bottle spilled down the front of him. I guess he was having trouble finding his mouth. I don't think he drinks the same kind of stuff you do. What's up?"

"Just a question, Jerry. Ever heard of a guy named Charlie Sales?"

"Charlie Sales? Of course."

"Who is he?"

"Who *is* he? He's a lawyer, Jack."

"What kind of work does he do?"

"Damned good work," Jerry said. "He's the one who got Tony Russo off for Murder One."

"Tony Russo . . . he works for . . . ."

"Tony works for Albert Mariani, Jack. Or at least he did. Nobody's seen him around lately."

"That's *right*. The trial wasn't in L.A. though, was it?"

"No, he got a change of venue. Too many victims here, too many memories. They tried it up north."

"But it was in the papers here."

"Sure. Maybe a year ago, a year and a half . . . ."

"Did Charlie Sales have a moustache, Jerry?"

"No, not Charlie. Hell, with a moustache he'd look like a used car salesman."

"Thanks, Jerry. That's very helpful."

"No problem. Hey, you want me to ask the wino what he'd recommend to you?"

"Maybe next time."

I hung up. "Charlie Sales is a mob lawyer," I said.

"That's funny," Diana said, "he looks like a used car salesman."

FORTY-THREE

"So what is this, progress?" Diana asked. She was wearing one of my tee-shirts and it was covering less and less the more she scooted around, pouring wine and reaching for pieces of paper.

"The picture's a lot clearer. What Cynthia was telling us was that a set of local mob hairballs had decided to stop competing and start cooperating. They put down their knives and shotguns and became investment partners. And they couldn't have chosen a more opportune moment. In hard times people buy more dope and play more numbers. They reach for pills and powder and needles and whores and get-rich-quick solutions. The people who sell those things suddenly have a lot of loose money. They look around for ways to spend it and they discover that the biggest bargains are in real estate. They find a lot of people on the ropes and they buy them out. Only this time they're doing it on a grand scale. They're building a self-contained empire, something they can mine on either side of the law for the rest of their lives."

"Assuming that's true," Diana said, "I've got three questions."

"What are they?"

"First, the point of the message seems to be that some well-known slimeballs suddenly have a new joint venture. If that's right, if the Alhambra project is the key, what *laws* are being broken?"

"Who knows? Bribery? Extortion? Money laundering? The possibilities are endless."

"Violation of building codes?" she said skeptically.

"Probably that too."

"All right, but there's nothing obvious that jumps out except for the source of the capital behind the project."

"That's true."

"OK," she said, "question two."

"Which is?"

"How did Cynthia Bladen find out about this?"

"Good question. That's what *we've* got to find out. Then we'll know why she was killed."

"Fine, but remember—the identity of the partners is no great secret. One of their lawyers is spread all over two and a half months-worth of the *Arizona Republic*."

"*We* didn't realize that right away."

"No, but we were only on the case here for about six and a half hours."

"OK. So what you're saying is that what Cynthia was telling us was no big deal."

"So it would seem."

"But we're just getting into it. Maybe the other three don't want anyone to know they're in bed with Mariani. Maybe Mariani's working one on one and the other three don't know who their partners are. Maybe this is some elaborate screw-your-buddy game and we're just looking at the first move."

"Maybe."

"You seem skeptical."

"I'm just thinking out loud."

"Didn't you have a third question?"

"Yes. Are you going to just sit there playing detective or are you going to help me out of this t-shirt?"

———

"How's the shoulder?" I asked, as the shirt sleeve slid over the florid remains of the wound.

"It's fine," she said, as she slid her arms around my neck and pulled herself onto my lap.

Her eyes were open as I kissed her. She held the kiss for what seemed like a full minute and then pulled her head back, searching my eyes for another minute as she touched the back of my head and neck with her fingertips. Then she kissed me again, this time longer and deeper.

When we broke the kiss her eyes were still open. She wasn't even blinking. "What are you looking for?" I asked.

"For you."

"I'm right here."

She held my eyes with hers and brought her lips closer. I felt the warmth of her breath as I moved forward, kissing and tasting her mouth as her hands moved down my back. I opened my eyes. Hers were still open. The lashes were aimed at me as her eyelids slowly rose. Her eyes were moist and full of longing, as if they were ready to speak and then to tear.

I opened my eyes at first light. The night air and the full-throttle air conditioning had lowered the room temperature. I looked at Diana and she was lying on her back, uncovered to her hips. Her nipples were puckered with the chill, her hands resting on the sheet and her eyes open.

I reached over and put my arm around her waist. It was cold and lifeless. She continued to stare at the ceiling. "What are you thinking?" I asked.

"Nothing, really."

"Nothing?"

"I'm just sorting through."

"Any ideas?"

"Not really."

"Tell me."

"I really don't have anything."

"Tell me anyway."

"OK. I was thinking about Bladen. Brandeis, Stanford Business School. A little gray at the temples, gray in the eyes, gray in the skin, gray in the suit, gray in the shirt and the socks and the tie. What would bring the demons out of somebody that gray? What would make him reach for something long and sharp? What would make him cut and what would make him kill?"

"We've talked about him," I said. "The problem is you also have to account for the woman in the Mojave—Margaret Watermann. Could Bladen really have killed her too? Where would he have known her? Why would he have killed her? There's no link between her and the wiseguys, at least none that anyone has found. There's also the mutilation pattern. One time this killer cuts breasts, another time he cuts bellies—why? There are just too many things that don't square."

"You're looking for logic and reason," she said, "but what difference do logic and reason make? Back in Washington—years ago—there was a man who worked at the Government Printing Office. He had worked there for thirty-seven years. His name was Terence Crispe. A little guy. Not in Bladen's income bracket, but just as gray. He had a watch and a medal and a wall of certificates and citations—the mainstay of the office: one-fourth of the fifth floor. All day long he worked as an editor and proofreader, checking commas and semicolons, making sure the senators' words were underlined and set in bold type, making sure the federal regulations were printed and promulgated, making sure the requests for grant proposals came out on time and the project reports were duplicated and filed promptly.

"He checked the vendors' invoices for paper and ink and he checked the dates on every new federal form. He supervised the offset printers and the secretaries and he handled the office hearts and flowers fund, never missing a birthday, a retirement, a hospitalization, or a funeral. One night one of his assistants went through his desk looking for manila file folders and found a small, black velvet box resting on a stack of flyers and pamphlets in the back of a drawer. It had a gold clasp. The assistant's curiosity got the best of him and he suddenly flipped open the clasp. Inside the box was a collection of human molars, arranged in converging lines, just as they would appear in your mouth. No canines, no incisors, just molars. Terence Crispe was a man of specialized tastes. And they later discovered that the set in the box wasn't from the same mouth. They were matched like pearls, each a perfect specimen, each drawn from a separate human mouth. The assistant thought this was strange enough to call the police and when they went to Crispe's apartment they found hundreds and hundreds of teeth, all sorted and polished and carefully labeled. The box in his desk drawer was his traveling set. He couldn't stand to be away from his collection."

―――

Diana's waist was still cold, even though she had turned her head toward me. "Where did he get them from?" I asked.

"Wherever he could find them. When the feds came in and checked all their records they realized what they had stumbled upon. Two years earlier, they discovered, Terence Crispe had been picked up outside the morgue at D.C. General, refusing to speak and refusing to leave, but there was no evidence of a crime and no charges were filed. A funeral director in Arlington later said that he recognized him and thought he had seen him before, though he wasn't sure where. Then there was a funeral director in Alexandria, then one in Fairfax, one in Bethesda, and one in Rockville. Always the same story—he looked familiar; they had seen him sometime in the past; one said he had seen him often. A young, homeless man in Southeast came forward and said he had sold Terence Crispe two of his molars for $75."

"Crispe extracted them?"

"Yes. He gave the donor a bottle of rum a half hour before he operated."

"Jesus."

"Then there were some scarier things. The police matched four of the teeth in the collection with the dental records of three homicide victims."

"Unsolved?"

"Yes. They also found that two of the teeth in the home collection belonged to Crispe himself. He apparently preferred seeing them in a display box to seeing them in the dark corners at the back of his mouth. They were lined and stained."

"Maybe he was ashamed of them from the beginning and wanted to find some that were better," I said.

"Something like that," Diana said. "The perfect molar. And when that wasn't enough the perfect set of molars on each side, and then the perfect set on top and bottom. Terence Crispe's quest. Terence Crispe's life's work."

"And how does that fit our case?" I asked.

"I don't know. I'm just looking at another gray suit and another gray face and I'm thinking there might be a lot of blood and pain and death somewhere in the back corners of that mind."

"Donald Bladen's gray as hell—I'll say that for him—but there's still no connection between him and Margaret Watermann."

"That we've been able to find."

"Right. But what would any of this have to do with Alhambra Enterprises, Inc.?"

"I don't know," she said, looking back at the ceiling and sliding her hand over mine. "That's what I'm trying to figure out."

"Donald Bladen is a very wealthy businessman," I said. "His putative line of work is capital formation. He had a lawyer wife named Cynthia with a home computer in a study just off the master bedroom. Cynthia was murdered and she left a message for whoever might look for one, but the message that Cynthia left was in her office computer, *not* in the one at home."

"She discovered something about her husband but recorded and encoded the information at her office in order to protect herself."

"Possibly. Perhaps she learned something *from* him."

"Or something *about* him. The mutilation's the problem," Diana said. "It's also the key."

"How so?"

"It's something personal. The mob doesn't kill that way. They kill hard and quick and they don't worry about cleaning up the blood or hiding the body."

I thought about that for a second, noticed the goose flesh on Diana's arm, kissed her on her shoulder, and slid my hand up to her breast. "Aren't you cold?" I asked. She didn't respond. I touched one of the bumps encircling her nipple and then stopped. Something deep behind my eyes suddenly clicked and everything around it fell into place.

"That's it," I said.

"That's what?"

"*Why* didn't I remember?"

"Why didn't you remember *what*?"

For a moment I stopped breathing. I hesitated to tell her.

FORTY-FOUR

I GOT OUT OF bed, slipped on a hotel terry-cloth robe, and got a glass of tap water from the bathroom. I sat down on a chair opposite the bed and took a drink.

"Well?" Diana said.

"Cynthia had a mole on her breast, next to the nipple. Whoever killed her and mutilated her removed the mole."

"Aren't we observant," she said. "And you had to get out of bed to tell me that. Why?"

"I don't know. I guess I didn't think you'd want to hear it."

"Give me a little credit," she said.

"I do. It's just not the sort of thing I thought you'd want to hear."

"Look, that all happened before you met me. Just don't expect to share my bed now and tell me about other womens' nipples . . . unless the other women are also *dead*."

She said it without a breath or a blink.

"So tell me, what are you thinking?" she asked. "Why would somebody go to the trouble to cut off a mole like that?"

"Maybe as a trophy?"

"To remember her by."

"Something like that," I said.

"What took *you* so long to remember it?" she asked. "Never mind, you don't have to answer that."

I didn't.

"It's the sort of thing someone might do who knew her well."

"Somebody sick," Diana said. "Tell me about it. Was it . . . was it more like a beauty mark or more like an imperfection?"

"It wasn't anything in particular. It was just a mole."

"Don't bullshit me, Jack. This isn't about you and me. This is about our case. Think."

"I'm serious. It wasn't anything. That's probably why I forgot it."

She didn't speak but her eyes were probing deep.

"Really," I said.

"So why would the killer also slice up Margaret Watermann's belly?"

"I don't know."

"I don't know either," she said.

I took another sip of the water. The drapes were brighter now with the morning light and I could feel some of the warmth along the edge of the carpet.

"It's something at least," she said. "I don't know quite what yet, but it's something."

"I think we should talk to Donald Bladen."

"I think so too," she said. "In the meantime, why don't you take off that ridiculous robe and come back to bed."

I put the glass back on the bathroom sink, slipped off the robe, hung it next to its mate in the closet, and walked back to the side of the bed. She raised her right arm to make room for me and I got in beside her. She covered herself with the double sheets and thin blanket between, turned on her side and held me in place with her left arm and left leg. Her hand and arm were still cold, but her armpit and the crease between her thighs were warm. She held me that way, making me aware of her moisture and her scent. I turned my face toward hers. Her eyes were closed and her lips were open, reaching toward me in the pale light. She had never shown me that kind of need. I kissed her and her body tightened around me. I kissed her again and everything began to open as I lifted her on to my legs and chest. She was like a missing part of me that suddenly returned and fit in its perfect way.

———

United flight 258 was a fifty-nine-minute 737 jump from Phoenix to Burbank with twenty minutes on each side for predictable delays. We had had a good breakfast, knowing that the sustenance on the flight would be stale pretzels and a soft drink. I opted instead for some Bloody Mary mix and the bag of peanuts I got from the airport newstand. Diana took orange juice and vodka. Her shoulder was bothering her and she washed down a handful of aspirins with the Smirnoff and O.J.

The Burbank airport is the original L.A. airport, the one Howard Hughes used, and if you look closely and feel for it you can be there—in the truly good days—for a moment or two. A few moments were all we really had. We threw our bags in the trunk of my car and took Hollywood Way to the Golden State Freeway. The midday traffic was heavy but it was moving briskly and I caught the Ventura without a pause and headed into Glendale.

"This is where your old girlfriend lives, isn't it?" Diana asked.

"How did you know that?"

"I'm a detective. I detect."

"Yes, it is," I said, "but she's not here very often. She's usually in Santa Monica at St. John's."

"That's a long drive. Especially if you're on call. What's she hiding from over here?"

"I don't know that she's hiding from anything. She lived here during her residency at County General. She just never left. It wasn't that she wanted to be near me. She was here before we met."

"Why do you say that—that she didn't stay here to be by you?"

"Because it's true."

"Maybe she thought about leaving and stayed because she met you."

"Possibly."

"You don't think you could be important enough to a woman to make her want to be near you?"

"I didn't say that."

"Didn't you?"

"No."

"Maybe you split because you wanted some signal like that from her and she didn't deliver."

"I told you. We had words, words she didn't like."

"That was just smoke. No grown-up with brains gives up that much because of a few words. You wanted to play a bigger role in her life and bent in the other direction to try and hide the fact.

You're caught between generations, Jack. You thought you were saying the right thing, but it wasn't what you really felt. When it backfired you started to drink."

"I don't think so."

"If you didn't really want her, why didn't you celebrate when she split?"

"Things are more complicated than that. She's a surgeon. She gets up every morning and stares into the eyes of people who expect her to cut them open and then make them whole again. That's her job and it's more than most people could handle. I respect that, and I don't mean that in some simpering modern-man sense. I've seen a lot of spilled blood and a lot of people cut open and I've seen the look in their eyes before they go under."

"Her *job*? You think a *job* should come between a man and a woman?"

"In the past—when it didn't—the women usually lost."

"Don't be so modern," she said. "I can't imagine a job more important than a man I really wanted."

"You certainly don't sound very modern."

"Modern? What good is modern?"

"You wouldn't be a police lieutenant without it."

"You don't really know much about women and life, do you?"

"I don't know; sometimes I think I know too much."

"Why do you think you lost those women, Bladen and, what's her name—Weeks?"

"We were moving on different tracks, in different directions."

"Different tracks? Different directions?"

"Yes."

"You don't get it, do you?"

"Get what?"

"This . . . ." Gesturing with her arm in a semicircle.

"What?"

"The job. The life. It's all shit. It's nothing more. It's just shit. If I walk through the wrong door or depend on the wrong person . . . bang, it's over. My face turns into hamburger. I piss all over myself, fall down, and it's done. Somebody calls my mother and father and asks them to come accept some bullshit medal. A couple of squads of cops are ordered to put on their blues. There's a parade. A few blank rounds are shot off. I take the dirt nap, everybody checks their watches, and then they all go back to work. That's it. The star of the show bows out. There's seven minutes of sustained applause and then nobody gives a rat's ass, except for my mother and father, who hate the system and their daughter for wanting to join it. That's all it is. A job? It's something you do because you're addicted to food and you don't have a life. And other people who don't have lives spend most of theirs envying you yours."

I didn't answer right away. We were coming into Pasadena and I was working my way to the right side of the freeway to turn off at Lake.

Finally I broke the silence. "That's a pretty heavy bottom line."

"What?"

"It *is* all shit," I said, "but that means that what happens between you and the person who matters has to make up the difference—all of it."

"That's what it means," she said. "Not that you don't have help. There's winter sunlight, pastel linens, warm air off the desert, San Diego sunsets, red wine, warm beds, blue pools, long nights with soft rain . . . lots of *things*, but they're all just props, just part of the set. The only thing that counts are the players."

"If there's so little, why risk losing it in a job like this?"

"Because there *is* so little," she said, "and because I enjoy taking out the people who want to take away what little there is."

"Why don't we get something to eat and do just that?"

"Do what?"

"Find the person who killed Cynthia Bladen and put the son-of-a-bitch on the gurney with the thin mattress and the thick needle."

FORTY-FIVE

The Crocodile Café is on the east side of Lake between Green and Cordova. A magnet for the young and the hungry, it features outdoor tables offering dining under the awnings and stars, with cool desert air and strategically positioned space heaters. In the afternoons it's quiet and you can usually find a seat. Diana and I stayed inside and took an inconspicuous table in a far corner. She ordered something healthy with four different kinds of lettuce and a green sauce; I ordered something spiced with chiles that was thick and meaty and came with a pile of potatoes on the side. It tasted good, even though I wasn't paying much attention to what it actually was.

She was eating and watching me.

"How's the cilantro?" I asked, as she took a bite.

"That isn't cilantro," she said, pointing at a corner of her plate with her fork.

"Sorry. It was just a guess."

"Playing the California odds instead of paying attention?"

"Actually, I was paying attention to something else."

"What?"

"You. And what you said—back on the freeway."

"I meant what I said. Remember our deal: we always tell each other the truth or everything's off."

"I remember."

"OK. So are you going to let what I said get in the way of what we have to do?"

"No."

"You're not going to let it break your concentration."

"No, I won't."

"Are you sure?"

"Yes."

"When we get down to it, both of our asses will be on the line. When that happens, I want to see fists and bullets, not tears and moony looks."

"You will. I want us both standing when it's over."

"Good. When do we start?"

"Now."

"Where?"

"With Bladen."

"I'll order some coffee," she said, "while you find him."

I sorted through the soiled notes I had stuffed in a pocket of my wallet and found Bladen's phone numbers. When I called his office his secretary dodged my questions. When I told her it had to do with his dead wife she told me he was at home for the day and I could reach him there.

"He doesn't really feel well," she said. "He hasn't been in for the last two days." Trying to discourage me.

I called his home number immediately, racing against the warning call I knew she would be making. He picked up the phone on the fifth ring. I told him I had made progress and needed to see him. He told me he didn't care and that I shouldn't bother. I told him the LAPD and San Bernardino PD were both involved and that if he didn't talk to me he could be charged with obstruction of justice. He told me not to try a cheap bluff like that or he'd have his lawyer down my throat before I could hang up the phone. I told him I still cared about finding his wife's killer whether he did or not. He said something under his breath like "I'm sure you do," but I let it slide.

"I've got a lieutenant from San Bernardino with me. We'll be at your door in thirty minutes."

"I won't open it," he said.

"Look," I said, "this isn't some goddamned game. You can talk to us in your living room or in the lieutenant's interrogation room, but you're going to talk to us."

He hung up without responding.

I went back to the table, sat down, and took a sip of my coffee. It was hot and strong, but not bitter.

"Good, isn't it?" Diana asked.

I nodded.

"Did you reach him?"

"Yes, but he didn't sound too willing to talk to us."

"He'll talk," Diana said. "Is he at his office?"

"No, at home. His secretary told me he wasn't feeling well."

"Better still. He'll talk even faster."

I left a twenty under the check and opened the door for Diana. A bank of clouds had covered the sun and the afternoon sky was lead gray, with suspended sheets of yellowish brown smog. We drove north on Lake and took the Ventura to Sherman Oaks, heading over the mountains through Beverly Glen. The Santa Monicas were brown and dry and there was a lot of dead palm leaf and dusty scrub on the road, especially just below Mulholland on the north slope. Nature's trash. As always, the Glen was full of For Sale signs, a meandering vein between the Valley and the platinum triangle where prices fluctuate with every turn in the road. Fred Sands was winning the current listings race. As we reached the bottom of the Glen and came into Bel Air the lawns and shrubs were suddenly as green as the fresh money that fed them. Bladen lived in Westwood, on Hilgard, just east of UCLA. I turned onto Sunset, immediately changed lanes, and then hung a quick left. Donald and Cynthia had shared a yellow frame cottage with a cedar shake roof and trellises of dark roses, narrow across the front but deeper in the back. Two bedrooms and an office with a low seven-figure price tag. The locals call Westwood the Village. You can walk to the stores and theatres if your Mercedes is in the shop.

Bladen's was in his driveway. It was burgundy. A convertible. It was also new enough to still hold its showroom smell; I wondered if he had bought it with Cynthia's insurance money. I pulled in behind him, just in case he had any thoughts about leaving.

I knocked on the door and there was no answer. I knocked again and tried the knob. It turned in my hand. "He should be more careful," Diana said. "Bad people open unlocked doors."

"Sometimes they're greeted with loaded weapons," I said, pausing before entering.

We stood on either side of the door. It was heavy oak, with a Judas window covered by an opaque curtain. On our side there was also some miniature iron grillwork with tamper-proof bolts. I turned the knob and gave it a hard push. The door swung open and I looked down the hallway. At the end was a large bronze on a marble pedestal illuminated with track lighting. It was some kind of junior Triton holding on to some sea horses.

I called out Bladen's name but there was no answer. Halfway down the hall I called out again but there was nothing but the whirr of a wall-unit air conditioner in the den and some street noise from Hilgard.

"Maybe he left," Diana said.

We kept looking. At the end of the hall I pointed to the living room on the right and dining room beyond. "Nice couch," she said. "What is that, silk?"

"Yes. It looks like it's been cleaned since the last time I saw it."

I opened the door to the powder room on the left but it was empty and the light was off. We went through the living room and into the dining room. The gold-flecked drapes across the windows on the east wall were pulled shut. I walked into the kitchen and then called to Diana, "He's out in the back." She was about to open the dining room drapes.

The kitchen was white with red accent pieces. It didn't look as if it had been used for a while. "Woman's kitchen," Diana said, lifting the corners of a set of designer potholders hanging on magnetized hooks on the side of the refrigerator. She opened the door; there was nothing inside but some eggs, some Chinese carry-out cartons, and a half-gallon container of milk that had started to turn.

The shallow backyard was mostly garden with roses, impatiens, and baby fan palms. In the center was an electric fountain that was pumping water through a tube connecting a set of terraced cement shells above a shallow pond. Opposite the fountain was a metal lattice-work table and chair set with a yellow and white-striped umbrella. Bladen was sitting at the table, watching the stream of water run from shell to shell before it fell into the pond at the base. He was also clutching a drink with both hands as if he was holding on to a lifeline.

I opened the kitchen door for Diana and closed it behind me, loud enough to announce our arrival to Bladen. His head turned a few degrees toward me and then turned back to his fountain and his drink.

I introduced Diana and he looked at us with eyes that were swelling with anger.

"You've got five minutes," he said.

"All we're trying to do is find your wife's killer," I said. "I don't understand why you wouldn't want to help us."

"It's too late," he answered. "When I hired you to find her you got there too late. What do I care about her killer? It was probably some punk killing her for drug money. If he's ever found, the social workers will defend him, the judges will let him off, and the taxpayers will look after his care and feeding until he decides to kill again. I don't even think about justice; I know I'll never see it."

"There's something I never told you," I said. "I'd like to get your reaction to it."

"What's that?" he sighed.

"After Cynthia's body was found you told me you didn't want to know any of the details. There was one key detail I didn't tell you. A small portion of her body had been removed—not randomly, but systematically. You could even say *surgically*."

There was nothing in Bladen's eyes yet but pain and further disbelief.

Diana spoke. "It was a rectangular piece of flesh from her left breast. It included the entire nipple and a portion of the areola."

"Jesus," Bladen said.

"Why would someone cut her there?" Diana asked, digging into his eyes with her own.

He just stared.

"Any ideas?" she said.

"No."

"Anything you can tell us at all?" I asked.

"Like what?"

"I don't know," I said. "What comes to mind?"

"Nothing," he said. "At least nothing useful. Cynthia had some breast cysts that needed to be aspirated. That was a year or more before she died. I can't think of anything else."

"Was there anything special about that part of her body?"

"Special?" Bladen said.

"Yes," Diana answered. "Something different. Something worth noting."

"She had a tiny mole on her left breast. It was almost like a freckle; it was nothing out of the ordinary."

"Let me ask you something else," I said. "Are any of the following names familiar to you—Arturo Santos, Antonio Brienza, Albert Mariani, and Donato DiStephano?"

"What are you getting at, Grant?"

"Have you ever heard of any of those men?"

"Of course. They're all known criminals."

"Do you have any reason to believe that your wife could have been in contact with any of them?"

"You son-of-a-bitch," he said. "Get the hell out of my house before I pick up something and hit you with it."

"Mr. Bladen," Diana said, in a prosecutor's voice, "those names appeared, in code, in your wife's office computer."

"What the hell are you talking about?" he said.

"You're an intelligent man," she answered. "Please act like one. Why would your wife go to the trouble to encode the names of those people and retain them in her computer's memory?"

"I don't know," he said, shoving the fingertips of his left hand through his hair, "I don't know."

"Wouldn't it seem reasonable to you that she knew something she wanted to preserve, something she couldn't leave out in the open, something to do with organized crime?"

"Yes," Bladen said, "but what purpose does it serve to list those names? Everybody knows who those people are, at least everybody does who lives in Southern California and reads the newspaper."

"That's not all that was there, Mr. Bladen," Diana said. There was also a word: Alhambra."

"Alhambra?"

"Yes."

"The castle in Spain?"

"You're an educated man, Mr. Bladen. Most people would have thought of the Alhambra section of L.A."

"It's a book too, I think—by Washington Irving?"

"A+," Diana said, and then paused.

"What does that have to do with the four criminals?" he asked.

"Good question," Diana said. "We've just been working on that and we think it refers to a resort complex in Scottsdale, Arizona."

"Big project," I said, "even for those people."

"I still don't see what that has to do with Cynthia." He seemed calmer now, even guarded.

"What do *you* do for a living, Mr. Bladen?" Diana asked.

"I bring people together. I broker business ventures. But I think you already knew that, Lieutenant. Are you suggesting that I had something to do with this mob deal in Scottsdale, that Cynthia found out and that I killed her?"

"Did I say that?" Diana asked.

"Like you said, I'm not stupid," he replied.

"I didn't say that," she answered. "I said you were an intelligent and educated man. Intelligent and educated men do stupid things . . . all the time."

"I don't work with gangsters, Lieutenant, and the last thing I would ever want to do is see my wife dead."

"I like your new car," Diana said. "I had a 190 once; it was second-hand. I didn't keep it. I couldn't afford the maintenance."

"That's not my car," he said. "It's my neighbor's. He loaned it to me."

"Generous neighbor," I said.

"This is Westwood, Grant, not Alhambra. It's his son's car. My neighbor's car is a Rolls Corniche."

"What happened to yours?"

"It's being repaired."

"What happened? It must have been something serious."

"Nothing happened. It's an old car. It needs care."

"Cynthia used to drive a Volvo," I said.

"It's Cynthia's car that's being repaired."

"What happened to yours?" Diana asked.

"There was an accident, shortly after her death. Fortunately no one else was hurt."

"What happened?" I asked.

"What happened? Nothing happened. I was trying to kill myself and I failed."

When we got up to leave, Bladen stayed seated. "There's just one last thing I'd like to ask you," I said.

He looked at me without speaking.

"Have you ever met a man named Charles Sales?"

"No."

"Are you certain?"

"Yes."

"He's a lawyer."

"I don't work with lawyers. I have lawyers who work with lawyers."

"Did Cynthia ever mention any of those four people to you?"

"No, she did not."

"Did she ever mention Charles Sales?"

"No. Never."

We each looked into his eyes, trying to sense any doubt or duplicity, but he returned the look, holding his expression. We let ourselves out and walked past the Mercedes. "Very neighborly place," I said.

"Yes."

"Do you think he's telling the truth?" I asked.

"Of course."

"Of *course*?"

"I told you earlier. Men don't know how to lie."

FORTY-SIX

I opened the car door for Diana and then walked around and got in the other side. "So," I said. "He doesn't talk to lawyers; he has lawyers who talk to lawyers. His *wife* was a lawyer. Maybe she talked to Charlie Sales."

"Let's find out," Diana said.

―――

On its face, the Law Office of Charles Sales, Esq. was a model of propriety. Sandwiched between two condo complexes on the east side of Doheny, Sales' base was a single-story, free-standing building with a small parking area in the rear. I saw the inconspicuous blue and gold business sign on the small blanket of lawn between the building and sidewalk and pulled into the driveway, but when I turned left at the rear of the building to park I suddenly confronted the full security setup: an electronic gate, the Caution: Severe Tire Damage mini shark fins, and the business end of a closed-circuit television camera.

Before I could back out of the driveway a voice came from somewhere in a hedge: "Good afternoon. Welcome to the Law Office of Charles Sales. May I assist you?"

"Just trying to turn around. Sorry."

"Good day."

I pulled back on the street, drove north toward Sunset for a half block, and parked in a one-hour zone. "He doesn't want to be surprised," I said.

"No," Diana answered. "You did the right thing. If you had tried to talk your way in he would have been gone before we could get through the door and his security people would have been right behind us. Better to walk in. Nobody expects that in L.A."

We waited ten minutes to gain a small edge of surprise and then walked back toward the building.

"Did you see any cameras in the front?"

"No," she said, "but I'm sure they've got something."

There was a small porch in the front of the building. We entered without knocking or hitting the bell. Inside was a hallway with a steel door at the end and a window on the left. It was set up like a bank teller's station with 2-inch plexiglas, a sliding tray, and a speaker slot. The plexiglas had the word MOSLER etched along the seam; I remember when all they made were safes. A middle-aged woman was seated on the other side of the glass. She looked like one of my grammar school principals: ready to hit anything that moved. On the left side of her desk was the closed-circuit TV monitor for the parking area. When she looked up at me she didn't try to hide the instant recognition.

"May I help you?" she said, her voice thick with disapproval.

"Yes. I need to see Mr. Sales. Immediately."

"Do you have an appointment?"

"Tell him there's a problem with Roy Hitchcock. I'll explain the situation to him face to face."

She got up, opened the door behind her, walked through and then immediately closed it. I couldn't see anything on the other side but blank wall. She was gone for at least two minutes. When she returned she said, "You may go through that door. Wait in the next room." Then she pushed a button under the rim of the window and the electro-lock buzzed. I opened the door for Diana. We walked into a small waiting room and the steel door locked behind us.

On the left side of the room was another teller's window, but this one had a deeper drawer. The woman appeared at the window and slid the drawer toward us. The top opened as it slid. "Please put any metal objects you are carrying in this drawer," she said, "particularly any weapons. The doorframe you just passed through has a metal detector and each of you set it off."

At that point there were a number of things I thought about saying: for example, "This has been fun so far, but when do we get to the part where you put on your rubber gloves and search our body cavities?" Or, "This has been a hell of a lot of trouble, but I just know our conversation with this asshole is going to make it all worthwhile." Or, "You give good frisk, but I bet you can't take 120 words a minute in shorthand."

I didn't say any of them because I figured that the sort of clients who showed up on Charlie Sales' doorstep wouldn't have been surprised in the least. He probably should have put a sign out on the porch: "Through these doors pass the biggest sleazoids in the world; the one thing they have in common is that each is capable of paying my fee."

I had left my .45 locked in the glove compartment of the rental, but I took my backup .32 out and put it in the drawer. I also dropped in a knife and a set of keys. Diana took her .357 from her purse and put it in the drawer along with something I hadn't seen before. It was in a nail file case, but it looked like an ice pick with a flat handle.

The woman slid the drawer back and removed the objects. Her expression never changed. We could have been giving her ten rolls of pennies, two weeks' allowance, and our paper route money.

She reached under the window. "Through that door is another metal detector," she said. "Walk through. If you're clean I'll open the door beyond it."

We did. We were. And she did. Finally we were in the inner sanctum and finally we met Charlie. The room was small, no more than twelve by twelve, with a single desk and two client chairs. Behind the desk was a small bank of file cabinets and a thick, squat safe.

Charlie had lost the moustache. He was about fifty and he was wearing a gray wool suit, burgundy tie, glasses with a slight yellow tint, and a rug that had cost him plenty. He was wearing a ring on each hand and both were encrusted with diamonds. He looked like a big city landlord.

"What the hell is this about?" he asked. "And who the hell are you two?"

"Nice receptionist," I said. "Is she on loan from the SS?"

"Cute," he said. "Who are you?"

"My name's Grant; I'm a private investigator. This is Lieutenant Craig, San Bernardino PD."

"I don't represent cops or private dicks."

"What a coincidence," I said, "we don't hire mob lawyers."

Diana leaned forward in her chair. "We do arrest them, however, so don't give us any more of your smartass bullshit."

Sales put his hands in the air as if to say Hold It. "Do you have a warrant?"

"No," she said.

"Do you plan to arrest me?"

"Probably."

"Probably? What the hell does that mean?"

"You're an accessory on the Alhambra project."

"The Alhambra project is clean. You're wasting my time. Get the hell out of my office."

"What makes you think it's clean?" I asked.

"I know it is."

"You think the people you represent tell *you* everything?" Diana asked. "You think all they're building is a hotel? You couldn't be that naive and still be alive."

"What do you want?"

"We want to ask you some questions," I said.

"Go ahead and ask. I'll give you three minutes."

Everybody was giving us time limits.

"Tell us everything you know about Cynthia Bladen," I said.

"Who in the hell is Cynthia Bladen?"

"She was a lawyer."

"So? What the fuck do I look like—the yellow pages? Do you know how many lawyers there are in L.A. County?"

"I didn't say she was from L.A. County."

"Don't be cute," he said. "What happened to her?"

"She was murdered."

"You have my condolences. Now what the hell does that have to do with me?"

"Before she died she left a message. It had to do with the Alhambra project."

"What kind of message?"

"A list of the investors."

"What kind of list? What names were on it?"

"Suppose you tell us who the investors are," Diana said.

"Forget it. Attorney-client privilege."

"Tell us how many at least," Diana said.

"No way. What do I look like—your assistant?"

"Was Cynthia Bladen involved in any way with the Alhambra project?" I asked.

"I just told you. I've never heard of any Cynthia Bladen. It's a big project. How the hell would I know who's involved? Maybe she represents one of the subcontractors. Maybe she represents some citizens' group."

"Past tense, Charlie," I said. "She doesn't represent anybody now."

"Yeah? Who do you represent?"

"Forget it," I said. "That's privileged."

He laughed.

"You think it's funny, Charlie? Let me ask you something—when the cops come to cart your ass downtown along with your wiseguy friends, who are you going to call? You're going to need the best, you know that, Charlie? This isn't some real estate scam; this is Murder One and your ass is right in the middle of it."

"Don't tell me about criminal law, dickhead. And don't try to threaten me. You haven't got the juice."

"I know," I said, turning toward Diana, "but *she* does, and she'll hit you so goddamned hard your fucking rug will fly off and land on the other side of the Sunset Strip."

"I'm terrified," he said.

"You don't know what that means," Diana said. "But I do. Have you ever been on the Universal tour, taken the walk through the sound stage?"

He gestured with his right hand, as if to say "Don't waste my time with such stupid fucking questions."

"It's all set up for the tourists—a lot of aisles and railings. You stay in your same relative place and just keep moving counterclockwise, checking the sets and the lighting and the blue screen effects."

"What the fuck are you getting at?" he asked.

"You probably never paid much attention to the sound stage itself. Basically you've got a hangar and a course of special insulation held in by chicken wire. It looks pretty primitive—like soft cement sprayed over plywood—but it works like a son of a bitch. You know where else they've got insulation like that?"

He just stared, bored out of his mind.

"I'll tell you. The bulls at San Quentin use it. They've got this little setup—right at the end of death row. They sit at their desks, watching the clock and the television monitors. Think about it. They spend a third of their lives there; it's only reasonable that they try to figure out how to make it bearable. One of the things they do is slap up the insulation. They surround themselves with it. It's their cocoon, Charlie. You know why? Because if they didn't have it, all they would hear would be cons yelling and crying and talking to themselves incoherently. Sometimes the cons scream for no apparent reason. They pound the cinder block walls until their hands turn to pulp and mush. Then they smash their heads against the bars trying to shake the nightmares loose from their heads. They pull on the bars and moan like puppies separated from the brood bitch.

"All they can think of is one thing: the pair of gurneys. Did you know there were two, Charlie? A and B: two movable beds, each with a steel support for the IV bottle. Every night the cons play the scene over and over again in their minds. Outside the glass box are observers, victims, reporters, the bulls who enjoy the end of the third act. The cons are strapped in. They can't move. The state doc hasn't even turned the switch to start the flow and already the air is getting thin and the lights are getting warm.

"Just a trickle. That's all it takes, Charlie. You feel the spike puncture the vein and then you wait for the poison to hit. It's hot when it mixes with the blood and the arm starts to shake, trying to hold off the inevitable. You know what? It never works. The poison always wins. Sometimes it takes as long as five or six minutes. You're lying there shaking against the restraints, rolling in your own sweat. Then of course there are the convulsions. And the wrenching and gasping. Even the old gunbulls turn their heads away. You know what really gets to them? The bare lightbulb and the baby-shit-yellow walls. Not a pretty place to die and not a pretty way to do it.

"When it's finally over, the duty officer turns on the full bank of lights. The M.E. comes in to check a few vital signs and that's it. Think about it. A guy in a cheap suit with blended whiskey on his breath and lungs sour with tobacco smoke lifts your right hand and lets it drop. Then he makes a mark on a form. He puts his stained index finger on your carotid artery, ticks off another box, and then puts on an antique stethoscope and listens for your heart. A little backup for the heart monitor the con wears.

"He doesn't hear dick, Charlie. He marks the last box and signs the form. Two trusties come in with one of the bulls and they roll what's left of you out. Your body's nothing but loose angles. It's scut work, Charlie. The trusties hate it, because you've got piss all over your pants legs and you've shit on yourself. They curse and complain to the bull but he doesn't listen. His friends haven't heard a word. They're back at their station, drinking coffee and listening to the radio—protected by their insulation and their chicken wire. You were screaming and begging and bracing your feet against the chipped plaster wall. Then you were praying and crying, shaking, waiting for the flow to start.

"They didn't hear a word, Charlie. The insulation worked. Nobody cared about your problems except for the two black men covering your body with the sheet and trying not to get their hands too dirty."

"Are you finished?" he said. "You think you can scare me with that cheap crap?"

She moved in close, with her eye no more than six inches from his face. "Listen, motherfucker, you'll *wish* you could be scared. You'll wish you could feel anything. And take this as a promise—if you're holding out on us, if we find out you had any knowledge—*any* knowledge at all—of Cynthia Bladen's murder, I will come after you with everything I've got and put you on that cheap bed and watch the blood flow from your eyelids when you cough and gasp for breath as your lungs explode with pain and you feel like your head is in a Mason jar with the lid being screwed down turn by turn."

"I told you. I don't know a goddamned thing. Now get out of here."

She fixed him again with that stare and raised a single finger. "Remember," she said.

———

The receptionist gave us back our weapons as if she was a hat check girl handing us our London Fogs. We walked outside, into the late afternoon light and the dusty air, churned by the line of cars heading north toward Sunset.

"I liked the bit about the insulation," I said. "I had never heard that before."

"I made that up," she said, "but he seemed to believe it."

"You think he was telling the truth?"

"Yes, I think he was."

"Then I think I know who killed Cynthia Bladen."

FORTY-SEVEN

"Who?" she asked. "Tell me."

"Just let me make one phone call," I said. I pulled out my cell phone, but the battery had run down and I had forgotten the recharging cord.

———

I drove north until I hit Sunset. Then I turned right and into a restaurant lot with a public phone. The valet parking shed was faded brown cedar, surrounded by banana plants with matching brown-tipped leaves. One of the attendants tried to take my keys but I told him I was just there to make a call. He told me I couldn't park there unless we were going to eat at the restaurant. I showed him my PI license. He told me I still couldn't park there, so I showed him the butt of my service automatic. He asked me if I needed any change for the phone and I said, "No, thanks."

I tried to reach Frank but he was already on his way to Hollenbeck to check on a multiple homicide. Instead the desk sergeant gave me Jerry Dailey.

"Jack, I'm glad I caught you. I've got some news."

"What, Jerry?"

"The hitter who tried to whack the lieutenant . . . ."

"What about him, Jerry?"

"We've got an I.D."

"Tell me, Jerry."

"Enrico Gutierrez."

"From where?"

"San Berdoo, Jack. A cousin of one of the dickheads she put away in the gang war."

"He was an amateur, then."

"That all depends on what you call an amateur, Jack. The guy tried to kill a police lieutenant. He just wasn't very good at it."

"How did you I.D. him, Jerry?"

"You'll love this, Jack."

"Try me."

"It was a stunning piece of detection."

"How did you do it, Jerry?"

"Consider this. The guy had no criminal record. There were no prints on file. And there were no dental records. No real surprise there—this guy never heard of Crest, Jack. I don't think he ever even heard of water."

"So how did you I.D. him, Jerry?"

"Simple. We just waited and checked the missing persons reports in San Berdoo. After awhile his family finally got around to asking about him. You can't show up for Saturday-night dinner when you're stretched out in a morgue drawer, right? We showed the anxious relatives some Polaroids, they gagged, and suddenly we had something to put on the blank line of his toe tag. So what do you think?"

"That helps me a lot, Jerry. Thanks."

"We're here to serve," he said. "Do you want me to try to patch you through to Frank?"

"How soon is he due back?"

"Maybe an hour. Maybe a little longer. He just wants to ask a few questions and look over the crime scene. It's nothing special—a sour drug deal with a couple of runners and lookouts caught in the line of fire. He wants to check it all out before they start scrubbing down the walls."

"Tell him I'll meet him downtown, Jerry. I'll probably get there before he does."

"No other message?"

"Just tell him I think I know who killed Cynthia Bladen."

"Anything certain?"

"Just adding it all up, Jerry."

"Anything else we can do in the meantime?"

"No. I just want to go over the case with him and get his opinion."

"If he gets here before you do I'll ask him to wait."

"I appreciate it, Jerry."

"Like I said, Jack—we're here to serve."

I got back in the car and told Diana the LAPD had identified Gutierrez.

"Never heard of him before," she said.

"And you'll never get to know him now."

"Maybe he died happy, thinking he took me with him."

"I don't know about *happy*. From what Jerry said about the shot group it sounds as if he died *quickly*."

"So tell me about your hunch on Cynthia's killer."

Diana was now using Cynthia's first name as if she knew her. Maybe after talking to me about her she felt as if she did. At least there was no hint of jealousy in her voice.

"It's more than a hunch," I said. "The evidence is pretty clear."

"Well?" she said. "Are you going to play coy or are you going to tell me?"

"I'm going to tell you," I said.

"Wait a minute," she said, looking into the rear-vision mirror on the passenger side.

"What is it?"

"Look for yourself. Don't be too obvious about it."

I looked into the center mirror without turning my head. It was the blue van and it was directly behind us.

"Our friends are back."

"Can you make out faces?"

"No. There are two of them, both with sunglasses and baseball caps."

"Facial hair?"

"No."

"What do you think?"

"I think I'm getting tired of this bullshit."

"What are you going to do?"

"I'm going to let them chase me. Then I'm going to lose them, double back on them, and chase them instead."

"That's not going to be easy."

"No, but I don't want us to catch four shotgun shells and the rear window of the car in the backs of our heads."

"Do it," she said.

———

So long as I was in heavy traffic I figured I was safe. If they shot me on Sunset, my car would plow into the car in front of me, the line of traffic would collapse like a dead accordion, the street would gridlock, and they would be stuck, with every tourist on the Sunset Strip suddenly looking into their faces. So I stayed in the center of the boulevard until I got within a block of La Cienega. Then I turned right, driving due south until I hit Santa Monica where I turned left. The traffic was still heavy.

I drove east on Santa Monica for a few blocks. Then I suddenly sent the message. I turned right on Sweetzer and abruptly left on Romaine and then left back to Santa Monica. Then I turned left on Laurel and right on Fountain and right again on Fairfax. They knew that I knew.

I looked in the mirror—obviously this time—and saw them jockeying through traffic, three cars behind me. As I headed south on Fairfax they were gaining on me but the traffic was still dense enough to make it difficult for them to take a clear shot.

This wasn't the first time we'd played chase-me and each time before they'd lost. It was probably starting to piss them off.

"What now?" Diana asked.

"Hold on," I said.

I crossed Beverly, hit the brake hard, and swerved left directly into oncoming traffic. The drivers in the northbound lanes slammed on their brakes and threw their passengers forward in their seats. Then they hit their horns and started shaking their fists and offering their middle fingers.

I drove into CBS Television City and down the ramp and into their underground garage. I hit the ticket button, grabbed it, and watched the wooden arm slowly rise to admit me. I hit the accelerator and drove to the back of the first level.

"Keep your eyes open," I said. "We'll wait for a few cars to exit first, then we'll find somebody ready to leave and we'll ride out with them. The hairballs in the van will be waiting for us outside; they can't come in here—not with us armed and with so many places to hide. Instead of driving out in the Taurus we'll go out in the back seat of somebody else's car. Then when we get outside we'll find them and follow them in another vehicle."

"You mean we'll commandeer one."

"Sure. That won't be any problem. Life is always easier when you're working with the real police."

"Out of her jurisdiction."

"Don't worry about it. All you need to show is the badge and the gun."

―――

No more than five seconds later I heard the thud of steel against wood and the squeal of tires as the van broke through the gate and hit the slick, sealed-concrete garage floor.

"What's your other plan?" Diana asked.

I hit the accelerator and circled in the opposite direction of the sound of the van's tires, heading for the exit. I didn't know what kind of weapons they had and I didn't want to be cornered. I saw the gate ahead, held my hand against the horn, and pressed the accelerator to the floor. I slowed for a second as I approached street level and then hit the accelerator again, careening into traffic.

I turned right on Beverly and sped past the Pan Pacific Auditorium, then took a hard right and headed for Hancock Park.

"What now?" she asked.

"Do you have to keep asking me?"

"It's my ass too," she said.

"And a very pretty one I have to say."

She just smiled skeptically.

"I'm going to Hancock Park."

"Why? To seek sanctuary in the mayor's house?"

"No. I'm going back to plan A."

It took me seven minutes to get to what the Chamber of Commerce calls the Rancho La Brea Fossil Pits. With the L.A. County Art Museum now next door and the tar pits doing their usual brisk business, the public parking lots on the north side of the complex are always filled with arriving and departing cars. I pulled in next to a Hertz Camry packed full with a family of tourists. I gave them the short version of our situation and asked for their car. "Call LAPD—downtown—and ask for Jerry Dailey," I said. "He'll take care of everything."

"Hell, it's a rental," the father said. "Enjoy."

He handed me the single key and its plastic tag and I slipped into the passenger seat. "You drive," I said to Diana, and slid out of sight.

She circled the edge of the lot and headed toward the exit. "There they are," she said. "They've spotted the Taurus."

"What are they doing?"

"They're both saying the F word."

"Good. Keep going."

Diana pulled out of the lot, turned onto a side street, and waited. A few minutes later the van sped out of the lot.

"Here we go," she said.

I slid back up in the passenger seat as we followed the van east to Fairfax. They turned right and we followed, keeping at least a half-block's distance between us. The traffic was heavy; that helped. As we got into Hollywood the skies turned to shades of dark gray and a thin sheet of rain spread over the car like sweat, cratering the dust on the hood and smearing the windshield.

"What do you think?" she asked.

"Hard to say. We're not really close to any freeways. Maybe they're going to hit a boulevard and travel east or west."

"Why don't you lean over," she said.

"What do you mean?"

"Lean your head toward the door. Don't make the outline of your body so obvious."

I slumped down in the seat and wedged my head between the window and the headrest. "How's this?"

"Better. If they take a side street I'm going to have to get much closer."

"I know."

They crossed Santa Monica Boulevard and suddenly turned left on Norton. Diana accelerated and cut the distance between the cars in half.

"How did you know they would do that?" I asked.

"I didn't. I was just anticipating."

They turned again, circling through the streets of West Hollywood.

"Cautious, aren't they?" Diana said.

She took some chances, laying back, playing the odds on short streets and alleyways, hurrying up and then slowing down. Eventually we picked them up again on Fountain.

"They can't seem to stay out of Hollywood," she said.

As they drove east on Homewood they started to slow. Diana pulled over to the curb and killed her lights. The rain started up again. "There," she said, as they turned left into a driveway, "they're home." She pulled back out from the curb and drove slowly down the street. The driveway was actually a narrow city street called Homewood Lane. We stopped at the entrance to the street. There was nothing on it but a single set of five connected townhouses seventy-five yards up the street on the right side. They looked like they had been transplanted from the East Coast. The facades were discount Tudor. We were looking at an angle, but as far as we could see, the windows were all dark and the van was nowhere in sight.

"What did they do with the van?" Diana asked.

"I don't know. They probably parked it in the back. If they don't know we're following them they're probably locking it up now and getting ready to go into one of the houses. You can't really tell from here. You stay with the car and I'll check it out."

"No way. I'm going too."

"So what happens if we both leave the car and the van suddenly comes tearing out from behind the building? You can't park any closer, not on a deserted street. If they make a break for it and we have to run all the way back to the car you can kiss them goodbye and write off all of this work."

"I'll give you three minutes."

"Make it five. There are a lot of windows there to look in."

"Five, then."

———

There was a semicircle of pine and scrub honeysuckle framing the rear of the buildings. I edged through it as quietly as I could. The other local vegetation consisted of thick undergrowth and high weeds, interspersed with trash food wrappers and crushed aluminum beer cans. As I worked my way toward the center of the tree line I saw what looked like the rear bumper of the van projecting behind a stake-fence enclosure for the units' Dempster Dumpster. In what remained of the twilight I could see some pigeons and gulls vying for the right to check out the garbage in the dumpster. There was also a squadron of flies flying in and out of the beam from a small floodlight that was bolted to the exterior wall of the center townhouse.

I stepped over something furry and indistinct and dead—I hoped it was a squirrel—and got a better view of the van. The windows were still dark in each of the buildings. The gulls were chasing away the pigeons and the flies were circling in tight formations. I wondered if they were trying to impress me or one another.

I stayed low to the ground and hurried out of the tree line, across the driveway and over to the back of the van. The rear windows were painted black. I lifted my automatic and tried the handle on the rear door. I was surprised when it opened. The inside of the van was empty except for a pile of dark cloth pads and some movers' straps. I felt around in the stack of pads but found nothing. Then I climbed in, closed the door behind me and worked my way forward to the driver's and passenger's seats. There was nothing there. No weapons, no cards or registrations, nothing in the glove compartment and nothing in the ashtray. Very antiseptic. I figured the van wasn't stolen. Other peoples' vans are always filled with something. This one must have been theirs; it was clean by design. If they had any weapons, and I was sure they did, they were now carrying them.

Before I left I reached under the dash with both hands and felt around for wires. I gripped as many as I could and pulled them loose. Then I took out a small knife and cut each of them at the base. I knew the clock was ticking and I had other things to do, but if the two from the van got out and I didn't, I wanted to help ruin their getaway plans and raise the odds for Diana. Ordinarily I would have pulled the plug wires and distributor cap, but I didn't want to make any unnecessary noise by raising and closing the hood.

I slid back through the van and out the back door. Then I closed it gently and moved around behind the fence which enclosed the dumpster. The smells of death and spoilage were no longer fresh but they were still palpable—flat, dull, gray smells that brought all the worst memories back to me but still managed to whet the appetite of the flies and gulls. I slipped inside the fence with my gun raised because it was the textbook move. Fortunately there was no one there. I lifted the lid on the dumpster and found some small garbage bags and fast-food containers. The beam of light addled the roaches inside and they skittered into dark corners, but except for their twitching antennae nothing else moved. I saw what remained of the rib cage of one of Colonel Sanders' chickens and a pile of baby back ribs in congealed goo in a styrofoam tray. The flies kept their distance but the gulls came in for a closer look.

I went back outside and looked up at the row of townhouses. The windows were still dark, except for a single gleam of light in the first floor window of the center building. I wasn't sure whether it was new or if I had simply missed it before. It looked like a reflection, possibly from some glass nicknack on a table.

Still holding my automatic, I hurried over to the door of the center building. I paused, took a breath, and twisted the knob. It turned as easily as the handle on the van. I stood away and pushed open the door. There were no muzzle blasts or pit bulls, just an old hallway with what appeared to be a chipped and yellowed linoleum floor. I closed the door quietly and stood there for a moment, breathing silently. The smell of the place was a blend of dried wallpaper paste, mildew, and musty, overstuffed furniture.

I turned to the right and walked into what appeared to be an old dining room. There was no table there now but the original chandelier was still in place: a crystal relic laced with cobwebs. In the mixture of moonlight and floodlight beam reflecting across the window, it looked like a large, inverted insect, clinging to the ceiling with several broken limbs hanging at odd angles.

Still curious about the tiny gleam of light in the window, I walked through the darkness toward the smudged glass. There was a table next to the window and on top a large piece of cloth breaking the outline of the object below. I lifted the cloth and found a rectangular box with a cylindrical extension facing the window. There was a circular hole cut through the table and a thick wire running from the back of the box down to the floor. A gull swooped across the window, through the searchlight beam, and the cylindrical object moved. The lens was focusing. Smile, detective. You've been starring on Candid Camera.

I remember trying to turn and I know I started to curse, but all I remember from the instant after is the feeling of something long and rigid striking me between the shoulder blades and across the back of my head and a red-black flash like a cheap aerial salute exploding in my head and eyes.

FORTY-EIGHT

The minutes that followed are lost. I remember waves of pain and static in the frayed space behind my eyes where I tried to form words. I started to turn my head to look for something, probably a clock, but the pain shot down my spine and I thought for a second I had been struck a second time. I closed my eyes, tightened my body, and tried to hide from the pain.

My body wouldn't buy it. Instead it sent fresh jolts through my arms and legs, this time a series of cramping pains mixed with hot needles at the joints and dull throbs along the veins and muscles. I started to move, very slowly, and nothing happened. My arms were locked in place and so were my legs. The pain was traveling from the top of my head to the base of my spine like the flash of cheap pinball lights.

Then I realized I was standing up. How could I be standing up? Every cell in my body wanted me to swallow two fistfuls of aspirin, wash them down with a quart of scotch, crawl into a warm bed, and not move for at least three weeks. Why would I be standing up when I was having difficulty even piecing together the fragments of words and thoughts?

I tried to take a step forward and nothing happened. I opened my eyes and turned my head, trying to block out the pain while I looked around for answers. The static started again behind my eyes but I saw enough to realize why I had been unable to walk.

I was clamped to two pieces of steel pipe, formed in the shape of a cross without a headpiece. The wrist straps were padded with fabric but reinforced with iron. I couldn't get a clear view of the restraints on my ankles but they felt like hard plastic. There must have been blood on the back of my head because my hair was damp, as if it had been rinsed and then toweled off. Whoever the meticulous son-of-a-bitch was who had cleaned me up had also removed all of my clothes.

The thought of Cynthia's scrubbed, bloodless body clicked in and began to drive out the sense of pain. I turned my head from side to side, trying to focus and get some sense of where I was being held.

I should have known from the dampness alone, but the smattering of low-wattage bulbs in corners and rafters removed any remaining doubts. I was below ground level, in the cellar beneath the townhouses. The windows that had once faced aluminum wells below the parking-lot level had all been bricked up. The walls that had originally separated the basement areas of the five townhouses had been removed and the floors above held in place by square wooden support beams that smelled heavily of creosote. The result was a large open space with rows of beams that shadowed the musty concrete floor. On the beam to my right was a small garden hose on a semicircular metal rack. Five feet in front of me was a floor drain—the drain that had carried off Cynthia's blood and the water that had been used to rinse her lifeless body.

Sitting beneath an isolated set of connected buildings, the windowless, silent cellar was a death factory. The victims were brought here in the van, taken down the stairs, stripped, killed, rinsed, dressed, and removed for final disposal. It made perfect sense. If the clothing were discarded it could be found. If it were burned the smell could attract attention. Instead it was buried with the body, stain-free. Very efficient, even if a little compulsive. The floor was rinsed and scrubbed and the blood disappeared into the sewers to mingle with human waste and dark water.

Behind me was a table or workbench, but I could only see a corner of it. There was no furniture in the cellar except for a single metal step-stool that was probably used to change bulbs. No boxes or stacks of old newspapers. No garden tools or mowers. No cans of automotive oil or lawn umbrellas. All very antiseptic. A dungeon fitted out like a field hospital.

A light flicked on in a far corner and I caught the scent of burning tobacco. It was familiar but I couldn't place it immediately. The man approached me but his body was back-lit by the ceiling bulb and his features were indistinct. I saw the smoke wisps float beside his face. He walked slowly, slipping his left hand in and out of a coat pocket. He stopped ten feet in front of me and I got a clearer look. He was about 5'9" and he was wearing a starched white lab coat. His features were bland and undistinguished: dark eyes, short brown hair, a flat nose, pouchy jowls, and a thin-lipped, expressionless mouth. He was smoking a pipe. He looked like a doctor who was used to losing patients.

"Where's your friend?" I asked.

He stared at me for a second before responding. "Looking for your friend," he said, "so that she can join us."

"Why do you need her?"

"Contract," he said, walking toward the bench behind me. He flipped a switch and a bank of lights came on. They were all focused directly on me. He then walked toward the floor drain. He was carrying a Polaroid camera. The One-Step. I remembered it from a thousand Christmas commercials. He looked me up and down for at least a full minute, focused, and then hit the shutter release. I heard the gears whirr and saw the photograph emerge from the base of the camera. Then he walked forward, squatted, and took a picture of my right leg.

He walked back to the table and I heard what sounded like the twisting of a jar lid. Then he opened a cabinet door, removed something, placed it on the workbench, and twisted another lid. Suddenly a second smell overpowered the scent of the pipe smoke. It was unmistakable. It was formaldehyde.

I needed time.

"I haven't smelled that in years," I said.

"What, the formaldehyde?"

"No, the pipe tobacco."

I was searching my memory for the name.

"You recognize it?"

"Yes. Isn't it . . . Three Star?"

"Yes. Not many people recognize it." He seemed pleased. There wasn't a lot of anger in him. I wondered if there was any humanity.

"It comes from Chicago," I said.

"Yes."

"Specialty of the house—Iwan Reis, right?"

"Yes."

"They made their reputation on it, then changed the titles of their other blends. They put different color stars on all the packages. The blue is the original."

"Yes."

"Do you have it shipped?"

"No. I buy it here."

"I grew up in Chicago. I haven't smelled Three Star in years."

He didn't respond.

"Did you kill Cynthia Bladen or did your partner?"

He walked around and faced me. "I don't remember," he said. "We take turns."

"How many have you done here?"

He didn't answer.

"What does it cost you to tell me now?"

"We don't keep count," he said.

"Hundreds?"

He didn't answer.

"What's your fee?"

He stared at me, shook his head, and went back to the workbench. He stayed behind me, in the semi-darkness.

"Satisfy my curiosity," I said. "Think of it as a final wish."

"$15,000," he said.

"Are the lieutenant and I a package deal?"

"We don't discount," he said.

"There's one thing that's been bothering me."

He didn't ask me what, so I kept on talking.

"When we were driving through Alhambra, checking on the local businesses . . . you stopped following us. Why?"

"You already had your final wish," he said.

"Give me a second one."

His pipe must have gone out because I heard him strike a match. Then I heard the sound of light tapping against the rim of the pipe as he tamped the tobacco down and struck a second match. The scent edged out what was left of the smell of the formaldehyde. Finally he spoke.

"There was no final contract then. In the beginning we were simply sent to follow you and only kill on command. When it looked as if you might not get close the client pulled us back. Following's less expensive than killing."

"And it doesn't carry the death penalty."

"None of *our* clients ever need to worry about that."

"You're very confident."

"We're very good."

"So why am *I* here now—because I was following you?"

"You're here now because you're stupid and inept. We were following you because you were getting too close."

"Then the contract's been activated."

"Yes."

"What makes your client think we're so close that we have to be killed?"

He didn't answer.

"Cynthia discovered it before we did, didn't she?"

He still didn't respond. He was just behind me, speaking softly into my ear like a bad conscience. Then suddenly he walked around and approached me. He was carrying something at his side. He stopped in front of me and lifted a dark leather box. He opened it and held it up before my eyes. It was lined with black velvet and it contained six surgical scalpels. They were all in a row, with their blades facing in the same direction. I had to admire his sense of neatness and precision.

"Any preference?" he asked.

FORTY-NINE

"How about a fresh one from the factory, made to order by old-world craftsmen and shipped by surface mail?"

He didn't smile, but I didn't really care. Any extra words meant extra seconds. My five minutes had been up for a long time and Diana wouldn't sit in the car waiting for news releases. If the other killer had found her, he'd be back here by now. If he hadn't, there was still a chance.

The dirtbag with the scalpels walked back to the workbench and I closed my eyes tight for a second, hoping to hear the slightest squeak of a floorboard or the creak of an old step. Instead I heard him pick up a phone and punch in seven digits.

"I'm calling from Hollywood," he said. "Yes . . . yes . . . we have one . . . we'll have the other soon . . . the man . . . no, there's no problem . . . yes, I understand." Then he put the receiver back.

"Phone calls can be traced," I said. "Aren't you taking a risk?"

"But traced where?" he answered, piqued by the suggestion that he could possibly slip up.

"You're wired into somebody else's line?"

He walked around and stood in front of me. His expression was ugly. "Your picture has already been taken," he said. "The condition of your body is now immaterial. Would you like me to do some preliminary work on other parts of you before I move on to the throat?"

"I'll pass. Thanks."

"You're a wiseass, aren't you, Grant? I don't much care for that."

"I'm not, really. It's just that I've gotten used to this brand of blood I have and I'd hate to lose any of it."

He shook his head, emitted a sound of frustration and disgust, and walked away. Then suddenly he stopped and turned. He was standing in the dark beyond the flood lights. I could see the color of his face, but only the bare outline of his coat and body. "I'll tell you your problem," he said. "You haven't learned a basic fact—you can't live if you can't let go of the past. You keep talking about the Bladen woman . . . you should have forgotten about her; you shouldn't have taken the case; you shouldn't have gotten involved. But you couldn't help yourself, could you? You were in love with her and even though you resented her husband you agreed to help him. You know why? Because you couldn't let go. Even if you found her dead it would be *you* who had found her. That would have closed the loop for you. You can't deal with incompleteness; you can't move on."

"That sounds like a diagnosis from an expert," I said.

"Me? No. Never. I like things tied up in neat packages but I don't give a damn about the past. I do my work, take my money, and walk away."

I thought I heard something on the floor above but when I tried to listen closely there was nothing there.

"Well, am I right?" he asked.

"If I hadn't taken the case I wouldn't be here, but I might have taken the case whether I knew her or not."

"Bullshit. You're lying to yourself. Missing persons is for the bottom feeders. You took the case because you couldn't forget her. You wanted it the way it was. You wanted the warm sheets and the slap and tickle. If you couldn't have that you wanted revenge. And you know what?"

"What?"

"You're not going to get either. You're going to follow her and some other asshole will have to worry about finding you. It's the oldest story in the world."

"What is?"

"People hanging on to the past. Don't you know where it takes you?"

"I didn't know it took you anywhere."

"How old are you, Grant, late forties?"

"Yes, and change."

"And you went to high school in Chicago?"

"Skokie, actually." I was still grabbing every extra syllable and second I could.

"Didn't they make you read *Macbeth*? Christ, junior year. Same damn textbook. Second semester. Every damn student, every damn year. Fucking *Macbeth*. 'And all our yesterdays have lighted fools/ The way to dusty death.' That's your life story, Grant. You worry about the yesterdays and you end up in the ground before your time's come. That's exactly what's happening to you. You're a fucking cliché, you know that?"

"You take pride in your work, don't you?"

"I haven't met anybody who does it as well."

"Maybe I feel the same. Maybe I'm just doing a job. The Bladen woman was an old friend; the husband found my name in a rolodex and called. I didn't have anything else on, so I accepted it. I figured from the beginning that she was dead. She was gone too long. They're always dead when they're gone that long."

"Why are you trying to convince *me*?" he said. "It's too late now anyway. You should have gotten out when you could. But you didn't. So now you're going to have your throat cut and I'm going to have to stand here and listen to you gurgle and watch you piss on yourself. It's not a pretty sight, you know."

"Well, you have to do something to earn your fifteen thou. By the way, where do you think your friend is?"

"He'll be back."

"You think so?"

"Yes."

"Don't bet the whole fifteen."

"Shut the fuck up," he said, and walked back to the workbench. For a moment I thought he might get a pistol or shotgun and look for his partner, but he was too smart for that. He came back toward me. This time I caught the gleam of the scalpel in his hand.

"Tell you what," he said. "You try to piss and gurgle by yourself here. When I finish doing you I'm going after the woman."

He walked around behind me and thrust his left hand under my chin, pulling up hard as he raised the scalpel toward my throat. "Try not to make too much of a mess," he said. "I've got another one scheduled after you." He tightened the grip. "What does she look like without her clothes? Never mind, I'll find out for myself."

When they talk as much as he did you know that no matter how skilled they are at what they do they're still amateurs at heart. Either they're in it for the talk as well as the money or they have to talk to break down some residual barriers deep in the gray matter. The real pros just kill and walk away.

I don't know why that thought gave me hope. I was strapped to a cross of steel pipe and a hired killer was lifting a surgical scalpel to my throat. He had also rolled up his sleeve so that he could just wash the blood off his arm and save on his dry cleaning bill. Anyway, he had cupped his left hand over my chin and his little finger was pressed against the top of my throat. When he pressed harder I started to cough uncontrollably. This time it wasn't an act or a stall. It was an honest, retching cough and for some reason or other it frightened him. He dropped his hand and stepped back.

The fear runs deep in some men and when it comes out they cover it quickly with anger. He stepped forward and hit me in the back of my head with his fist. It was a good shot, more or less in the same spot as he hit me earlier, and the lights flashed again in my head and eyes.

I think I lost consciousness for an instant, but I heard him say "Son of a . . ." and then there was another flash, but this time I didn't feel anything. And with it a noise. And something warm and wet on my shoulder, like a garden sprinkler catching you as you tried to hurry by. And then a searing pain in my back and hip. And then a slumping sound.

And then Diana's voice. "Whose sins are *you* dying for?" she asked.

"Probably his. What took you so long?"

"I had to lose the friend first."

"Is he dead?"

"No, I think he's outside waiting for me."

"You just blew out this one's brains and they splattered all over my shoulder, didn't they?"

"I didn't get to the shoulder yet," she said, patting me on the belly. "Nice outfit."

She walked behind me. "Oh shit," she said. "He caught you with the scalpel when he fell."

The pain came back with her words. "Funny about adrenalin," I said. "It kicks in and then it kicks right back out."

"We've got to get you stitched up," she said. "This is pretty nasty."

"The hell with it. We've got to visit the person who hired these assholes."

"Wait a minute," she said, unstrapping my wrists and ankles. "Just stay still." She went over to the workbench and looked for something to use to patch me up. I could hear her opening drawers. I turned and saw her lift her skirt and cut a strip from the lining with one of the leftover scalpels. Then she came back, stretched the piece of material across the wound and attached it with some furnace tape.

"Talk about field expedients . . . ." I said.

"It'll hold until we can get you to an emergency room. Put the rest of your clothes on. We can run up to Kaiser in Hollywood. It's not far from here."

"I told you, we've got something to do first."

"There's plenty of time for that," she said. "If you bleed to death you won't be worth a damn to anybody."

"What about the dickhead outside?"

"I'll take care of him."

———

We dragged what was left of his partner up the stairs. "There," Diana said, "let's sit him up in that one." We put him in an overstuffed chair and propped him up as best we could. His head was turned slightly so that anyone coming through the door would not see his closed eyes or the missing right side of his head, just the left profile, resting comfortably against the wing of the chair.

"Sit down somewhere out of the line of fire," Diana said. She turned on the chandelier light. "Now moan a little for me."

It didn't take a lot of acting. My back and side hurt like a son-of-a-bitch and I could feel the moisture seeping against my back. I looked up at the chandelier. It was ugly as all hell but it served its purpose. After a minute or two there was the sound of light footsteps just beyond the door. I moaned a little. The door opened slowly. I moaned again. Then there was a voice. "Larry . . . ?" Then the door closed and then there was the voice a second time. "Larry . . . is that you?"

"No, it's not," Diana's voice said, and the three muzzle flashes followed in due course. The body hit the door hard and then slid slowly to the floor. It didn't move. Not with three rounds forming a perfect, tiny triangle in the center of the forehead. His mouth was open, as if he was trying to form a word no one would ever hear.

We had to step over him to leave. "How do you get the shot group so tight when the head jerks with the impact of each round?" I asked.

She just smiled, looked down, and said, "Jesus, what an amateur."

"We've got one more stop," I said.

"You don't have that much time," she said.

"It won't take that much time."

FIFTY

DIANA AND I CLOSED the door behind us. My back was wet with blood and my head was cobwebbed with pain and static. I noticed that the steps were wet.

"It rained again while I was inside," I said.

"Yes, just lightly."

She had her hand around my waist, supporting me but trying to make it seem as if it were a romantic gesture. I leaned toward her and kissed her. "Thanks for showing up when you did," I said, "I was starting to miss you."

"Any time," she answered. "How do you feel?"

"I'll be OK. I just need to sit down for a few minutes and stop looking over my shoulder."

―――

We got in the tourists' rental Camry. "Try not to bleed on Mr. Hertz's seat," Diana said. I produced the beginnings of a smile.

She started to drive north, toward Sunset.

"Where are you going?" I asked, leaning forward for a second until the pain pulled me back.

"Let's let it be a surprise," she answered.

"I told you I don't want to go to a hospital. We'll do all that later. After you turn right on Sunset, head toward the freeway."

"Where are we going?"

"Downtown."

"To see Frank?"

"Let's let it be a surprise," I said.

The Hollywood freeway was jammed in both directions. We inched forward for a few hundred yards. Diana tightened her grip on the steering wheel. "Should I get off of this?" she asked.

"No, stay on for awhile, I'm just starting to get comfortable."

"So tell me," she said, "what were those dirtbags doing with the lights and cameras and all that other crap?"

"I was pretty groggy at the time, but I'll give you my best guess. The way I figure it, it was all very simple. What they were doing was providing proof to their clients that they had completed their side of the contract."

"What do you mean?"

"Before they cut their throats, they stripped their victims and looked over their bodies for noticeable marks or scars—anything that was out of the ordinary. They took a photograph of the full body and then a photograph of the particular feature that was unique."

"And then showed the pictures to the people who bought the hits."

"Yes, but that wasn't all. After they sliced a victim's throat they outlined the part of the victim's body that could be identified as unique. Then they cut that section of flesh from the body. They put it in some formaldehyde and showed it to the client. The client saw a picture of the whole body, a close-up picture of the section in question, and the section itself."

"Jesus."

"Visual proof, as it were. The guy in the white coat took a picture of me and then a picture of my right leg. I figure he was focusing on all the criss-crossed scars from the operations I've had."

"That is really disgusting. And I'm not easily disgusted."

"Very efficient technique, though. And very convincing. If you want to take hold of somebody's attention there are few things in life that work better than a cloudy glass jar containing an unfamiliar object floating in a pint or two of formaldehyde."

"And after you've made your point you can dispose of the evidence easily. The client gets all the proof he needs and the rest of the body is buried a hundred miles away in the desert."

"And the killers collect a cool fifteen thou."

"With minimal risk."

"Exactly."

"Then that's why Cynthia Bladen's nipple and areola were cut off."

"To get the mole."

"And Mrs. Watermann's navel was cut from her belly to show the location of a nearby incision scar or birthmark."

"Yes."

"So the murders didn't have anything to do with sex or psychology."

"No," I said. "All they were interested in were cold-blooded business transactions."

The traffic was still heavy on the Hollywood. We crawled past Silver Lake and then Echo Park. As we got closer to downtown we saw the flash of roof lights from a line of cruisers and realized that the problems were on the Pasadena and that whatever had happened there had clogged all of the on and off ramps and gridlocked the Hollywood.

"Get off of this wherever you can," I said.

"How do you feel?" she asked. "Do you want me to take you to County General?"

"No."

"You didn't answer my first question."

"I've felt better. There . . ." I said, raising my hand and pointing, "turn off there." My back suddenly felt as if someone was driving miniature spikes into my open wound. I put my arm down quickly.

"Careful," she said.

"I'm OK," I said, wondering how she knew exactly how I felt.

"Where do you want me to go?"

"Bunker Hill."

"Cynthia's office?"

"Yes."

The last time I was there the etched-marble facing of Cynthia's building appeared to ripple and glimmer in the sunlight. Now, in the evening sky of thick clouds and bright moonlight, it was a flat black obelisk dotted with small rectangles of light. The vertical, parallel ridges of rough stone merged into a common blackness and the windows that were masked by darkened glass in the daylight broke up the planes of the building like barred openings in a dark tower.

The guard at the sign-in desk was flipping through a year-old copy of *Newsweek* from one of the waiting room stacks.

"Put the current time next to your signatures," he said.

Diana showed him her badge. "We're here on business," she said. "Don't make any phone calls or set off any alarms."

He looked at the floor behind me and then back at Diana. His expression dropped. I looked down and saw some drops of blood on the black marble tile beside my right foot.

"Are you OK?" he said to me.

"I had an accident. I'm here to see a lawyer."

"There are plenty of them here."

"I only need one," I said.

"Use the last elevator on the right. We shut down the rest of them after eight o'clock."

Diana and I walked across the lobby to the bank of elevators and punched the UP button. The rear elevator door opened immediately and we got on. She punched the CLOSE button and flipped the toggle switch that locked the elevator in place. She turned toward me and said, "Are you really all right? Tell me the truth. I don't want any bullshit."

"I'll make it," I said, leaning against the carpeted wall of the elevator and bracing myself on the teak rail.

"Then let's do it," she said, flipping the toggle switch and poking her finger into the number 18.

FIFTY-ONE

The double doors of the Briggs and Billings suite were secured by a vertical floor bolt. The lock looked impressive but it had been opened and closed so many times by so many inattentive people that Diana was able to coax it open with one side of a miniature pair of scissors and the point of a nail file. We took out our guns and walked in.

The lights in the suite were dimmed. No one was in sight. We listened for a moment but heard nothing. We walked down the nearest passageway between offices and workstations and I clicked the light switch on the nearest wall. One of the offices had a band of light at the bottom of the door. I switched the hall lights back on.

"That's Cynthia's office, isn't it?" Diana whispered.

I nodded yes.

We approached the door and stood on either side of it. I put my ear to the door but heard nothing beyond the steady whirr of the hallway ceiling vent. The air from the vent was cool and as my damp shirt clung to the tape and blood around my wound I felt a chill all along my back.

Diana snapped her head in the direction of the office and raised her weapon. I raised mine, turned the doorknob with my other hand, and threw the door open. We stabbed at the air with our weapons but there was no one there who could shoot back. Directly opposite us, sitting behind Cynthia's desk and holding a blue steel .38 special in his lap, was Donald Bladen. His mouth and eyes were open and his clothes smelled of the refuse of his bowels and bladder. His teeth were visible, as if he were showing them to an animal or small child. His eyes were fixed on us but they stared through us. His brown suit and dark brown tie were neatly tailored and conveyed a certain dignity. They were conservative but cut with a touch of style. I noticed some circles among the geometric patterns of the tie. They seemed to be looking at us too, like his eyes. His left hand rested peacefully on his left leg as if positioned by a thoughtful passerby. His nostrils seemed flared but he wasn't breathing. He hadn't heard me open the door. The left side of his head was gone and the freshly painted rich gray wall of Cynthia's office was speckled with dark globs that ran in dry red lines toward her lavender carpet.

I closed the door behind us and looked at Diana.

"Surprised?" she asked.

"Yes," I answered.

We holstered our weapons and approached Bladen's body. There was some blood on his shoulder, but none on Cynthia's desk. That was just as she had left it, with her notepads, pencil box, scissors, letter opener, brass ruler, tape dispenser, stapler, and blotter all in place.

"Look," Diana said, as she walked around the desk.

"What?" I asked.

"Look," she said again.

Cynthia's computer was on. I looked at the screen. The Rolo-List package was on, with its list of coded names.

"What do you make of that?" Diana asked.

"I don't know," I said. I took out a handkerchief, lifted the phone from its cradle, and started to punch in Frank's number. Just then the door flew open. A man in a dark suit, silhouetted by the hall light, stood in the doorway. He was holding an automatic pistol aimed at my face.

FIFTY-TWO

HE LET THE GUN drop to his side. "Lieutenant Craig? Mr. Grant?"

"Hello Bart," I said. "That's a very nice 9 mm automatic pistol you're carrying."

He looked at it as if he was embarrassed to be holding it and put it on the corner of the desk. Then he spoke.

"I heard voices. I was in my office. I was just about to call the police department."

"Why were you going to call the police?" I asked.

"To tell them about Donald Bladen, of course. Isn't it terrible?"

"What happened?" Diana asked.

"He came here just before you did. He told me that you and Mr. Grant had asked him about his wife and about some criminals."

"And?" I said.

"He mentioned several names. I recognized two or three of them. They were people whose names are in the paper all of the time. He asked me if Cynthia could have been representing them. I told him I didn't know but that I would find it very difficult to believe. I told him that she had never mentioned their names to me."

"Did he threaten you?" Diana asked.

"No, of course not. Why do you ask?"

"He asked you a question. Generally we don't ask people a question unless we believe they know the answer. When you said you didn't know, he might have thought that you were lying."

"I *was* not lying, Lieutenant, and he *did* not threaten me."

"I think that's a sign of very good breeding," I said.

"What do you mean?" he asked.

"You said that you *were* not lying and that Donald Bladen *did* not threaten you. Most people would say 'was *not*' and did *not*'. You put the accent on the verbs. It's a small point but the mark of an educated man."

"Why, thank you," he said.

"There you go again," I said.

"What do you mean?"

"Most people would just say 'thank you' rather than add the word *why*."

He looked at me quizzically.

"Let me guess," I said, "Choate, Yale—certainly Yale—and Harvard law. Probably not Skull and Bones. Snake and Book?"

"Actually I attended the Claremont School, Yale, and Stanford law. Father's health was failing. He wanted me in California."

"But he made an exception for Yale."

"Everyone in our family has gone to Yale," he said.

"Yes," I said, "but I doubt that any other members of your family have represented dirtbags in the Mafia."

"What *are* you talking about?" he said.

"Please Bart, we're all intelligent people here. Let's not play pretend."

"I'm quite serious," he said.

"So am I. The men you hired to kill us are dead. You were waiting for their call. Bladen's been dead for a long time. His blood is dry and his body's rigid. He came here to confront you and you killed him. Then you tried to make it look as if he killed himself."

"*That* is ridiculous," he said.

"I told you, Bart. We're past pretending. You bought the hits on us and you bought the hit on Cynthia. And for a mere fifteen grand. She made *that* much for you in a week."

Diana took out her gun and held it on Briggs.

"That's true. She did. Why would I *possibly* want to kill her."

"Because she found out the kind of clients you were representing, Bart, and you couldn't stand to see the firm's name associated with organized crime. Your father and grandfather and great grandfather would have looked down from the heavens and puked all over their clouds. More to the point, Bart, you couldn't stand to see the firm scale back its lifestyle in tough times. The economy's in the toilet, Bart. Companies and law firms are going under. People are being terminated. What happens when times are hard? People sell their property for a fraction of its value. And who has the money to buy that property, Bart? You know, don't you? The people who sell the dope and recruit the twelve-year-old prostitutes, the people who *always* make money, especially in tough times. They buy up the land, they throw up legitimate businesses, and then they launder the dirty money. But they can't do it alone, they need lawyers to help them, Bart. And what kind of lawyers do that dirty work for them? Not the lawyers from Briggs and Billings. At least not until recently. We met Charlie Sales. He's *their* kind of lawyer, Bart. But there's only one problem. Charlie's a criminal attorney. He couldn't read a plat book or check a title if his life was hanging in the balance. We saw his office. There weren't any blueprints or surveys or appraisals. There were hardly even any file cabinets. Charlie's a courtroom lawyer, Bart. He's a mouthpiece, pure and simple. He couldn't handle the Alhambra project. For that they needed somebody from a different world. Somebody from your world, Bart. And when they called, you said Yes. Donald Bladen figured it out too, didn't he?"

"I'm not going to listen to any more of this," he said.

"There isn't any more, Bart. The only thing that's left is for the lieutenant to read you your rights. And that really shouldn't be necessary, should it? Not for somebody who's supposed to be an officer of the court. She'll do it anyway, Bart, just to be on the safe side. The only thing *I* have left to say is that I'm looking forward to seeing you strapped down on the gurney and watch the executioner shove the needle into your arm. That should be a family first too, Bart. You killed my friend to save your name and your bank account, you sleazebag son-of-a-bitch. She's not here to do anything about it, but I am."

I was going to add something else but my head was clouding up and the pain in my back was increasing with every syllable. I started to feel faint and rested my hand on the desk to steady myself. Diana must have sensed it, because she turned to me for a second. It was all that Briggs needed. He was through the door and gone. The round that Diana fired only caught the door frame and the wall beyond.

"Sit down," she said. "I'll get him."

"Wait a minute," I said. "He may have another gun."

"So?"

"I'd like to see better odds." I started to straighten up. The blood was heavier now and the whole back of my shirt was soaked. I reached for the automatic he had placed on the desk and checked to see if it was properly loaded. Before I could say anything else Diana was through the door.

FIFTY-THREE

I put the 9 mm in my belt and checked my own automatic. The clip was full, even though its image was blurring and doubling. I wanted to help Diana but I didn't want to get in the way. I didn't really trust my vision or my coordination, but I went out in the hallway anyway, working my way from door to door and trying to hear the sound of footsteps.

When I got to the end of the hallway I looked around the corner but saw no one. A long, second bank of offices paralleled the west wall of the building. Each door was closed. I hurried across the open area and braced myself against the wall for a second to catch my breath and try to focus my vision. The bright hallway lights were reflecting in the polished walnut paneling. At least it was an upscale place to die. I tried the first door. It was locked. Then the second. And the third. All of them were locked.

I tried to be as quiet as I could but the carpet was thick and every time I touched something I gave myself a shock from the static electricity. "God *damn* it," I said, aloud. Bart probably would have put the accent on *God*.

On the south side of the eighteenth floor was a set of numbered conference rooms and the firm's law library. The numbers were in antique brass, affixed to each door at eye level. I remembered the second conference room as the one in which we had all met earlier. Diana had had previously uncapped Perrier and I had had the sense that Bart Briggs was not the kind of person I'd ever want to see on my own time. I also remembered that hidden bar at the end of the room and I wondered how many more sliding doors and moving panels there might be. The suite looked simple enough, but I reminded myself of the fact that what looked like a straightforward set of rooms could also be a deadly maze. After checking each of the conference rooms I hurried across the hall to the law library.

From the light in the hallway I could see that the library contained a row of floor-to-ceiling stacks. I listened carefully but heard nothing. Then I flipped on the light switch and checked each row as quickly as I could without exposing myself unnecessarily. At least the books were thick enough to slow down a bullet if Briggs opened up on me.

I went back out in the hallway. As I had done with all of the other open rooms, I closed the door behind me. If Briggs was doubling back on me I wanted to force him to make as many sounds as possible. I also left on the hallway lights on the off chance that if he was looking for some darkness to cower in it might make his job a little more difficult.

The east side of the floor contained the partners' offices. The executive washrooms were both locked but I didn't spend any more time on them than I had on the locked offices. I was worried about Diana and I wanted to help her.

The corridor was long and I didn't want to risk anything unnecessarily. If Briggs was able to kill both of us now it would be all over. No one but Bladen, Diana, and I knew what had happened. And Bladen was already gone. Diana and I were the only thing standing between Briggs and a successful escape. If he got away he would go first-class. He had the money for it now.

Each of the partners' offices was also locked. As I reached the end of the hallway I paused. The only part of the office suite left was the reception area to the northeast and the bank of offices and workstations where we started. In the hallway on the other side of the glass doors were the public washrooms and the elevators.

I checked my automatic again and took a deep breath. I was ready to go around the corner. Suddenly the central air conditioning system shut down for a second and the floor was quiet. Then I heard a sound. It was faint. It was a sound of anguish and pain.

FIFTY-FOUR

For a second I thought Briggs might be trying to decoy me, but the sound came again. It was Diana. She was laying on the floor behind the receptionist's desk. Her body was hidden by the modesty screen and it took me a second or two to find her. There was a bright red mark on the side of her forehead where she had been struck and there was a pool of blood on the floor, next to her side.

A decorative black marble obelisk was laying on the floor a few yards away. Briggs must have dropped it there after he struck her with it. The mark on her head was swelling but the skin wasn't broken. I tried to lift her up and she cried out in pain.

Then I saw why. After striking her, he had taken a small metal letter opener and plunged it into her back. I ripped her coat and blouse and she moaned. Then she got out a single word, "No," and raised her right hand, pointing at the far wall.

"Don't worry. He's not going to get very far."

"No," she said again. Her voice was hoarse this time and the word came out as an urgent whisper.

I ran down the hall to the conference room with the hidden bar, found a quart of bottled water, and ran back. My vision was still blurred but my head was somehow clear. I turned her on her belly, rolled up my jacket and put it under her head, being careful not to allow her to lay on her head wound. Then I removed the letter opener and she breathed in deeply with the pain. I poured the bottled water on the wound and covered it with a piece of blouse and some adhesive tape. "Hang on," I said, "this isn't going to be precision work."

It's funny how things come back to you. As I put the tape across her back and saw the blood oozing from beneath it, I remembered the voice of an old Army medic repeating the same words over and over. "Step One: Stop The Bleeding." I used the letter opener to slice open the cushion on the receptionist's chair. I took out the foam pad and laid it over the wound. Then I looked for something heavy enough to keep it in place and apply pressure to the wound without making it difficult for Diana to breathe. There was nothing handy. Finally, I picked up the receptionist's phone directory and set it on the pad on Diana's back. It looked ridiculous, but all I cared about was whether or not it would work.

I got back up on my feet, lifted the receiver of the receptionist's phone, and punched in 911. I wasn't sure whether or not anyone would respond, but it was worth a try on a night of gambles and long shots. I found four other phones in adjoining workstations, lifted the receivers, and hit 911 on each of them. Then I looked at the wall toward which Diana had pointed.

Above the paneling was a small, unlit EXIT sign that I had missed before and at waist level was a vertical brass handle that paralleled the paneling seam. Unless you looked closely you would never see it. Appearance was more important than function at Briggs and Billings.

I opened the door carefully. The stairwell was serviced by an auxiliary power system and the lighting was minimal. There were two signs on the gray cinderblock wall opposite the exit door. The one on the left pointed to the stairs and said: TO ROOF. The one on the right said: EXIT TO LOBBY AND PARKING LEVEL. NO ACCESS TO INTERMEDIATE FLOORS AFTER 6:00 P.M.

I hobbled back inside, got on the elevator, and pushed the button marked L. When the door opened I flipped the lock switch and stumbled into the lobby.

I yelled to the guard: "Has anybody left the building in the last few minutes?"

"Not through here," he said. "Why? Have you got a problem?"

"Call the police and an ambulance. There's an officer hurt on the eighteenth floor."

"What do you mean, hurt?"

"Just do it," I said. "Has anybody left the parking lot lately?"

"Not that I noticed," he said.

The bank of monitors at his station was glowing brightly but so was the screen of his portable television and he was holding a cup of coffee and a sweet roll. Our first and last line of defense. If we were invaded he could always scald them with the coffee and pummel them with the sweet roll. I got back on the elevator and went down to the parking garage.

I heard the signal ring as the elevator stopped and I moved over to the side of the car. I didn't want the doors to open and my already-bloodied body to be greeted by a splash of automatic weapons fire. Nothing happened, so I walked into the garage, looked, and listened. The exit door was secured by a ceiling-to-floor steel gate that was operated by a card reader. The gate was down. If Briggs had driven out, or even walked out, the moving image of the gate would have registered on the monitor in a way that would attract the attention of most guards. And Briggs could not have walked out without raising the gate. There was no pedestrian door.

If he *was* gone there was nothing I could do about it but make some calls and hope the police could find him. The odds wouldn't be good. The City of the Angels is not an easy place to seal. Too many roads, too many airports, too much water.

I decided to check one last possibility and got back on the elevator. At least I had forgotten about my own pain. The adrenalin was helping, even though I was lightheaded. I rested against the elevator rail and breathed deeply. I rode back to 18, went through the glass doors and into the office suite, and checked on Diana. She was breathing but the blood was still seeping from her back and pooling on the carpet beside her. The red mark on her head was blackening and the swelling was the size of a golf ball. I touched the top of her head gently but there was no response. Then I went back to the stairwell and climbed the stairs to the roof.

I had already gone through more doors in the last hour than an Avon Lady, but I tried to be careful as I opened the door onto the roof. It was heavy steel with a panic bar, and there was really no place to stand in the stairwell that would take me out of the line of fire. I did the best I could, leaning against the wall and opening the door quickly. The swirling winds on the roof made that more difficult, but I managed to get the door open and walk out onto the roof without being shot.

The skies were dark and there was a light rain coming through again with the front. I hurried around a pile of old construction materials and ran toward a steel structure that enclosed the heating and air conditioning units for the building. Then I caught my breath and started to look around. The moon was a little brighter now and I stayed in the shadows as I walked on the light gravel and tar, trying to make as little noise as possible. The winds and the traffic sounds eighteen stories below helped. There was also the muffled sound of a large motor that I couldn't quite identify.

I could see the Hollywood freeway's interchange with the Pasadena and the meandering Golden State a little to the north. The rows of red and white lights bobbing through the valleys and canyons have a beauty all their own, providing you're not caught in the middle of them.

I kept walking, hugging the green steel wall of the mechanicals' structure, and looked south toward the center of the roof. There was Briggs. He was pacing wildly and holding a cellular phone to his left ear. I didn't see a gun.

As I approached him, ready to take him down, I realized who he was talking to on the cellular. A black helicopter with no commercial markings rose over the south side of the building like a very large and very dangerous marionette, hanging in space, ready to make abrupt moves. As it came closer I could feel the wind from its blades. Briggs' hair was blowing around his ears and forehead.

"You're not getting on that," I yelled.

He turned to me, surprised and angry.

"Lay down on the ground and put your hands over your head."

He just stared at me.

I fired a round a few inches from his feet. His eyes flashed but he still didn't move. The helicopter came closer. Briggs was yelling into the cellular phone now. Suddenly there was a burst from the right side of the chopper and the rounds hit just beyond and to the side of him. He stood there, panicked, and then fell to the ground.

"You're playing with the wrong boys, Bart," I yelled. "They don't want to save you. They want to shut you up permanently."

He turned his head toward me in anger.

"You should have called Yellow Cab," I said.

Suddenly the chopper shifted and was pointing at me. A second burst came, striking the green steel and sparking on impact. I aimed at the shaft below the rotor with my automatic and squeezed off three rounds. The chopper was too far away and I was too dizzy to make the shot. I put my automatic in my belt, reached behind me, and took out Briggs' 9 mm. A second burst came from the side of the chopper. This time a piece of the metal from the edge of the wall caught my cheek and creased it with a searing pain.

I braced my right arm with my left hand, aimed, and emptied the clip into the housing of the helicopter. It hovered for a second or two as I threw the 9 mm on the ground and took out my own automatic again. Then it listed to the side and crashed into the corner of the roof. At first there was no flame, just the violent crunching of twisted metal. Then came the flash and the heat blew across the roof like an invisible fireball.

I turned toward Briggs but he was gone.

I looked around the roof in every direction but I couldn't see him. I circled back around the green structure that had given me cover and concealment but Briggs wasn't waiting for me there. I didn't want him to escape and I didn't want him near Diana. I ran over to the door to the roof and pulled hard on the handle. The door swung open but before I could hit the step I was struck in the corner of my stomach with something very long and very hard. Briggs had been hiding on the other side of the entryway structure. I fell back on the roof, clutching my chest and belly and pulling up my knees in a futile effort to relieve the pain.

Briggs was standing above me. He was holding a piece of discarded pipe that had been left on the roof. I had seen it laying there a few minutes before, but I had been more worried about knives and automatic weapons.

"Thank you for disabling the helicopter," he said.

"You're welcome," I said, but before I could say anything else Briggs swung the piece of pipe at my head. I turned just in time to catch the brunt of it with my right shoulder. My back and arm screamed out in pain.

"Why are you protracting this?" Briggs said.

I didn't answer. Instead I braced my right foot against the roof and tried to forget the fact that my body felt as if it had been broken in half and dropped into a metal press. The blood was flowing heavily again from my back. Briggs hadn't noticed that; he was more concerned with crushing my skull. He lifted the pipe again and as he leaned forward to swing I pushed as hard as I could with my foot and rolled out of the way. The pipe thudded against the roof and some of the gravel struck me in the face. I rolled a second time and somehow made it to my feet.

Shuffling and stumbling, I got to the pile of old construction materials and reached for my own piece of pipe, but the one I tried to lift was too long and Briggs caught me on the arm with a second blow. I fell back and tried to keep from crying out. He smiled, and as he stood there enjoying the moment, I picked up a short piece of 2 x 4 with my left hand.

"That's not going to do much good," Briggs said, his hair blowing about his face and his forehead and face wet with the light rain.

He swung again, more viciously this time. I blocked the pipe with the 2 x 4, but it fell out of my hand on impact.

"You see what I mean?" he said.

I kept my eyes on him as I bent down to pick it up a second time.

"I'm starting to rather enjoy this," he said, accenting the *joy*.

———

From the streets below I could hear sirens.

"They're here, Bart," I said, coughing out the words. "Do you really want to face another murder charge? You know they're going to get you."

"What *I* want to do," he said, pausing, "is stand here and watch you die."

I let him talk.

"You've ruined everything—all of my plans, all of my hopes, my family name, my reputation . . . at least I killed that bitch downstairs . . . at least I got some small portion of revenge. Now I'm going to have more."

He started to raise the pipe for one last swing. He struggled a bit. I had been holding the 2 x 4 like a baseball bat, but this time I kept my right hand on its base and cradled it at the center with my left. As he came forward I thrust it upwards and into his throat. His eyes popped and his cheeks filled with air as he dropped the pipe and began coughing uncontrollably. He was holding onto his throat now and staggering with the pain.

The right side of my body had given all it had, but I braced the end of the 2 x 4 against the roof and kicked him with my left foot. I caught the center of his right kneecap with the toe of my shoe. As he cried out in pain I stumbled toward him and swung with the edge of my left hand, shattering his nose against his right cheek. The blood poured over his mouth and chin as he fell backwards.

Now I was standing uncertainly between him and the roof door. There was no other way down, but he kept backing away from me and looking toward the edge of the roof.

"You want to go down that way?" I asked. "Go ahead; I'll watch."

He caught his breath and started moving quickly, sputtering blood but turning his head back and forth to fix me with an angry stare. He looked along the edge for a ladder or fire escape, coughing and spitting. I came closer.

Suddenly he lunged at me and tried to turn my body in the direction of the edge. The fear and terror added to his strength and he was able to move me closer to the darkness. I tried to plant my right foot but there was no strength left in it. I grabbed his neck with my hands and butted his shattered nose with my forehead. He cried out again but didn't release his hold on me. Dragging me toward the edge he swung wildly at me, but I slipped the punch and staggered away from him.

I stood next to the edge of the roof, tempting him to rush me. I wasn't sure I could get out of the way in time. We stood there, eye to eye, separated by no more than a few yards, both of us covered in blood.

For a moment I could feel my right foot again and I turned it slightly, bracing myself. He stepped forward and I drove my right fist into his left cheek. His head snapped and I drove my left fist into his belly. He staggered and I moved around him, my back turned toward the roof door. There was nothing beyond him but the Hollywood Hills in the distance and eighteen floors of dead air.

He turned and faced me. I listened to the sound of the cruisers' sirens and thought about court rooms and holding cells and endless appeals. Then I thought about Cynthia and her husband, of all that she might have done and all that he lost. And finally I thought about Diana, her head crushed by a piece of stone and a letter opener driven into her back. Then I drove my right fist into the center of his face.

He stumbled to the edge, collapsed at the rim, and almost as an afterthought reached out in the darkness to find something to grasp in his desperation. I stood above him, watching.

Later, Frank explained the architecture of the building to me. Frank knows about those things. He kept using the word *Mayan*. The building didn't look Mayan to me, but what Frank meant was that the building sloped. That's why Briggs didn't immediately fall. He slid, grasping at the etched marble through eighteen floors as it flayed the skin from his hands and face.

———

The roof door flew open and a squad of blue uniforms appeared. Shotguns and pistols were pointed in all directions as Frank came onto the roof. He ran toward me.

"What happened?" he asked.

"Did Diana make it?" I asked, ignoring his question.

FIFTY-FIVE

"She was still breathing when they took her out."

"Where?"

"County General."

I started to walk toward the roof door but my right leg gave out before I could get there.

"Holy Christ, Jack, your back looks like something out of a slasher movie. Lay down, we'll get a stretcher for you."

"Look over there on the roof, Frank. Toward the center. There should be a cellular phone somewhere. Briggs dropped it. I need it." I put all my weight on my left foot and tried to steady myself.

Frank said something to one of his uniforms and then went over and picked up the phone. "Here," he said, handing it to me. "Who are you going to call?"

"Laura."

I punched in the number at her apartment and got her answering machine. I called her office and got her service. They told me she was at St. John's. I called the surgical floor. It took them several minutes to find her.

"This is Dr. Weeks," the familiar voice said.

"Laura this is Jack. I need your help. Who is the best trauma person at County General?"

"I miss you too," she said. There was an edge to her voice.

"Seriously, I don't have the time."

"What kind of trauma?" Her voice changed back to professional.

"Head injury and stabbing."

"What kind of head injury?"

"A blow from a blunt object."

"Joel Levinson, but he doesn't do neurosurgery."

"I need a favor," I said. "I want you to call County General and ask them to have him standing by. There's a police officer coming in."

"They won't do that, Jack. They have wounded police officers coming through their turnstiles all night long. If Joel's not on duty you have to take whoever they've got."

"I said I needed a favor," I said. "I want you to make this happen."

"Did something happen to Frank?" she asked.

"No. He's all right."

"It must be somebody important to you." The voice changed to personal.

"Laura . . . please . . . we don't have the time."

"I'll see what I can do, but you know I can't promise."

"Thanks."

I handed the telephone back to Frank. "Here . . . evidence. He used it to call the helicopter."

"Jesus, they had a rough landing," Frank said.

"Mob guys. Briggs thought they would swoop down and save him. He didn't know how they deal with liabilities."

"And you shot them down?"

"With one of Briggs' guns."

Frank shook his head. The roof door opened again and two paramedics came through carrying a stretcher.

"Your vehicle has arrived, sir," Frank said.

"I don't need that," I said. "Just get me something to balance my right leg."

"What do you think this is, a mime act? Lay down on the damned stretcher. We'll take you to County General too."

The twelve steps between the roof and the eighteenth floor felt like a hundred as I rocked back and forth on the wound in my back. One of the paramedics had put a towel under me and it had helped, but not enough. When we got to the eighteenth floor they flipped me off of the stretcher and onto a gurney. Frank rode with me on the elevator.

"So what was the deal?" he asked.

"Long story," I said, coughing intermittently. "Diana and I found the men who killed Cynthia and the Watermann woman. They probably killed a lot of others too. They had a nice little death factory in the basement of a row of townhouses in Hollywood. They took their victims there, photographed them nude, and then took pictures of identifiable physical features. They sliced off those parts of their victims' bodies, popped the evidence into a jar of formaldehyde, buried the bodies in the middle of nowhere, and showed their clients the pictures and the severed skin."

"Cute," Frank said.

"Then they could burn the pictures and flush the skin. The buyers saw enough evidence to convince them they were getting value for dollar. Then they promptly disposed of it. All very businesslike, and you've got to give them credit—they did know how to impress the kind of customers they wanted to attract."

"And Briggs hired them."

"Yes. Probably on a mob referral. It was obvious from the beginning that Cynthia's death wasn't a mob hit. Too complicated and convoluted. This was murder among the civilians."

"And you came here and found Briggs."

"Right. One of the killers called him from Hollywood and told him they'd captured me but not Diana, so I figured he'd be in his office, waiting and sweating. It's not the kind of business you'd want to transact at home, in front of the wife, kids, and housekeeper."

"But we found Donald Bladen downstairs too."

The elevator stopped. They rolled me through the lobby and out to an ambulance parked on the sidewalk. Frank got in with me.

"Bladen got to Briggs before we did. He confronted him and Briggs pulled a gun. I figure he told him to sit in a chair. Then he walked over and blew his brains against the wall and set it up to look as if Bladen had committed suicide. That happened earlier, but Briggs couldn't leave because he was waiting to hear from his boys in Hollywood. He wanted to make sure that they had Diana and me, but by then the two of them were already dead and we were on our way to take him down."

"He could have used those two to dispose of Bladen's body. Then he'd have a lot less explaining to do."

"That's right," I said. "A little Lysol and paint and nobody'd be the wiser. Unfortunately for him they were no longer in business."

We drove through the wasteland north of downtown on the way to the hospital, the siren blaring and the motorcycle escort surrounding us on all sides.

"Traveling in style tonight," I said.

"Nothing rare around here," Frank said. "They hear more sirens than the air raid wardens during the London Blitz."

I turned on my side and noticed the men on the street corners, smoking cigarettes and watching, unconcerned. Some of them were holding brown paper bags that flared at the top. Others were picking at their faces and forearms.

"Who sliced open your back?" Frank asked.

"One of the Hollywood boys. It was actually an accident. Diana took him out with a head shot and he got me as he fell."

Frank looked out the window. "You walk these streets and they'll slice you like that, but it won't be an accident."

As we drove past a row of street lights I blinked my eyes and suddenly things started to go black. I dropped back and tried to raise my left hand over my eyes but it wouldn't move. I felt like I did when I was a kid, going to the dentist for an extraction. It was downtown, just a block from the Chicago River. Dr. Franklin. I don't remember the nurse's name, but she always put her hands on my shoulders. He'd put the rubber mask over my face and tell me to count backwards from 100. The thick smell of the gas would hit me and I'd never make it past ninety-nine.

I awoke sometime later in a double room filled with sunshine. The bed next to mine was vacant. I turned on my side and felt a line of thick bandages up and down my back. There was an IV in my left arm. I was groggy but I didn't feel a bit of pain. I knew there was something in the IV pouch besides sugar water. Something strong.

I hit the button for the nurse. It took her at least four minutes to get there. "Yes?" she asked.

"I have to get out of here," I said.

"What do you mean? You just had two units of blood. You're lucky you even woke up."

"Thanks, but I feel fine. I have to check on somebody."

"You feel fine because you've got enough medication in you to sedate a stegosaurus."

I swung my legs over the side of the bed and sat up. "Please remove this IV," I said.

She walked over toward the bed and held up her hand with the palm facing me. "Put your hand against mine and push."

I lifted my arm and placed my hand against hers. I tried to push and nothing much happened.

"Push," she said.

I tried again and again nothing happened.

"If you try to walk," she said, "you will fall flat on your back. You will then be hurt as well as embarrassed. Believe me, you are not ready to get out of that bed."

"Then do me a favor and check on the person for me."

"Is he in this hospital?"

"She. Yes."

"What is her name?"

"Lieutenant Diana Craig."

"Where is she?"

"I don't know. She came in just before I did, with a head injury, a stab wound, and loss of blood."

"I'll see what I can find out," she said.

———

It was at least five minutes before she returned. "Lieutenant Craig is in the ICU," she said.

"What is her condition?"

"Her condition is listed as *grave*."

"I have to see her."

"She's unconscious."

"I still have to see her."

"I'll see what I can do."

———

This time it was ten minutes before she returned. She was holding something at her side.

"What's that?" I asked.

"Medication."

She lifted my hospital gown, raised the syringe, and stuck it in my hip. I don't know why I let her do that. In a matter of seconds I could feel that rubber gas mask coming. This time it was covering my whole body and as I breathed in I sank deeper and deeper into the bed, every part of me wishing me a pleasant and irrevocable good night.

———

I should have looked at the clock before I fell asleep. I think I was out for at least ten hours. The sunshine was gone. The clock face on the far wall was blurry, but it looked as if it read 9:45.

I figured I could live without the painkiller for awhile, so I removed the IV from the back of my left hand. I pulled the tape over the insertion point. There was some bruising there but no blood. I sat up and checked the drawers of the chest next to my bed. There was a set of paper slippers in a cellophane bag. I got them out and slipped them on.

Then I tried to stand up. My legs were rubbery but they held me upright. Using the bed and guest chair for support I made it to the closet behind the hallway door. There was a green cotton robe there and I slipped it on, covering the back of my hospital gown. The robe felt good. The room temperature must have been about 62 degrees. They say it makes it easier for the patients to breathe. I'm sure that's true. With your mouth frozen open the air travels in and out much more easily.

―――

I was halfway down the hall when one of the nurses stopped me. I didn't recognize her.

"Shouldn't you be in bed?" she asked.

"I certainly should," I answered, "but my doctor wants me to get up and move around as often as I can."

"It's almost ten o'clock," she said.

"Yes, I usually do this earlier, but they were thirty minutes late with my enema."

"Well, we're a little short of staff," she said.

"That's all right. I understand," I said. "Budgets are tight everywhere."

She went back to the nurses' station and I made my way to the house telephone next to the waiting room. I had to put my hand against the wall to maintain my balance. I picked up the phone, got the operator, and had her bounce the call to Maintenance.

"Hi," I said. "This is Roy Jenkins from A & A Lighting. I've got the bulbs for the monitors in the Intensive Care Unit. They told me to go to three, but there's no Intensive Care Unit there. Where should I be?"

"Fourth floor, North," the tired voice said.

"Thanks a lot," I said, hanging up and heading toward the elevator. It took a few minutes for an UP elevator. When I got on there were two residents there who looked me up and down as if I was a leper. They had plaid shirts and dark knit ties under their white coats and they were wearing their stethoscopes between their necks and shoulders. I guess the decision on how to wear those plays a fairly large role in the training of a modern physician.

I got off at 4 and checked the color coding on the floors and walls. Then I headed north. The nurses at the ICU station were settling in for the night. The patients had been pumped full of medication and the lights had been dimmed. The smell of coffee was eclipsing the smell of disinfectant.

The station was in the center of a large rectangle. I made my way around the periphery, trying to appear as inconspicuous as possible as I looked into the rooms. As anxious as I was, I didn't want to be hustled back to the second floor without finding out how Diana was doing. I knew these people by now. I knew they wouldn't hesitate to stop me. They were armed with very large syringes and they'd go for the fleshy part of my ass with very little provocation.

Most of the cases on the corridor were beyond *grave*: bodies bent into impossible positions, with tubes and wires and collecting bags everywhere. I could never understand why they put the catheter bag on the door side of the bed. Are the nurses too lazy to walk around? It's bad enough to be pissing uncontrollably into a plastic bag. Why do they set it up so that every visitor and passerby can watch the process?

I was three-quarters of the way through the unit when somebody stopped me. It was a male nurse: very short and very officious. "May I *help* you?" he said, with more than a little touch of sarcasm.

"I have a message for one of your patients. We came in together."

"And what is the patient's name?"

It was clear that any messages were going to go through him.

"Lieutenant Diana Craig."

"She's no longer here," he said immediately.

My heart sank as I imagined her being wheeled off to the morgue while I was in a drug-induced sleep only two floors away.

"How long ago?"

"About an hour."

"Can I talk to the nurse who attended her?"

"He went off duty at 9:30."

"At least tell me what happened."

"Nothing happened," he said. "Her condition improved and she was taken to a semi-private room."

"Where?"

"I can't give you that information now," he said. "She's resting comfortably and shouldn't be disturbed."

"Is there someplace quiet where we could talk?" I asked.

"I have work to do," he said.

"Just for a moment."

"All right. Come this way; 427A is vacant."

I followed him into the room. He turned impatiently and said, "What?"

That's all he said: "What?"

"Let me make this brief," I said, trying hard not to mumble the words. "Lieutenant Craig and I have been working on a case. So far six people have lost their lives in connection with it. I am usually a far less pleasant individual than the one you see before you. That is because a professional murderer recently opened up my back with a surgical scalpel. I have been assured, however, that I will recover fully. If you do not give me Lieutenant Craig's room number immediately I will make it my business to heal even more quickly and return to this ICU, where I will find you and put you in this hospital as a consumer rather than a deliverer of health services. If Lieutenant Craig is available to aid me in that process I can promise that you will still be in this hospital when the national debt has been retired, the British people have accepted the Euro, and the Congress has legislated strict term limits."

"Don't be silly," he said.

"I'm not being silly. I'm being polite." I moved closer to him so that our chests touched. "Even in this condition I could break most of your fingers and turn your sex life into a distant memory."

"Just a second," he said, bending around me and heading for the door.

"No. I'm going with you," I said.

We walked over to the nurses' station. He looked at a sheet on a clipboard. "She's in 321 South," he said, dismissing me.

I reached out and put my hand on his shoulder. "Why don't you come along?" I said, knowing that hospital security was only a phone call away.

We walked down the hallway until I could find a utility closet. "Let's go in here," I said.

"Why?"

"Don't ask," I said.

We went in and I told him to take off his clothes.

"Why?"

"Because I don't like your attitude. I want you to know how you make your patients feel."

He took off his clothes.

"Now what?" he said.

"Give them to me. As soon as I've seen Lieutenant Craig I'll return them to you."

"And what should I do if someone enters this room."

"Do what the patients do—try to hide your ass and hold onto your dignity under difficult circumstances."

I closed the door, walked down the hall, threw his clothes into a housekeeping bin, and pushed the DOWN elevator button.

———

The south wing was dimly lit and the door to 321 was closed. I eased it open. The table light was on but I couldn't get a good view of Diana. There was a short bald man standing in the way, making notes on a chart. He turned to me, surprised.

"And what do we have here, the Ma Bell man?"

"I beg your pardon," I said.

"You put phone books on the backs of my patients—is that what you do? I thank God there was no mainframe computer nearby."

"I thought it would stop the bleeding."

"I'm teasing you," he said. "It *did* stop the bleeding. Don't you have a sense of humor? You saved the lieutenant's life."

I liked the sound of that.

"And now you'll expect money and medals."

"No."

"I'm teasing again," he said. "How long have you been in this hospital?"

"I don't know. They keep knocking me out. I think about a day or so."

"That's enough," he said. "First the sense of humor goes. Then the rest of you. And you need your sense of humor here; did you know that?"

"Yes."

"So you came to see the lieutenant? She told me that that's exactly what you would do."

"Then she was awake."

"No. We communicated through a medium, a very nice gypsy lady who works Hollywood Boulevard and the south wing of County General Hospital."

"You're teasing again."

"Of course I'm teasing. Stop with that silly smile already. Give the lieutenant a kiss. The woman is in pain and she has been looking for her Ma Bell man."

"I will."

"But stay out of the bed," he said.

"OK," I said. "And thanks."

"Don't mention it. And don't ever come back here again. People die in this goddamned place."

"I know. Could you do me a favor?"

"What is it?"

"There's a male nurse in a utility room on the fourth floor. He gave me a hard time so I put him in there without any clothes."

"Short, with a bow tie and a voice like a soprano?"

"Yes."

"I never liked that son-of-a-bitch. Let him try to cover his *shvontz* with the Ajax cleanser can awhile."

"I saw the can. I think it's a small size."

"For him that will be plenty," he said, smiling and extending his hand. "Joel Levinson," he said.

"Jack Grant."

"Ten minutes," he said, professionally. "Then let her rest."

"I will."

He left. Diana was looking up at me. There were tubes in her arm and back and a bandage on her head.

"How do you like my doctor?" she asked.

"I do."

I bent down and kissed her. "I knew you'd make it," I said.

"I knew I would too." Her voice was fainter now. "I wasn't ready to say good-bye."

"Neither was I," I said, kissing her again. "Did they tell you about Bart?"

"Just that you took him down."

"That's one way of putting it."

"I didn't think he'd be able to move his arms fast enough to stay aloft. How does it feel?"

"What's that?"

"Justice."

"Great," I said. "The best."

"You know what?"

"What?"

"If you give me a chance," she answered, "I bet I can move it into second place."

"In a heartbeat," I said.

EPILOGUE

THREE DAYS LATER LAURA came by to look in on Diana. I was sitting in the visitor's chair wearing a robe that exposed my legs. When she walked through the door my lips froze. "Don't get up," she said. "Joel told me that you were hurt too."

I got up anyway, with some help from the corner of the bedframe.

"He's always like this, isn't he?" she said to Diana, as she walked over to the side of her bed.

"Laura Weeks," she said, holding her hand for a second and resisting the impulse to take her pulse and do the whole doctor thing.

"Thanks for your help," Diana said. "You picked the right doc."

"You're welcome. How do you feel?"

"For somebody with a concussion and a stab wound . . . I feel surprisingly good."

"How about you?" she said to me.

"I feel pretty good too. And I appreciate your coming by."

"I was in the neighborhood," she said. "Besides, how could I miss a soap opera scene like this. You know," she said, turning to Diana, "he hates these kinds of moments."

"I know. He thinks there must be some kind of script and he's not perfectly sure of his lines and that drives him crazy."

"You've got him pegged already," Laura said. "It took me weeks to figure him out."

"Sweet though, isn't he?" Diana responded.

Laura bent down and whispered something in Diana's ear. I couldn't hear it, but Diana started laughing and nearly pulled out her IV tube. Then Laura walked over and kissed me on the cheek and said, "You two get some rest now."

"Thanks again," I said, as she walked out the door. She didn't answer, but she turned and gave me a smile.

"That was nice of her," Diana said. "Classy lady."

"You can see how consistent I am in my tastes," I said.

"You *do* feel better, don't you?" Diana said.

"I do," I said.

"It kind of wraps everything up nicely. She still likes you. She's still there if you need her, even if the two of you aren't an item anymore. And even if you couldn't bring Cynthia back you were able to do what you knew she would have wanted you to do. The Alhambra project died the moment its backers' names hit the front page of the *Times*. There's talk of converting part of it to a model homeless shelter and returning the surrounding desert to its natural condition. I even got flowers from David, the kid who peed on their sign; he read about what happened. You did good, Colonel."

"You did most of it," I said.

"Oh, I know, I know, but you were thinking that the world was coming to an end and now you can see that we all still love you and you're still capable of saving us when we're in distress."

"Laura told you I'd feel like that, didn't she? You laughed because she predicted it so perfectly."

"That's not what she said."

"I'm not going to say anymore, because she probably told you that I'd try to wheedle it out of you."

"Oh, you think *that's* what she said?"

"I'm not going to ask," I said. "I'm going to plan your recuperation."

"Dr. Joel's already done that."

"No, I mean the real recuperation. I'm thinking maybe a lodge somewhere, with a lot of trees and sky and sunshine. Someplace with a lot of exposed wooden rafters and handmade carpets on polished wooden floors. Fresh air. Fireplaces. Cool mornings and long sunsets . . . ."

"And what, elk steaks?"

"Don't you like elk steaks?"

"No."

"Then no elk steaks. And no lodge, unless that's what you would like. Your call. I just want to be there with you."

Suddenly she broke into a broad smile.

"What? Did I say the right thing?"

"Laura said you'd try to please me by planning something lovely, but then letting me decide what I really wanted."

"So that's a bad thing?"

"No, it's why we love you."

"I don't understand," I said.

"I know," she answered, smirking like a devil in a tight red suit who had just signed her name on the dotted line of a very important pact. "So tell me more about this lodge . . . ."

Richard B. Schwartz is the author of *Nice and Noir: Contemporary American Crime Fiction*, a memoir, *The Biggest City in America*, four novels in the Jack Grant series, and numerous other books. He is Professor of English at the University of Missouri-Columbia.

If you enjoyed *Proof of Purchase*, read on for an excerpt from

The Devil's Pitchfork

by Mark Terry

PROLOGUE

Iraq—1991

DEREK STILLWATER AND RICHARD Coffee crouched on a desert ridge, peering across the expanse of sand toward an Iraqi ammunition depot. Dressed in biological containment suits camouflaged for night work with black face paint and tight black gloves, they watched the target site through night-vision goggles. They hated the suits. They were clumsy, bulky, and hot. Sweat soaked their skin and rolled down their backs and sides. Both men were thankful they didn't have to wear the gas masks unless all hell broke loose. They were both Special Forces. Above them the desert night was overcast, cloud cover at a maximum, no stars or moon visible. A Special Forces kind of night.

Coffee went about setting up a laser targeting system. Somewhere overhead flew an F-117A Stealth fighter. Once the ammunition depot was targeted and Stillwater gave an okay, the fighter would take out the depot, leaving a massive gaping hole in the Iraqi supply line.

Twenty miles away coalition troops were ready and waiting to break through the Iraqi defense.

Stillwater didn't like it. Through his night-vision goggles the desert glowed green. Two miles north he could see the shapes of men guarding the depot. Off to his left, much closer, was an Iraqi patrol. They were noisy and used flashlights; he found it hard to believe they would be so careless. But so far everything about the Iraqi army had surprised him. It had been amazingly easy to slip through its patrols in a specially equipped dune buggy, driving in the dark while wearing night-vision goggles.

Quickly Stillwater went about laying out his equipment. He was a specialist in biological and chemical weapons. The first thing he set up was a miniature weather station. Whether the Iraqis knew it or not, they had picked a good spot for their ammunition stores; the weather conditions here were unpredictable, particularly the wind, which shifted and veered and swirled around a series of low and high ridges on three sides of the depot.

The anemometer began to spin. Wind speed: 15 knots. Direction: unstable. Mostly a north or northwest wind. Stillwater grimaced. *Bad, bad, bad*, he thought. The Iraqis were known to have large stores of biological and chemical weapons. Saddam Hussein was a big fan of sarin and cyclosarin gas. If the bomber nailed the depot and the wind was blowing toward the U.S. and coalition troops, even at a distance of twenty miles there was likely to be fallout with unpredictable results.

In a briefing regarding the mission, Stillwater had recommended that allied troops stay even farther back. The answer: greater distance was not tactically efficient. Meaning when the depot was blown, the troops would advance quickly.

So now, on the front line, Stillwater had to make a decision. Were the weather conditions going to allow this bombing? Derek felt sand peppering the back of his neck. That was fine. If it began to hit his face, they were in trouble.

Suddenly, behind them appeared two Iraqi soldiers, also wearing night-vision goggles. They began to shout at Coffee and Stillwater in hoarse Farsi and point their guns.

"Dast kasidan! Payin! Payin!"

Not seeming to pay attention, Coffee clicked one more switch and gave Stillwater a thumbs-up.

Shit, thought Stillwater, and he hit a preprogrammed sequence on his radio, giving the all-ahead. His mission was clear. The targeting laser took priority over the safety of the troops.

The wind direction suddenly shifted from the west. If only it would hold. He watched the vane shift: north, west, north, north, west, south, west...

The soldiers barked orders, clearly wanting the two Americans to surrender. Slowly, eyes on the vane, Stillwater placed his hands on top of his head.

In a rough voice Coffee snarled, *"Madhar eta coon mae kun um!"*

The Iraqis began to scream at them.

"Offering to buy the beer?" Stillwater asked.

"I was suggesting that I would like to have anal sex with their mothers," Coffee said.

"Oh, good. I was worried you'd say something that might make matters worse." Stillwater didn't take his eyes off the weathervane.

West, west, west.

"Just buying time."

"I would prefer they didn't kill us—"

They didn't hear the F-117A fly overhead or see its batlike shadow blot out the sky. But Stillwater had a sense of the five-hundred-pound bombs coming down just prior to impact. The roar, even from two miles away, was deafening, setting off other bombs, a chain reaction of explosions. The ground shook, seemed to undulate like a writhing snake. For a moment it felt like the end of the world. Dust rose like flies from a corpse.

Stillwater, thrown to the ground with Coffee, kept his eyes on the weathervane.

An alarm went off in his ear, the small earphone connected to a chemical agent monitor, the second piece of equipment that was his responsibility. It was rigged for audio alarm only. The display that would indicate intensity and type of gas was blacked out for covert night action.

"Gas!" he shouted at Coffee.

But Coffee was rolling on the hard desert floor, handgun pulled, firing at the Iraqi soldiers, who had also been flung to the ground by the force of the shockwaves.

In the distance the depot continued to explode, armaments going off from the compression caused by the U.S. bombs. In comparison, Coffee's .45 seemed like a popgun.

Stillwater pulled his gas hood over his head and ran to Coffee, staggering as the ground shook beneath his feet. Coffee was gasping for air, scrabbling for his own hood. Snatching it from his hands, Stillwater yanked it over his head. *Antidote, antidote*, he thought, quickly grabbing for the kit attached to his belt.

With practiced hands he slammed together the ampule of atropine and injected it into Coffee's thigh. Coffee slumped to the ground, chest heaving. Turning, Stillwater saw that the Iraqis were on the ground, gasping for breath, clawing with bleeding fingers at their throats, dying for air. They would soon be dead.

Stillwater's gaze returned to the weathervane.

A gust of wind struck the helmet of his gas mask, sand making skittering sounds against the shield.

North, north, north.

The wind had shifted. It was blowing the poison gas and whatever else Saddam Hussein had in that depot. It was blowing the fallout toward the waiting troops.

He glanced at the Iraqi soldiers. Both were still, skin blistered, faces swollen, lying in pools of vomit and blood and shit.

Lugging Coffee onto his shoulders, Stillwater carried him to their dune buggy and dropped him into the passenger seat. Stillwater felt for a pulse beneath the hood.

Weak. But steady.

He'd live.

It took Stillwater only minutes to load their equipment into the dune buggy and haul ass out of there, back to the troops. As he drove, he radioed a warning of the cloud of toxic waste that was coming their way.

He hoped he wasn't too late.